Praise for the "hot and steamy"★ romances of Susanna Carr

"Be sure not to miss out on this one. After all, being wicked and being in love can fall hand in hand. This is a keeper, definitely."
—★The Romance Reader's Connection

"Entertaining. *Confessions of a Wicked Woman* proves that not only is being wicked good, but shows us how much fun it is."
—Romance Reviews Today

"Delightfully humorous, with sizzling chemistry between the characters, great secondary characters, and a love story that won't be soon forgotten. A definite recommend!"
—Love Romances

"A hilarious romantic read that will have you turning page after page . . . a must-read story."
—Romance Junkies

"Hilariously entertaining."
—Fallen Angel Reviews

"Jack and Stephanie's sizzling chemistry keeps the steam rising in this latest 'Wicked Woman' romp. As an added treat, Carr infuses this fun romance with a megadose of sidesplitting humor and irrepressible, eccentric secondary characters."
—*Romantic Times BOOKclub*

"Witty and sexy."
—Just Erotic Romance Reviews

"Sexy, sassy, delicious fun."
—Shannon McKenna

Also by Susanna Carr

Pink Ice

BAD GIRL BRIDESMAIDS

susanna carr

A SIGNET ECLIPSE BOOK

SIGNET ECLIPSE
Published by New American Library, a division of
Penguin Group (USA) Inc., 375 Hudson Street,
New York, New York 10014, USA
Penguin Group (Canada), 90 Eglinton Avenue East, Suite 700, Toronto,
Ontario M4P 2Y3, Canada (a division of Pearson Penguin Canada Inc.)
Penguin Books Ltd., 80 Strand, London WC2R 0RL, England
Penguin Ireland, 25 St. Stephen's Green, Dublin 2,
Ireland (a division of Penguin Books Ltd.)
Penguin Group (Australia), 250 Camberwell Road, Camberwell, Victoria 3124,
Australia (a division of Pearson Australia Group Pty. Ltd.)
Penguin Books India Pvt. Ltd., 11 Community Centre, Panchsheel Park,
New Delhi - 110 017, India
Penguin Group (NZ), 67 Apollo Drive, Rosedale, North Shore,
Auckland 1311, New Zealand (a division of Pearson New Zealand Ltd.)
Penguin Books (South Africa) (Pty.) Ltd., 24 Sturdee Avenue,
Rosebank, Johannesburg 2196, South Africa

Penguin Books Ltd., Registered Offices:
80 Strand, London WC2R 0RL, England

First published by Signet Eclipse, an imprint of New American Library,
a division of Penguin Group (USA) Inc.

First Printing, May 2007
10 9 8 7 6 5 4 3 2 1

SIGNET ECLIPSE and logo are trademarks of Penguin Group (USA) Inc.

LIBRARY OF CONGRESS CATALOGING-IN-PUBLICATION DATA

Carr, Susanna.
  Bad girl bridesmaids/Susanna Carr.
    p. cm.
    ISBN: 978-0-451-22120-9
1. Bridesmaids—Fiction.   2. Weddings—Fiction.   I. Title.
PS3603.A77435B34 2007
813'.6—dc22   2006031957

Set in Bembo
Designed by Spring Hoteling

Printed in the United States of America

To Leena

SERIAL BRIDESMAID ON THE LOOSE

CHAPTER ONE

"KELSEY!" MIMI CALLED OUT. "Get over here. I need your help!"

Kelsey Morgan tucked her shoulders a little bit deeper into the corner. "Do you notice that she doesn't even ask anymore?" she said to Hannah.

The fellow bridesmaid shrugged and made a stealthy sideways move to block Kelsey from view. "Mimi is the bride."

"So what?" She shook her head in disgust. "You know, that's the problem with weddings these days."

"Here we go," Hannah muttered and took another sip of her drink.

"Weddings are turning into false advertising for these brides. It convinces a woman that she's going to be the center of attention for her married life. That whatever she wants, she's going to get."

"Not necessarily."

"That she suddenly steps up from common woman to a princess. No, queen." Kelsey tapped Hannah's arm with the back of her hand. "Did you see the tiara Mimi is going to wear for this wedding?"

Hannah rolled her eyes. "It's bigger than what she wore for her first wedding," she admitted.

"It's bigger than the one Princess Diana wore!"

"Yeah, but Di's tiara had a better design. Anyway, this is Mimi's day and she wants it bigger and better than her first wedding. She can have it if she wants to. She's marrying up."

Kelsey placed the rim of her glass against her lip. "She's marrying old, that's what she's doing."

"Ssh." Hannah looked over her shoulder to see if anyone heard.

"Old money, old guy—"

"Kelsey?" Mimi's voice was closer this time. "Where are you?"

Kelsey fought the urge to pop out of her corner and see what needed to be done. She took a deep breath and steadfastly kept her eyes on her friend. "But just because she's getting married," Kelsey said in a low voice, "doesn't mean she can mistreat her bridesmaids."

"Sheesh, I haven't heard you talk like this before." She clucked her tongue. "You should have never made those video scrapbooks."

"Are you kidding? I wish I had made them sooner." That night changed everything. All Kelsey wanted to do was burn CDs as presents for the bachelorette party.

It hadn't dawned on her that the *bride* should have been working on them instead of her. She was used to going the extra mile, coming up with the additional touches and seeing it through for her friends' weddings.

She didn't have a lot of time or a disposable income like her sorority sisters, so she did what she could to be a part of the gang. After years of being the only scholarship kid in a sorority of privileged women, she had done her best to become indispensable.

Just like everything else, Kelsey met that goal too well. She never would have noticed that while she was invited to all the events and asked to be a part of the bridal party, she was treated very differently from the other bridesmaids.

By the third wedding video, an alarming pattern had emerged. While the giggling bridesmaids were basking in the glow of camaraderie, Kelsey had inevitably been taking care of a problem. Guests would be eating and she was in the back dealing with a prima donna wedding planner. The other bridesmaids were guests, and she worked her fingers to the bone.

Over and over and over. She'd already been a bridesmaid for twelve sorority sisters, and Mimi was on her second wedding. She could have been living in a nicer place with all the money she spent on bridesmaid dresses, shower presents, and travel costs.

But, no, she poured all that money into each wedding. Paid for the privilege of standing by a sorority sister who treated her like unpaid labor.

"Don't be bitter," Hannah pleaded.

"I'm not. It's my fault. I let them treat me this way." She had never once received a thank-you card acknowledging her hard work. Probably because she hadn't organized it so all the brides had to do was sign it. "But that's all going to change."

"Now you're talking." Hannah pumped her hand in the air. "What are you going to do?"

"First, I'm saying no to anyone who asks me to be a bridesmaid. Except for you," she assured Hannah, who would get married in eight months. "I wouldn't miss that for the world."

"I don't expect you to lift a finger," Hannah promised. "What else?"

"I'm not going to go above the call of duty for this wedding. Don't worry, I won't ruin anything." Kelsey placed her hand over her heart like a pledge. "Sabotage isn't my style."

"Glad to hear it."

"But the plan is harder than I thought. Do you know that I had to fight the habit of coming down early? The buffet was being set up here and I had to force myself to lie down in my room until I knew the prep work was done."

"Good for you. What else?"

"Well, I'm going to need your help on this one." She felt kind of selfish for asking. "But I don't want to pull you away from your fiancé."

Hannah held her hand up, stopping Kelsey's list of all the reasons not to do the favor. "What do you need?"

"I need to fill in some gaps on my wedding video." She looked off into the distance as she imagined what she wanted. "I don't have any footage of dancing. Celebrating. Having fun."

"No problem!" She snapped her fingers. "I didn't bring a video camera. Do you have one?"

"It's up in my room." She gestured in the direction of the sprawling farmhouse. "It's small and fits in the palm of your hand."

"Give it to me tonight and I'll keep it in my purse." Hannah waited expectantly. She frowned when Kelsey didn't say anything else. "That can't be it."

Kelsey had planned this to the finest detail. She knew she didn't miss anything. "What more is there?"

"You need a hot guy at your side," her friend insisted.

"Where am I going to find a hot guy? We are in the middle of nowhere on a farm."

"This is no ordinary farm."

That was true. The place may once have been a farm nestled in the valley of the Cascade Mountains, but today it was a hotel that exclusively handled weekend weddings. Romantic and intimate, the attention to detail was evident in the gourmet meals and a fantasy country house atmosphere. Only the very wealthy bride and groom could afford a weekend wedding here.

"It's too late to find a man," Kelsey said.

"No, no, this is crucial. Don't you get it?" Hannah asked. "If you're with a guy, you don't have free time to give to the bride."

"Yeah, that's why I never brought a boyfriend to a wedding." After having a few wedding dates complain about feeling neglected and ignored, she stopped inviting anyone she was dating to the weddings.

"See? You need to correct that habit. A bride isn't going to bang on your bedroom door or call you in the middle of the night if you're with a guy. Trust me on this."

"I never thought of that, but you're right." She leaned her head back on the wall. "Well, I can't do anything about it now. Every one of these guys is attached to someone else."

"Not every one," Hannah disagreed. "There has to be at least one hot, unattached guy at a wedding. Just look around and keep an open mind."

Kelsey cast a glance over Hannah's shoulder, but she saw the same guys she always did at these weddings. The men were either too old, too young, or with a date. Sure, there was always at least one guy on the prowl for one desperately lonely bridesmaid, but Kelsey already managed to offend the one at this wedding.

Kelsey looked back at her friend. "Does that statistic theory of yours apply to destination weddings?"

"Don't worry." Hannah patted her arm. "Not everyone is here. I'm sure there's a hot guy on the groom's side."

Kelsey looked at the groom in question. She could spot the pure white hair from across the room. Thin, gaunt, and slightly hunched in the shoulders, she couldn't imagine what the man looked like in his twenties. "I'm not going to hold my breath."

"You know, Shirley"—Zack looked over at his godmother, who continued to primp in front of the tiny mirror of the windshield visor—"I appreciate you taking me on this short vacation."

"My pleasure." Shirley Harrington readjusted the floppy brim of her hat. "You work so hard and you give so much to the family. It's the least I could do."

"Uh-huh." Zack returned his attention to the country road as night began to fall. "But can you explain how I'm supposed to find it relaxing watching your old friend Max marrying a gold digger?"

"Oh, hush." Shirley snapped the visor back into place. "Mimi has money of her own."

"Earned it the old-fashioned way?" Zack drawled.

"Of course." Shirley tugged on a hot pink kid glove. "Inheritance and alimony. But her wealth isn't nearly as large as Max's."

"I'm not surprised. Max is in his sixties and Mimi is what? Eighteen?" he teased.

"Twentysomething." Shirley sighed and slapped her hands onto her matching leather purse. "Okay, fine. Mimi is marrying Max for his money. So what?"

"Why the pretense? Let's call it what it is: a deal. They should go to the courthouse and sign on the dotted line instead of putting on a pointless ceremony."

"Mimi should have some fun before she signs her independence away."

Zack gave a look of surprise at his godmother. "It sounds like you have more sympathy for the bride than you do for your friend. Just remember that the gold digger sunk her claws in Max and is going to bleed him dry."

Shirley pointed a finger at him. "You are letting your past experiences color your judgment."

"That is what past experience is for," Zack said as he felt the muscle in his jaw bunch. "It keeps you from repeating your mistakes."

"Max isn't a love-stricken groom in need of saving. He knows perfectly well why Mimi is marrying him. And in return, he gets a beautiful, elegant trophy wife who is at his beck and call. You don't get that for cheap."

"It's the minimum he should get considering how much he's probably paying," Zack argued. "I bet she gets a million for every year she sticks with him."

"Believe me, Mimi will have earned it. Max is a good friend, but from what his five previous wives have said, he's a lousy husband. Probably a lousy lover. Most multimillionaires are."

The car swerved and Zack gripped the steering wheel. "Say what?"

She lifted her hand as if she were making a decree. "All

I'm saying is that when one person holds all the money in a relationship, they think they have all the power, and they abuse it."

"Shirley, I have never treated any of my girlfriends badly." He couldn't stand men who abused or mistreated women. It made him physically ill, and now he was being lumped into that category. To top it off, he was being called a lousy lover.

"You treat them like mistresses." She rolled her eyes at his incredulous look. "Oh, like this is some surprise that you use your money to get your way in relationships."

"Where are you getting this stuff?"

"Don't worry, sweetie. No one talks about you. You pay them off too well."

"Shirley," he said through gritted teeth, "if you don't stop talking like this, I'm going to turn this car around."

"See?"

Zack growled low in his throat. Shirley always managed to drive him crazy. How did he get roped into taking her to this wedding?

"You should remember that those women were attracted more to my money than to me. They had no complaints about the gifts." They didn't have any complaints about his skills in the bedroom either, but he wasn't going to discuss it with his flaky godmother.

"Mm-mm." Shirley's murmur was smug.

"How much do you want to bet that all of Mimi's gold-digging friends are going to swarm me like a flock of vultures?" The tension started to creep up in his shoulders. "Some break this is going to be."

"That's not going to happen, I promise. I won't tell them who you are. I'll just call you Zack."

"It's not that simple."

"I hate to break it to you, sweetie, but you aren't that famous. You may have made millions zapping computer viruses, but that's not as sexy as real estate."

"Thanks, Shirley," he said dryly. "You know how to stick it to a guy."

"Any time. Ooh, we're here!" She pointed at the discreet sign by the road. Shirley leaned closer to the windshield and peered out at the bright red barn. The doors were open, showing a very elegant and comfortable interior. "Looks like the festivities have already started."

He turned onto the private lane and drove to the big farmhouse. Zack parked and got out, rounding the car to assist Shirley. There was nothing but land stretching out until it hit a huge, black mountain. Maybe this was a good place to rest and relax.

From the corner of his eye, he saw a young woman walking out of the barn. She seemed to be sneaking out, doing her best to meld into the growing shadows.

"Yoo-hoo!" Shirley called out and the woman froze. "Could you tell me where I'm supposed to check in?"

The woman approached them. "This is it," she answered with a slow smile.

Zack ogled the brunette. The rich brown hair against her pale skin made him think of caramel and vanilla. He felt the unexpected bite of intense yearning.

That didn't make sense. This woman was not his type. She was too nice—too sweet—for someone like him. He liked his women spicy. The hotter the better.

His gaze lingered along the pale green shirt that hugged her ripe curves. His cock stirred with interest as he looked at her white wraparound skirt, the flirty bow on the hip taunting him to give it a firm tug.

Zack dragged his gaze back up. He didn't know why he was responding to this woman like this—hot and fast like he'd never seen a woman before. Especially when this woman was a refreshing mix of natural beauty with hints of sophistication. He looked into her eyes and couldn't look away. They were the color of dark cinnamon.

Maybe she wasn't so sweet . . .

"Good. Thank you," Shirley said to the woman. "So, tell me, are you on the bride's or groom's side?"

"I'm Kelsey Morgan, one of the bridesmaids." Kelsey offered her hand. "Mimi was my sorority sister."

"Shirley Harrington. A friend of Max's." She shook hands. "This is Zack."

"Hi." He grasped her hand and felt the jolt. A light, sparkly sensation washed over him and danced through his veins. He didn't want to let go.

And then Shirley latched her hand on his butt. He dropped Kelsey's in shock as his godmother gave him a hard squeeze.

"Grab my bags, sweetie," Shirley said and gave him a wink. "Or is that going to cost me extra?"

Chapter Two

"SHIRLEY," ZACK SAID AS he paced the hotel room fifteen minutes later when they were finally alone. "Don't ever grab my butt again."

"Oh, please." She plopped down on the sofa. "It was probably better for you than it was for me."

"What's with this?" He gestured at the large room. It took over most of the attic of the farmhouse, but it felt like it was closing in on him. The chintz patterns were beginning to spin before his eyes. "You reserved one bedroom for the both of us?"

"Calm down," she said as she removed her hat. "I swear I'm not interested in you that way."

Ew. He tried but failed to contain the shudder rippling through him.

Shirley narrowed her eyes. "Same to you, sweetie."

He folded his arms across his chest. "I don't know what you're up to, but I want no part of it."

"Zack, you're too young to understand. When I was eighteen, I was a knockout." She tilted her head as a secretive smile played on her lips. "Movie stars courted me. Sultans tried to seduce me. Back then, I had the image of a sex kitten." She raked her hand in the air. "*Meow.*"

He gave her a long-suffering look. "Shirley, please."

"Those years are long gone," she admitted with a soft sigh. "But every now and again, I get a chance to play pretend. I become *the* Shirley Harrington who took part in the sexual revolution."

"And the way to achieve this is by announcing to the world that I'm a gigolo?" He shrugged and threw his hands in the air in disbelief. "How does that work?"

"I never said the word 'gigolo.' You can use the term male escort, or friend, if you prefer. Just wink when you say it." She winked hard and dislodged one of her fake eyelashes.

Zack groaned and rubbed the heels of his hands against his eyes. "You're killing me."

"You should be thanking me," she insisted. "Once word gets around, no woman will be after your money."

"You better pray that no word gets around." Zack strode to the picture window that looked out onto the mountains. The view that had once seemed restful now felt like a trap.

"Why couldn't you have done this with one of your other godsons?" He paused as the answer came to him. Zack slowly turned and stared at his godmother. "This is why Zane refused to take you to the wedding, isn't it? You pulled this stunt on him."

Shirley gave a Gallic shrug. "Your brother has no sense of humor," she said as she pulled a compact from her purse.

"You'll find that he and I have a lot in common."

"Well, there's nothing we can do about it now." She winked at herself in the mirror, but the spidery eyelash caught with her bottom lashes. "There are no vacancies."

"I'm not going anywhere with you." Zack leaned against the window. "We are staying put and first thing tomorrow morning, we're going home."

Shirley looked up in surprise, one eye still shut. "I can't miss Max's wedding!"

"You've been to five of them, and I'm sure you'll catch the next one."

"But I have to be at this one," she insisted as she fiddled with the eyelash. "I'm Max's lucky charm."

Zack rubbed the spot on his forehead where a headache was brewing. "I'm not even going to respond to that."

"Anyway"—her eyelashes fluttered apart and she blinked rapidly—"I'm hungry."

He could see that ploy a mile away. "We'll order room service."

"Great idea!" She closed her compact with a snap. "Now, you're getting into the swing of things."

"You've lost me." He often felt that way when he spoke to his godmother.

"If we hole up in this room all night, the other guests will think I couldn't keep my hands off of you." She rubbed her palms together and chortled with glee.

Zack bolted for the door. "Get your purse. We're going to the party barn."

"But your idea is so much better."

He swung the door open and stepped into the hall. "Come on, Shirley." He impatiently watched her rise and shuffle across the threshold. "Don't you dare introduce me as anything but Zack."

Shirley patted him on the cheek. "If you insist, sweetie."

"And keep your hands to yourself."

Kelsey ran back to the party barn. She stood on her tiptoes and surveyed the crowd before she saw Hannah watching the guys play darts. Kelsey maneuvered her way through the crowd and tapped her friend's shoulder. "Guess what?"

Her friend whirled around. "What are you doing here? I thought you snuck out." She tilted her head. "Mimi found you, didn't she?"

"No!" she said over the music. "I was sneaking out and I found him."

Hannah squinted. "Him *who*?"

"The hot guy I need by my side." Zack is going to be perfect. Okay, normally she wouldn't even attempt to flirt with a man like that, but he was hers for the asking price. Her stomach did an excited flip at the idea.

"Already? Who is he?" She looked around the crowded party barn. "Where is he?"

"His name is Zack. He just arrived and I'm sure he'll be down here any minute."

"You'll have to point him out to me. Now, for the important stuff. How sexy is he?"

"Very." She didn't know what made him so attractive. She usually didn't like a crew cut on a man, but it worked for Zack. The aggressively sharp planes of his face countered with his full lips. She could sense his sensuality and strength just as much as she saw the cunning glittering in his dark eyes.

"No need to say another word. That look on your face tells me everything." Hannah's smile was wide. "I told you there had to be at least one of them at every wedding."

"There's just one itsy-bitsy problem." She gestured with her thumb and forefinger, barely holding them apart.

Her friend grimaced. "There always is."

"He's with someone."

Hannah smacked her forehead with the palm of her hand. "I told you to look for *unattached*."

"But this one is different," Kelsey said as the excitement hitched in her voice. "He's a gigolo."

Hannah's chin dipped. "A what?"

"A gigolo. What's another word for it? Male escort? Um...uh...huh." Kelsey put a hand on her hip. "There aren't a lot of words to describe his job. Plenty of words for the women, but—"

"Are gigolos still around?"

"I guess so. He seems to do very well with this career." It was more than the good quality clothes he wore. The guy had an aura of success about him.

"Maybe he doesn't have a lot of competition. Wait a second. Are you sure this wasn't a pickup line? Did he walk up to you and say, 'Hello, I'm Zack and I'm a gigolo'?"

"No, nothing like that," Kelsey said with a laugh. "I'm sure that is what he does. He seemed very unhappy that Shirley Harrington let it slip out."

"Oh, Shirley Harrington? I've heard about her." Hannah nodded her head. "This Zack is definitely a gigolo. She brings those guys to weddings, funerals, bar mitzvahs, you name it."

"Then other people will know he's a gigolo," she nearly squealed. She grabbed Hannah's fingers and tried not to jump up and down. "This is perfect!"

"How is it perfect?" Hannah pulled her hands away. "He's paid to cater to the highest bidder. That would be the woman who brought him."

Kelsey knew her friend brought up a major point. "That doesn't mean I can't flirt with him."

"In case you didn't notice, Shirley is supposed to be in her late sixties, early seventies. She's not going to let him hang around a young brunette."

There had to be a way to get to Zack. "Do you think gigolos have an exclusivity clause?"

Hannah held her hands up. "How would I know?"

"Maybe I can cut a deal with him," she said, mulling over possibilities as they formed in her head. "Get him on the off-hours. If I don't ask for the sex, he might give me a discount."

"Look at me." Hannah grasped Kelsey's upper arms and pointedly stared in her eyes. "Do you think this Zack gives Shirley a senior citizen discount? No, he does not." Hannah slowly shook her head. "I say pay full price and get the full service."

"You're right." The naughty thought tugged deep in her belly. "If I'm going to rebel, I should rebel all the way." She glanced at the door. "There he is!"

She watched Zack walk into the party barn. His stride was powerful and almost regal. It made her think of an emperor visiting a coliseum.

His chambray shirt stretched along his wide chest and flat stomach. The dark chinos showcased the compact, powerful muscles of his legs.

Kelsey's breath staggered slowly out of her lungs. She bet he'd look even better in a toga. Or nothing at all.

"Whoa," Hannah said, low and long. "He is so hot."

Kelsey nodded.

"So go after him." She gave Kelsey a little push.

"Now?" She hung back as uncertainty exploded inside

her. "Don't you think it would be bad form to approach him when he's with a client?"

"Yeah, he probably won't be as agreeable in front of his client." Hannah studied Shirley and Zack. "Okay, this is what we'll do. I will distract Shirley and you lure Zack away."

Kelsey gave a sharp nod. "Okay."

"Then I'll take pictures for your wedding video," Hannah said, "so try to look sultry."

"Got it." She snapped her fingers. "I forgot the camera!" She had gone to her room, but had felt so jumbled by Zack, that she didn't even remember why she had gone there in the first place.

"Wow, that is so unlike you. Are you feeling all right?" Hannah asked with a teasing grin.

"I'll go get it now." Kelsey backed away.

"And avoid Mimi," she said. "If she spots you before you hook this guy, she'll put you to work."

Kelsey turned and made her way to the exit. "Why couldn't this be a simple 'Hi, how much?'"

Zack glowered at a blonde as she looked him up and down like a cut of meat. He was going to give the party another five minutes and if it didn't get any better, he and his godmother were leaving the grounds. Immediately.

It didn't matter that Shirley was on her good behavior and introduced him solely by his first name. The damage had already been done. Everyone knew that Shirley brought "gigolos" to special occasions.

He started walking around the party barn the moment he could get away from Shirley without being rude. Grabbing a cold beer, Zack took a swig of the bitter brew and studied the guests. No one looked familiar, but they were only an hour or two away from Seattle. He prayed that he didn't recognize anyone who could witness this particular brand of humiliation, yet at the same time being recognized would save him from this mistaken identity.

Although the treatment he was receiving with the ladies at this party wasn't all that different from what he usually dealt with. If they weren't watching him and talking to other women while shielding their mouths, they were boldly running their gazes over his body. He was no model, but he'd like to think he was no slouch, either.

Still, it felt weird being looked over. Whether they thought he was a millionaire or a man for hire, he still felt like he was being appraised and valued. It all came down to money.

"He has good legs, but they aren't as good as my husband's."

Were they talking about him? Zack looked out of the corner of his eye and saw two young blondes in ladylike dresses and pearls. They were staring at his legs.

"He needs to pump more iron," the one with the shorter hair said, not bothering to lower her voice. "Look at that chest. I wouldn't pay money to see it naked."

"Now if he was built like Vin Diesel," the one with longer hair said, "then I'd pay."

"Ignore them."

Zack turned and saw the brunette by his side. Kelsey something. He couldn't get the idea of velvety caramel out of his mind.

"I'm used to it," he said gruffly, thinking of how people compared his stock portfolio with other millionaires in Seattle.

"They can be a little catty when they drink," Kelsey admitted.

"Aren't these women your friends?" he asked her, noticing how she came only to his shoulder, but she didn't seem petite.

Kelsey paused. "They are my sorority sisters."

He wondered what the distinction meant. Zack scanned the room and could easily pick out which were part of the sorority. They were about mid- to late twenties, and they came in different shapes and sizes, but each had a feminine grace. They had the look of refined ladies.

"Are they all bridesmaids?" he asked.

She sighed. "Yes."

"What's wrong with that?"

"My job as bridesmaid usually means herding them from one spot to the next. One would think that after twelve weddings, these women would know what to do."

Zack choked on his beer. "Twelve? You must love weddings."

"You have no idea," she drawled with sarcasm. "This is our thirteenth. And my friend Hannah over there is getting married soon."

She indicated her friend and Zack looked over just in time to see a redhead videotaping them. Hannah had a man beside her—presumably her fiancé. The man tilted his head and pursed his lips, like he was trying to place Zack.

Zack instinctively turned. If this guy knew who he was, he looked like the type to shout it out. "Why do you do it? Be a bridesmaid?"

He could tell the question surprised her. "The first time I was so flattered to be asked," she admitted ruefully. "Then around the second and third time I liked being a part of the festivities. It sucks being left out."

Zack saw the hint of loneliness dash across her face, and the old hurt it had caused, but the look was gone in an instant.

"But by the sixth time," Kelsey said, forcing the brightness in her voice, "it became a habit. If I ever get married, I can tell you right now that I'm eloping."

"No wedding for you?"

Kelsey gave an exaggerated shudder. "I've suffered enough."

Zack smiled, enjoying Kelsey's refreshing candor. He didn't have many conversations with women about weddings. He usually avoided the subject at all costs, and when he stumbled into it, he spent most of the time looking for hidden meanings, traps, and a way out.

Maybe there was something good to be said of masquerading as a gigolo—not that he would let Shirley know that! "What do you do when you're not a bridesmaid?"

"I'm an art buyer for corporations."

Why wasn't he surprised? Art buying was a very proper, ladylike profession that required connections.

"Kelsey? There you are!" A woman, about five people away, suddenly veered toward them. He remembered that blonde was Mimi, the bride.

Kelsey cringed. It looked like she wanted to make a run for it. "Zack, can I ask you something?"

The urgency in her voice intrigued him. "Sure."

"Are you . . ." She paused.

He leaned closer, inhaling her faint scent. It made him think of hot summer nights. "Am I what?"

"Are you taking on any more clients?"

Chapter Three

HOURS AFTER THE PARTY, the farm was dark and silent. Zack sat on one of the chaise lounges around the swimming pool. The underwater lights were on, casting eerie shadows. He peered into the water as Kelsey's question still echoed in his head.

"Are you taking any more clients?"

He was being propositioned. Was offered payment for sex. *He* was. And by the sweetest-looking woman he'd ever seen.

It was probably a good thing Mimi hustled her away, yapping about wedding favors. Zack knew he had looked shell-shocked. He also knew he hadn't given an immediate no.

Not that he would accept Kelsey's money, Zack thought as he leaned his head back and closed his eyes. He didn't need it and he didn't want it.

He didn't like it when women tried to pay for his meals. Sure, it was flattering that Kelsey wanted to sleep with him enough to pay him, but the same principle applies. He paid his own way.

Would she have approached him if she wasn't going to offer him money? Would she have approached him at the party?

He didn't think she would have. Women like Kelsey cut a wide path around him.

Zack shifted uncomfortably on the lounge chair and crossed one ankle over the other. Many women thought that sex was the great equalizer, but they eventually found out that wasn't true. Money held all power—or it gave the illusion. That illusion could shatter once you realized the woman you wanted wouldn't stay with you for all the money in the world.

That's when you realized you never had a chance to begin with. The money just made you believe you did.

Zack opened his eyes when he heard a sliding door open nearby. He watched a woman step out of a first-floor room in the farmhouse and walk toward the pool. The shadows made it difficult to tell who it was, but he knew it was Kelsey by the way she walked.

He got a look at what she was wearing and a burst of heat flashed through him. It felt like his tongue swelled inside his mouth, and he couldn't swallow all because of a swimsuit. The one-piece was modest, but the way Kelsey filled it out was indecent.

The neckline scooped low on her full breasts. His palms itched as he imagined cupping them in his hands. He clenched his hands into fists when he noticed that her nipples poked against the greenish blue fabric.

She was trim and athletic. The cutaways on the sides showed a hint of waist and gentle swell of hip, but what really caught his attention were the legs. Long and slender, they seemed to go on forever. He never considered himself a leg man until now.

Kelsey kicked off her flip-flops and tossed a fluffy white towel on a nearby chair. She dove into the pool, the move clean and barely making a splash. She resurfaced halfway through the pool before swimming to the other side. Her strokes cut through the water with mesmerizing speed.

When she got to the other side, she paused and pushed back her long, slick hair. It was a natural, simple gesture, but the innate sensuality in Kelsey's move sparked another white hot surge inside him.

"Didn't anyone tell you to have a swimming buddy?" Zack asked.

She turned quickly and the water splashed around her. "I'm sorry," she said, sounding slightly out of breath. "I didn't see you."

Zack believed her. He'd dealt with enough of the I-didn't-see-you ploys to know what was real and what wasn't.

"I didn't mean to disturb you." She made a move to the pool steps.

"You're not." It was lie. Her presence disturbed him. He didn't play with women as sweet as Kelsey, but something about her also seemed hot and spicy, and that whet his appetite.

"What are you doing out here late at night?" she asked as she treaded water.

"I could ask you the same."

"I just finished putting together the wedding favors." Weariness invaded her voice. "It took me forever."

"I'll be sure to enjoy mine, then."

"You'd better." Kelsey arched her neck and groaned. Zack's body clenched at the sight. "I just need a few minutes to do what *I* want to do."

"Same here." He'd start by wrapping her wet hair around his hand until he could cup the back of her head. Then he'd tilt her head back and give her a kiss that would rattle his bones.

"You get time alone?" she asked.

"I need it. Shirley can wear any person out." The woman never stopped talking, moving, or coming up with crazy ideas.

"Really?" She sounded almost scandalized.

"Not to mention that she snores." It was just one complaint on his list.

Kelsey laughed, the sound making him think of something light and floating. "Occupational hazard, I guess."

Zack lifted his head. Kelsey thought he meant . . . He shrugged and relaxed against the chaise. It wasn't worth trying to explain. He had considered sleeping on the floor when he had heard the god-awful sound coming from the bed. It was enough to drive him out of the room.

Kelsey lay on her back and floated. The water bobbed against her breasts and dipped around her thighs. Zack rubbed his hand against his chest, finding it difficult to breathe. Did Kelsey have any idea what she was doing to him?

"I guess you and I are a lot alike," she mused as she gazed up at the moon.

That comment surprised him. They were polar opposites. "How's that?"

"We give more than we receive."

"That's one way of looking at it." Great, now she thought he was some gigolo with a heart of gold. A victim. A lost soul. Well, the last part might not be far off the mark.

"With one noticeable difference," Kelsey admitted. "I pay for the honor, and you get paid."

"Getting paid isn't a sign of appreciation. People expect more when they are shelling out the money. The more it costs, the more they expect."

Kelsey rolled over and started to tread again. "I don't know about that."

"Take my word on it." Kelsey didn't need to know which side of the coin he was on for this hard-won experience. "They want to get their money's worth."

"But if you don't set a price, you're bound to be disappointed. People give you a token of appreciation because it's required, but most of the time it doesn't begin to cover all you've done for them."

Zack's memory flashed back to the time he gave one of his ex-girlfriends flowers as a peace offering and she threw them back in his face. She had expected more and the flowers had thorns.

"You should see some of the bridesmaids gifts I've received. They didn't show any hint of appreciation." She held up her hand. "Don't get me started."

"I'll try not to," he murmured as she pushed her feet off the wall and swam to the other side.

She swam a couple more laps and Zack leaned back to watch. She was beautiful. That combined with her athletic grace was an irresistible combination. The reaching arms and powerful kicks caught his attention, but her turns were downright sexy.

By the time she stopped, she was gasping deeply for breath. The scoop of her swimsuit seemed lower than before, and each intake of breath teased Zack with the sight of her deep cleavage.

"By the way," she said as she leisurely swam to where he sat. "I'm sorry."

"For what?"

"For asking if your services were available." She rested her arms on the edge of the pool.

Her apology surprised him, but he didn't know why. Kelsey seemed the type to go out of her way to make amends. "Why are you sorry?"

She bit her bottom lip. "I had a feeling I offended you."

"You didn't."

"I admit, I don't know the proper etiquette for this sort of . . ." She rotated her hand as she tried to come up with the word.

He raised an eyebrow.

"Thing," she finished lamely. "I'll be quiet now." She took a breath and dunked her head in the water.

He waited until she resurfaced to continue. "So why did you proposition me?"

"Well"—she paused as she wiped the water from her eyes—"it seems kind of selfish now."

"I'm intrigued."

"You seemed to have been my best bet." She stopped and grimaced when she realized how that sounded. "Not that I don't find you attractive."

"Oh, right. Of course not."

"I'm sure you have all sorts of women falling over themselves throwing money at you."

"More than you can imagine." He didn't like where this conversation was going.

"But only a few can afford you?" she asked, almost hopefully.

"*You* couldn't afford me."

"Is that right?" Annoyance flared in her eyes. "How much do you charge?"

"I'm worth millions."

"No, seriously. Why won't you tell me?"

"It's hard to say." How much would a gigolo charge wealthy women? "I work on a case-by-case basis."

"Oh, so it's not like a buffet where it's all you can eat on a set price?"

Zack swallowed back a groan as the vision hit him. Kelsey naked and spread out on the buffet table . . . Her body arching as she splayed her legs open . . .

"It's more à la carte?" Kelsey asked. "Like a woman with a fetish might have to pay more to play out her fantasies?"

"Mmm-hmm." Zack closed his eyes as he imagined Kelsey with a secret fetish. She didn't seem the type who'd beg to be tied up, but she wouldn't be against it. He could see it perfectly. Her arms would reach above her head like a swim stroke, but her wrists bound to the bed. She'd writhe and give that sexy half turn . . .

"Well, I don't have any fetishes," Kelsey insisted. "In fact, you wouldn't even have to touch me."

Suddenly the image transformed. Her hands were free, but she was somehow bound to the bed. She was reaching for him, her powerful muscles straining under the sweat-slick skin, but he didn't touch her.

He cracked an eye open. "Isn't that a form of a fetish?" he asked hoarsely.

"I don't know," she said, tilting her head as she pondered the question. "Is it? You must have a price list. I guess you wouldn't carry that sort of thing around with you, huh?"

He pulled a price out of the air. "One thousand dollars." It was a nice, even number.

"What is?"

He leaned back with his hands behind his head. "My price per day. Plus expenses and add-ons." The negotiator in him couldn't help but include that.

"One thousand dollars a day?" Her voice came out in a squawk.

"I'm worth it."

Her gaze traveled down the length of his body. "I'm sure you are," she said softly.

Had he really been a gigolo, he would have knocked down the price for her just for that look.

"Do you accept cash or check?" she asked. "Credit card?"

He wanted to gloss over the details, but Kelsey was one to get nitpicky. "I send itemized invoices afterwards."

"I don't know if that's a good idea." She propped her chin on her hands. "What you might think is an add-on, like snuggling, the woman might consider part of the package. And wouldn't women stiff you with the bill?"

His cock was getting stiff now. "I haven't had any problems. Considering the nature of the services, there has to be a level of trust."

"Okay, it's a deal." She lifted herself out of the pool.

He sat up abruptly. "Excuse me?" She was really going for it. He should quit this now. Tell her it was all a joke. Ignore the anticipation pounding through his veins.

"I'll hire you for the next two days," Kelsey said as she walked over to him. "Oh, what about Shirley?"

He was getting lost again. "What about her?"

"Won't she feel like I'm taking you over?"

Taking you over . . . Whoa. His cock swelled and pressed against his shorts. Maybe he *could* pretend to be a gigolo. It would work in everyone's favor, and no one would have to know the truth. "Don't worry about it. I'll talk to her."

"Because, honestly"—Kelsey pressed her hand against her chest—"I don't want to get into a bidding war."

"I wouldn't want that to happen, either." There was no telling what Shirley would do. "Anyway, she'll be more than happy to share."

"Huh?" Kelsey had a look of horror and took a hasty step back. Her foot slipped on the puddle of water behind her.

What was her problem? Oh . . . Oh! "No, not like that." How did she get the idea of threesomes from one innocent statement? Kelsey's spicy side was getting stronger and stronger. "I meant that the less time she has with me, the more time she has to seduce someone else."

"Oh, okay. Good. Whew." She stretched her hand out. "We should shake on it."

Zack rose from his chair, wondering what got into him. Yeah, just the sight of water dripping from Kelsey's body made him sweat, and he hadn't felt an instant attraction like this in a long time, but he knew the sensations could explode into trouble.

What he was doing was crazy. He had to be careful. This might be a game to him, and a fling to her, but she was still way out of her league. He had to be careful.

But not *too* careful. Zack grasped her hand. "Wouldn't you rather seal it with a kiss?"

Her fingers tensed under his. "The deal doesn't start until tomorrow."

Zack dipped his head. "Consider this a sample of what to expect."

CHAPTER FOUR

THE MOMENT THEIR LIPS touched, Kelsey knew the agreement was a bad idea. A wild sensation rushed through her. It was hot and jagged, but it didn't hurt. Far from it.

She drew back, startled. It was as if she had been hidden from view and a heavy veil had been lifted from her face. She was aware of every droplet streaming down her body. Her swimsuit felt almost minuscule, but her breasts felt full and heavy.

What was going on?

Zack cupped the back of her head with one large hand. He drew her closer, ready for another kiss. Kelsey splayed her hand on his hard chest to stop him.

He looked into her eyes, as if he were waiting for her to call it all off. She saw the challenging glint. He thought she wasn't ready for a man like him.

The problem was: she wasn't! She might have some sexual experience, but that didn't mean she was anywhere near Zack's caliber. She didn't know all the games and rules his circle played.

But she didn't want to know them, either. This was her time to call the shots. If she was over her head, she had the power to call it all off.

"Uh-uh." She lifted her hand and shook her finger at him. "I'm in charge now."

The dark look on his face made her pause. It was as if he wanted to wrestle the control away from her. And he could. They both knew that. She could sense that with any given moment, he could seize control and take her any way he wanted.

The only thing that held Zack in check was their agreement. That gave her such a rush, and she felt the folds of her sex swell in response.

"Don't move," she murmured. His muscles flexed but he remained still. She sensed that Zack's acquiescence cost him, but that couldn't be. It was what he did every day, wasn't it? Or was she doing something different than he was used to with his usual clients?

Maybe there was something good about not knowing the rules. She liked the idea that she was different from the other women he had. It made her feel like she stood out in the crowd. She only hoped it was in a good way.

Kelsey pressed her lips against his. His mouth was firm and unyielding. She hid a smile. Zack was really taking this "don't move" request too far. She grazed her lips across his, tasting him. Testing him.

His stubble rasped against her face. It didn't sting, but it pricked at her like a warning. She inhaled his scent. It was masculine and elemental. It smelled exclusive and pricey.

She stepped back and looked at him. She didn't know many gigolos, but something about Zack made her think that he had more layers than the usual player. The way he spoke—or chose not to speak. Even his manners as he had looked after Shirley made her take notice. It was these little things that didn't add up.

Zack Cooper fascinated her like a painting from one of the masters. She could stare at his face for hours and wonder what happened in his life that shaped every line and angle.

"Is that it?" he asked.

She guiltily jumped back. Yeah, that was it. Sample time was over.

She wasn't expecting much from him. She still wasn't sure if she planned to have sex with him. As much as she'd love to act on the reckless impulse, she knew better. One encounter with him would fundamentally change her.

"Were you planning to show me more?" she teased him. *See*, she wanted to say, *I can be as sophisticated as the next woman.*

Zack silently studied her, but she caught the sly look before it disappeared. She wasn't sure what it meant until he reached up with both hands. He grabbed the back of his collar and shucked off his shirt.

He was a celebration of muscles and golden skin. The fine dusting of hair against the solid muscle made her think of silk and stone. "I didn't ask you to do that," she said in a wispy, ragged voice. So much for her sophistication.

"I know." He placed his hands on his lean hips.

She reached out and ran her finger down his sternum, before dragging it along his defined ribs. He felt warm and sleek under her hand. She reached up again and flattened her hand against his chest. She couldn't help it; the feel of him was almost addictive.

Kelsey liked how his muscles bunched underneath her hand. He took a breath as her nail grazed his flat brown nipple. She watched as it pebbled in response. Without a moment's thought, Kelsey stepped forward and licked his nipple.

She teased the nub with the tip of her tongue, and found her own nipples puckering. She drew him in her mouth and her breasts tingled. When she gently bit down on Zack's nipple, she felt the sting as well.

His sharp intake of breath warned her, as did the jerk of his muscles. She ducked under his arms and stepped around him just as he tried to clasp her against him.

She skimmed her hands along his back, imagining what it would be like to rake her nails against his flesh in the heat of the moment. Leaning against him, Kelsey flattened her breasts in the middle of his back. Her tight nipples poked against her swimsuit and she wondered if he could feel them.

She curled her arms around his sides and smoothed her hands against his chest. In this position, she was in control. He couldn't touch her, and the naughty power consumed her . . .

Only to evaporate with a poof the moment Zack dropped his shorts.

She froze as the panic crawled up her chest. She had a hot naked Adonis in her hands. He was willing to do anything. He was ready to fulfill her fantasies.

And that idea scared the hell out of her.

She dropped her arms and took a hasty step back. Kelsey immediately regretted that move. Her eyes traveled down his sculpted buttocks and powerful, muscular thighs.

Oooh . . . wow . . . Her sex was slick with anticipation.

"Now it's your turn," Zack informed her, looking over his shoulder.

What? She wasn't ready! No, she was going to let him know that. He would stop, and she didn't want to call it quits.

"No," she said, pleased at her firm tone. She pressed her hand against Zack's shoulder to prevent him from turning. "You're playing by my rules. I stay dressed."

His shoulder tensed under her hand.

"Now, Zack, don't move."

She wasn't going to take her clothes off? At all? He was standing in front of her buck naked, his cock hard and ready, and he couldn't get the woman to take her clothes off?

He glared at the stars. Why was he being punished this weekend? Why?

He flinched when he felt Kelsey's hand glide over his butt. It was like she was palming an object of art. Was she appreciating it or determining the value?

Zack clenched his teeth, doing his best not to flex any muscle in his butt. He wished she would move around and face him. Then he could see if she was feeling anything. He could tell if she liked what she saw.

He shouldn't have started this. Zack refrained from closing his eyes and shaking his head. Kelsey didn't play by the rules. She didn't know there *were* rules. This is why he didn't mess with women like Kelsey Morgan. They did nothing but cause a man to wander into dangerous territory without knowing it.

Kelsey's hand slithered over his hip and she palmed his cock. He clapped his hands over hers without thinking about it.

"I'm sorry." Her breath wafted against his back. "Am I going too far?"

Was she kidding? She wasn't going far enough! "No," he said and slowly released her wrist.

"Maybe you should put your hands behind your head."

Say what? His eyes bulged out at the request. Why would

he do that? He fought against the instinct to argue and reluctantly complied.

He gritted his teeth as she reached under and cupped his balls, testing the weight in her hands. If she so much as gave him a good squeeze or twist, all bets were off.

She did something with her fingers that made his eyes cross. Zack carefully exhaled. Okay, maybe his first mistake was thinking she was an innocent young thing. The feel of her hands exploring him had gotten him hot and hard faster than he could remember.

When she gripped the base of his cock, Zack braced his knees. Kelsey was pressed tight against his back. Her wet suit felt cold, but he didn't seem to notice that as much as her breasts cushioning his back and her pelvis snug against his butt.

She was so close, so tantalizing, and he couldn't touch her. When she began to pump his cock, he dug his fingers into his hair, but he didn't feel the bite. His world was centered on Kelsey's hand. He didn't think he could take much more.

No, he was strong. He could wait her out.

If matters were reversed, she would be flat on her back, naked and accepting him. She'd beg him to slide into her hard and fast.

Zack squeezed his eyes closed but the image popped into his head. Moisture beaded at the engorged tip of his cock. Kelsey's thumb captured the drops and smoothed it along his length.

Kelsey slowly turned and stood by his side. He opened his eyes and gave her a sideways glance. She seemed fascinated by his cock.

That only made him swell more.

"Do you want me to stop?" she asked.

What kind of question was that? Especially while she was still pumping his cock? He should tell her to stop, if only to show his self-control. Over his body.

"No." He would turn this into his favor. He would make her wet and ready and in need of his touch just as he felt right now. And then when she was right about to come, *he'd* ask if she wanted him to stop.

He watched her hand as it went up and down, faster, faster, until his heart couldn't keep up anymore. He felt the sweat beading at his hairline. How much longer before she gave up and decided to sink onto him? He didn't think he would last much longer.

Was she close? Would she be able to catch up, or did she think he could rebound fast? Did she feel *anything* other than a hard cock in her hand?

He looked at her and their gazes collided. He wanted to look away. He felt vulnerable. Needy and powerless.

Zack dropped his hands from behind his head and slapped his hand over hers. She stopped as his fingers flexed. He wrestled for self-control, breathing deeply. For one brief moment he waited for her next command.

Zack swallowed hard when he saw the dazed look in her eye. She wasn't going to make a move.

He tore his gaze away. Angry at himself for that moment of indecision, Zack curled his hands over hers and pumped his cock. Tight, hard, just the way he liked it, until he felt the release boiling inside him.

He glanced at her. He hadn't planned to. She watched every instinctive, primal move he made. She caught the emotions race across his face before he could hide them. She saw everything as he let go.

Zack felt the orgasm from the soles of his feet. It kicked him, sparking a wildfire. It roared through his blood until it poured out of him.

He held back the guttural cry as his legs shook. His head spun and the black dots swirled before his eyes. He stumbled against something solid before realizing it was Kelsey. She stood by his side, propping him up.

He reluctantly let go of her hand that held his cock. He wobbled as each breath burned his lungs. Zack didn't look her in the eye. He felt too exposed because of that one glimpse of weakness.

He didn't say anything, either. Even if he could put two words together, the ones he chose would be too telling, or too misleading.

Kelsey's arm around his waist tightened. It was almost like a hug before she withdrew. She moved away, her mouth brushing against his shoulder. Was that a kiss?

"I'll see you tomorrow, Zack," she said as she walked away. "Good night."

He stared at her, dumbfounded, as she walked away. Those touches couldn't have been from tenderness, he decided as he watched her slip on her flip-flops before grabbing her towel. She returned to her room and slid the door behind her without a backward glance.

Zack waited until she disappeared into her room before he staggered to the pool and fell in with a loud splash.

CHAPTER FIVE

ZACK NEEDED COFFEE AND lots of it. He glared at the morning sun with bleary eyes, and decided he needed to get off of this farm. He was hungry, grumpy, and in need of a certain woman's companionship.

At least he found the food. It was a country breakfast set outside on gingham and fine lace tablecloths. The picnic table groaned and buckled under the amount of mouth-watering food, but the buffet style was a bad stroke of luck. His mind superimposed Kelsey—naked, wet, and arching over the fine china—and he had to leave before he sampled the gourmet meal.

He was sure his grumpiness would disappear once he found Kelsey. That proved more difficult. He had called her room, but there had been no answer. A knock on her door an hour later offered no results.

Now he was searching for her. He shook his head in self-disgust. This did not bode well. Usually the women were seeking *him* out.

He wasn't going to worry. Once he got Kelsey into bed

and gave her the kind of pleasure that had her clinging, the roles would reverse. She wouldn't stray far after one night. He was sure of it.

"Zack! There you are."

Zack froze when he heard Shirley calling out for him. He did not want to deal with the woman first thing in the morning. Or the afternoon . . . or at anytime now that he thought about it.

He reluctantly turned around and narrowed his eyes when he saw Shirley approach him. She wore a scarlet and black kimono, but what really got his attention was the scarlet turban.

"Are you feeling all right?"

Shirley seemed to bristle at his concern. "Yes, of course." She twitched the hem of her kimono so it would hang straight. "Why do you ask?"

"You're walking around in your bathrobe."

"This is what I wear around my house every morning," she informed him as she patted her turban.

"If you insist."

"I want you to know that this isn't working out," she announced.

Zack frowned. "What isn't?"

"This"—she paused delicately—"*arrangement* we have."

He closed his eyes. "Never say it like that again."

"I need a guy who can perform."

The waiter walking by them stumbled and darted a glance their way before hurrying away. "Shirley . . ." Zack warned.

"A guy who is up and ready for action twenty-four, seven."

He felt the guests' attention zooming in on him. "What are you doing?" he asked through clenched teeth.

"Zack," Shirley lowered her voice, her scarlet mouth barely moving, "you are ruining my reputation."

He stared at the older woman with incomprehension. "Therefore you feel a need to ruin mine?"

"I brought you here to remind people of my sexual allure," she whispered. "You are not helping when you run after a sweet young thing half my age."

Zack felt a stab of guilt. "I'm sorry. I hadn't considered that." He never combined the ideas of Shirley and sex to begin with, and he didn't want to start any time soon. "Kelsey—"

"Say no more. I got an idea." Her eyes gleamed with anticipation. "Just follow my lead."

His gut instincts were sounding all the alarms from that suggestion. "Do I have to?"

She shrugged. "I've thought this through. It's either that or Kelsey and I will have to fight over you. Don't worry about me. I may have had a hip replacement, but I still can take her down."

"I'm following. I'm following," Zack promised. "But up to a point."

"Now, Zack, honey," she said a little louder. "I understand that when I took you on that you were new to your . . . career."

Already he wasn't sure where she was going with this, but it didn't look good for him.

"You needed someone with vast experience." She placed her hand over her heart. "Someone like me."

"Spare me the details," he said under his breath.

"I'm going to come right out and say it."

Zack braced himself. "You're enjoying this, aren't you?"

Shirley's eyes sparkled. "You need more practice."

He remained still as her words echoed in his head. "Excuse me?"

"Increase your stamina."

"This is your bright idea?" he asked in a low, dangerous growl.

"Add some more moves to your repertoire," she suggested with a dismissive wave of her hand.

His gaze locked with hers. "You are pushing your luck."

"In fact, I don't want to see you again until tonight," she declared before looking out from the corner of her eye to check on their audience. "Then you can show me what you've learned."

"Shirley," he said softly, "you should count your blessings that you are my godmother. If anyone else . . ."

"No!" She held her hand up. "No amount of begging is going to change my mind. If you want me—if you really, really want me . . ."

"I really, really want you to stop."

"Then you will go right now and learn some moves to dazzle me." She flicked her wrist, the sunlight catching her jeweled rings. "Be gone."

"Oh, I get it," Zack said as he folded his arms across his chest. It was either that or wrap his hands around Shirley's neck and squeeze. "You found someone else to hook up with and you don't want me hanging around."

"Now, now." She patted her hand against his cheek. "Don't be jealous. I never promised to be faithful."

"He can have you."

"Zack, don't give up. You can still win my affections. May the best lover win."

He watched Shirley stride off with a regal air, her pride

fully restored. Zack wasn't sure how his godmother did it, but the woman always seemed to get the best of him.

He wasn't going to hang around to see the reaction of the wedding party. He didn't care what they thought about him, but he didn't trust how he would respond to the stares and remarks. He knew he wouldn't maintain the cover story Shirley concocted.

Anyway, he had more important things to do. Like find Kelsey. He strolled around the party barn and the farmhouse, but Kelsey was nowhere to be found. Zack walked along the wraparound porch and looked out into the acres behind the house. He wanted to find her before the wedding started.

"Zack?"

Zack stopped at the sound of a male voice. He turned and found a man standing behind him. The guy wore what appeared to be de rigueur for this social set—a polo shirt, long shorts, and a pastel sweater tied at his shoulders. He didn't look familiar, but then, these guys were all beginning to look alike.

The man approached him in a friendly manner. "Zack Cooper?"

"Yeah?" he asked carefully.

His eyes lit up. "The guy who developed the software patch for—"

"Ssh!" He covered the man's mouth with his hand and looked around. No one else was on the porch, but that didn't mean the solitude would last long. "Don't announce it."

The guy's eyes widened. "It is you!" His voice was muffled from Zack's hand. "I knew it!"

Zack tightened his hold and dipped his head so he could lock eyes with the guy. "What part of 'don't announce it' do you not understand?"

The man's eyebrows crinkled. "Sorry."

Zack lowered his hand. "What do you want?"

The guy rubbed his mouth with the back of his hand. "Why are you acting like a male escort?"

"Long story." A thought occurred to him and he grabbed the guy by the collar. "You haven't told anyone, have you?"

"And let everyone try to sell you their product?" His voice was high and rushed. "Why would I do that?"

Zack gave the collar a warning twist. "What's your name?"

"Sam Japp." His cheeks were turning red.

The name meant nothing to him. "Why are you bothering me?"

"I'm with a start-up company. Japp & Associates? Maybe you've heard of us?" His expectant smile dimmed when Zack shook his head. "I've been trying to meet with you in Seattle for weeks, but I can't get past your receptionist."

Zack let go of the collar. The guy had the goods to give *him* a twist. He needed to contain the problem with a minimum of fuss. "Do you have a card?"

Sam produced one with the mind-boggling speed of a magician.

"Here's the deal." Zack swiped the card from Sam's fingertips. "If you can keep quiet about me for the weekend, then I will meet you next week at my office. You'll get twenty minutes to pitch whatever you want."

Sam perked up. "Okay."

Zack looked at him from the corner of his eye. Sam made him think of a golden retriever ready to chase the ball. "I'm not promising you anything." He felt it was important to make that clear. "Nothing is guaranteed. Got it?"

"Got it."

Already he could tell Sam didn't have a cutthroat mentality. If Zack had been in Sam's position, he'd have been making the most of the guy's uncomfortable situation.

Zack started to walk away and tracked back. He narrowed his eyes as he stared at Sam. "Do you know Kelsey Morgan?"

"Of course." Sam looked momentarily confused by the change of subject. "She and my fiancée are best friends."

"Don't say *anything* to Kelsey."

"Oookay." Sam grabbed his collar before Zack could try to get it again. "But seriously, what's the big deal? So what if you're dating an old lady? That doesn't automatically make you a gigolo."

"Old lady? I'm not dating an old lady." Had he cut off the oxygen to Sam's brain? "Oh, yeah. *Shirley.*"

He was going to get even with Shirley. He didn't know how, or when, or what could match the aggravation he was going through now. All he knew was that he would get his revenge.

Zack knew his mood was darkening. He needed to find Kelsey and set his seduction before all he did was growl and bark. "Do you know where Kelsey is?"

Sam pointed to the back of the house. "Yeah, she's hiding out in the gardens. It's way back there." He made a face. "I forgot. I wasn't supposed to tell anyone."

Zack felt his eyelids lower. "That doesn't give me a lot of confidence that you'll keep my secret."

The guy was taken aback by the connection but he quickly recovered with a smile. "That's different."

He scoffed at the answer. "Yeah, how?"

Sam's smile widened. "I'll profit from yours."

"True." Zack patted him on the back. "Very true. Thanks, man."

Zack headed for the trail that led to the gardens. The riot of colors and blooms made a romantic backdrop for wedding photos, while the old trees and large plants shaded strolling guests.

That garden was also a good place to hide. Why had Kelsey felt the need to disappear? Was she getting away from the wedding activities or from him? Or was she feeling shy about what they did last night?

If that was the case, then that was a good sign, Zack decided as he strode past a lush, dark green hedge. If Kelsey was avoiding him because of last night, then it meant she felt something more than a cock in her hand.

He was going to drag her out of her hiding place and show her how to have fun. This time around he was going to gain control.

"Can you believe Kelsey?" Zack heard a woman on the other side of the shrubbery say. "What is she doing hanging around a gigolo?"

Zack slowed down and tilted his ear in the direction of the hedge.

"Well, Margot," another woman who spoke through her nose said. "She is the last of us to get married, and there's no man in sight. That's why she's being so difficult. I'm sure of it."

"I heard she's blowing off everything," Margot said. "She always handles the behind-the-scenes stuff. At my wedding she was the liaison for that horrible florist."

Zack stopped walking. Kelsey was trying to get out of doing stuff for the wedding? There had to be a good reason.

Kelsey Morgan was a woman who was generous with her time. He got the impression Kelsey was always willing to push up her sleeves and dig in as an act of friendship.

"Mimi was counting on her," the other woman complained. "The only reason she asked Kelsey to be a bridesmaid is because she does the work. That's why I had her as my maid of honor."

Zack drew his head back sharply. Kelsey was always asked to be a bridesmaid because she was *good at it*?

"Why did any of us ask her? She doesn't need any direction, she doesn't complain, and she doesn't expect anything out of it." Margot's voice faded as they moved further away from the hedge. "So what if she's a sorority sister? She doesn't belong."

"She'll figure that out once we're all married and she wants to use us as contacts."

Kelsey couldn't see Zack's expression as he listened to Pinky's remarks. When she had seen him stop, a part of her wanted to shoo him away. Divert his attention. Anything that would keep him from finding out how much she didn't fit in around here.

But nothing brilliant came to mind, and then it was too late. He heard everything. She took a fortifying sip of the cold Bellini in her hand, wondering what Zack was going to think of her now. She knew she sounded like a pathetic loser. A victim. The underdog.

She was doing her best to appear unaffected and unconcerned by her sorority sisters' words. They didn't burn, which was a pleasant surprise, but she still felt the sting. At least she had figured this out before overhearing conversations like that one, otherwise it would have been devastating.

Zack looked away from the hedge and continued his walk. She knew the moment he saw her lying in the shade on a colorful hammock. He hesitated and peered at the cluster of trees before veering off his path.

She felt jittery as she watched him approach. Zack's stride made her think of a warrior. Proud and aggressive as he conquered the distance between them. She'd like to think she looked like a seductive empress, waiting for him to impress her, but she probably looked as vulnerable as she felt.

"I guess you heard that," he said, showing no expression.

She shrugged. "Pinky's voice can bend steel."

He motioned toward the hedge. "Why do you put up with it?"

She took another sip of her drink and savored the taste of peach and champagne. "When I rushed the sorority, I had heard rumors that I was going to be blackballed because I wasn't anywhere near their social sphere as they originally thought, so I did everything in my power to become indispensable. It worked and I've been using that method ever since."

"Until this wedding."

She felt the wry tug of her mouth. "I watched a bunch of wedding videos and found myself a second-class citizen. The Cinderella to the ugly stepsister, only this was of my own making."

"What do you plan to do about it?"

"I'm going to be selfish and attend as a guest." She snuggled deeper into the hammock, feeling decadent. All she needed was a few pillows and some half-naked guys fanning her with giant leaves, and she'd be set.

"Where do I fit in?" A look of uncertainty swept across his face. "Please tell me I'm not the Prince Charming."

Kelsey smiled at that, although the idea made her heart thump. "Hannah suggested I wouldn't be bothered if I had a hot guy at my side."

"And you picked me?"

"You were the only one that was remotely interesting," she admitted. It was the understatement of the century, but he didn't need to know that.

Zack crossed his arms. "I'm also more expensive."

"So?" Was he going to give her a discount because he felt sorry for her? "Hey, don't pity me. I knew what some of these women were like. I thought I could bide my time, work around it, and they would admire and respect me. I was wrong. Now, I don't know why I even bothered."

"Won't it hurt your work?" Zack leaned against one of the tree trunks next to her feet. "An art buyer needs clients. The wives of CEOs would be helpful."

"Do you think they would help me?" She rolled her eyes at the thought. "Not without getting something more in return."

He gave a slight nod. "You seem to understand the system."

"For an outsider looking in?" She bit her tongue, disliking how she let the bitterness creep in.

Something dark flickered in his eyes. "I'm saying it as one survivor to another."

"Cheers to that." She raised her glass before taking another healthy sip. It was strange that in all her years with the sorority, she never felt like she was part of a team as she did right this moment with Zack.

"But Kelsey, if you're going to pay a thousand dollars a day—plus expenses and add-ons . . ."

She groaned. "I think it's very sweet that you're worried about my spending."

"I am not sweet!" He stepped away from the tree. "Wanting you to get your money's worth doesn't make me sweet."

Kelsey cocked her head to one side and studied Zack. "Does my not having sex with you make you nervous?"

"No." His voice sounded hard and final.

"If you say so," she murmured against the rim of her glass. She choked on her next sip as Zack reached out and grasped her ankle.

"The point of our agreement is getting the both of us naked and thoroughly—"

"Am I complaining?" she asked as she watched his large hand glide toward her knee.

"No," Zack said, "but you aren't fully satisfied, either."

"I'll keep that in mind." Her voice sounded high and tight. She kept her gaze on his hand as he skimmed her kneecap with his palm. Hot, tingly sensations pricked the back of her knees. She wanted to wiggle underneath him but kept still.

"Have you met your goal?"

"Pretty much." She didn't look away from his hand. "I haven't lifted a finger this morning, and I'm swinging on a hammock, drinking a Bellini"—she raised her almost empty glass—"and have the undivided attention of a hot guy."

His fingertips flirted underneath her thin shorts. "Is that all you wanted?"

No, she wanted him to slide his hand in her shorts and push her underwear aside. Rub the callused heel against her swollen clitoris before sinking his finger into her wet slit. Even then, that wouldn't be all she wanted.

Zack made tiny circles with his fingertips on her soft inner thigh.

"What do you want to do," Zack asked in a deceptively lazy manner, "to make this wedding better?"

The question doused her back to reality. She didn't want to think about the wedding. She didn't want to be here anymore. All she wanted to do was go back to her room with Zack and forget everything.

Kelsey looked away from Zack's intent gaze. "I wanted some video clips that showed I was the life of the party," she said in a rushed mutter before moving her leg out from under his touch. "That was an unrealistic part of my plan."

He clamped his hand on her hip, preventing her from turning away. "No, it's not."

Kelsey wanted to scoff at Zack. "How can I have candid shots of my wild center-of-attention moment when I'm not a party animal?"

"I'll teach you everything I know."

Her sex clenched at the promise. His rough and sexy voice made her edgy. Kelsey took a steady breath. "I was hoping to keep my clothes on during the making of this video."

Zack took her drink and set it down on the grass. "Kelsey, I will make sure you have the time of your life this weekend. The camera will capture nothing but images of you laughing, smiling, and enjoying the party."

She tried to figure out his angle. No one did anything for her without expecting something in return. "Why do you want to help me out?"

He leaned over her, his hands bracketing her head. She inhaled his scent as his gaze snagged hers. He was so close that all she had to do was tip her chin and she could brush her lips against him.

"My goal," he said in that husky, low tone that made her toes curl, "is to give you pleasure."

Oh, wow. Did he have any idea how potent those simple words were? He wanted to give her pleasure. Pleasure her. Make sure that she was having the time of her life. She wanted to grab the promise and hold it close, but at the same time she wanted to inspect it for hidden strings.

"This is an add-on, isn't it?" She slapped her hand against her forehead. "I knew I should have looked at the price list."

Zack's lopsided grin mesmerized her. "No, Kelsey. Consider this part of the package. Now come on"—he grabbed her hands and pulled her off of the hammock—"it's time to do whatever you please."

CHAPTER SIX

KELSEY'S SQUEAL—PART FEAR, part laughter—alerted Zack and he turned to find her. The world stopped, his heart dangling in his chest, as he watched Kelsey toss in the air.

He saw it all in slow motion. Kelsey's arms splayed out wide, but her legs pressed firmly together. Her hair floated around her face in waves. Her eyes grew wide when she began to fall. The squeal dragged out of her mouth as she tumbled down from the air until she landed on the huge, sturdy blanket surrounded by young men.

Zack smiled as he enjoyed the pleasure shimmering from her eyes, the high color racing across her cheeks, and the smile stretching across her face. His chest swelled to the point of hurting, knowing that she was having fun because of him.

The music in the background suddenly blared to full volume. The world moved again. It was like someone hit the PLAY button again.

"Okay, Zack, give it to me straight," Hannah said as she turned off the small video camera. "How many Bellinis did it take to loosen Kelsey up?"

Zack shook his head. "That is all Kelsey." Why was everyone surprised? Was he the only one who knew Kelsey was just waiting to have fun? That she was more than willing to test her wild streak if given the chance?

"She hasn't asked the time? Or if the flowers were in place? Or"—she pointed her finger in the air, as though this was the real test—"if Mimi was mad at her?"

"Not for the past hour."

"Amazing." Hannah smiled as she watched Kelsey scramble inelegantly off the blanket while the men threatened to toss her higher. "Too bad you won't be on call for future bridesmaid gigs."

That made Zack pause. What was he doing? He wasn't going to be there for the next wedding. Sure, Kelsey wouldn't need him, but he'd like to be there. He felt very protective of Kelsey and wanted to be her backup.

Possessive, too, he realized when he saw one of the groomsmen getting close to Kelsey. Zack strode toward them. He must have flashed a threatening look because the guy hastily dropped his hand and was long gone by the time he was at Kelsey's side.

"Zack," Kelsey greeted him with a smile as she grasped his arm. "You know how to throw a great party."

"Kelsey?" Pinky's voice screeched and the party went silent. Zack turned to see the woman stomp down the stone steps and confront Kelsey. "Mimi is very upset with you. She needs you to help her get ready right away."

"The wedding is in four hours," Kelsey reminded the other bridesmaid. "What's the problem?"

"Mimi can't find her shoes," she announced.

Kelsey blinked. "I didn't take them."

Pinky gave a long-suffering sigh. "We *know* that. We want you to find them."

Kelsey didn't move, and Zack knew she was debating on keeping her goals or surrendering. He placed his hand on her back, silently letting her know he was there for her. He knew it would be easier for her to do what was asked than make waves. He would understand if she made that decision, and help her if she needed it, but he hoped she wouldn't.

"I don't know where to look," Kelsey finally said. "I'm sorry, but I can't help you."

"Excuse me?" Two spots of anger burned on Pinky's cheeks.

"I can't help you." She said it louder. Zack also noticed the words came out easier.

Pinky huffed. "I can't believe you're acting this way."

Kelsey shrugged. "Get used to it."

Okay, Kelsey, time to pull back. If he knew Morse code, he'd tap the advice against her spine.

"You're dumping your friends who need you for a guy?"

Kelsey's back went rigid. Zack could tell that the accusation went against everything she stood for. "No, I'm—"

"A guy you have to *pay* for him to show you a good time?"

Zack stepped in front of Kelsey and glared at Pinky. "You need to watch what you say."

Pinky shoved her hand a few inches from Zack's face, but didn't look at him. "Excuse me? Am I talking to you? Do you have anything to do with this?"

For one brief moment, Zack wanted to tell Pinky exactly who she was talking to. No one had dismissed him like that for a long time, and the last person who did so was still regretting it. Zack reached out and lowered the woman's hand with all the restraint he could muster. "What was that?"

Kelsey stepped into the fray, as if his lethally soft voice alerted her. She pulled Pinky to the side so hard that Zack was surprised by the speed and strength Kelsey displayed. He watched as she said something fierce and obviously upsetting to Pinky.

Pinky reluctantly walked back with Kelsey right behind. "Sorry," she muttered. "That was uncalled for."

"Yeah, no problem." It was weird now that he thought about it, but the only one who treated him with respect was Kelsey. She didn't think any less of him than everyone else.

He sensed Kelsey by his side. "What did you say to her?" Zack asked as they watched Pinky's angry retreat.

"It doesn't matter."

He looked down at Kelsey, wondering how often her efforts had gone unappreciated. "It does to me. Thanks."

She gave him a shy glance. "You're welcome."

"Hey"—his gaze snapped back to where Pinky had been— "she didn't say sorry to you."

"Don't hold your breath on that."

"Kelsey, we need to work on you." He draped his arm around her shoulders. "You have to stand up for yourself. Tell people what you want. Don't take no for an answer."

"It's harder than you think," she complained.

"Give it a try." He felt her burrow into his side and realized he could get addicted to the feeling. "Practice on me."

"Zack?" she asked dutifully.

"Yes?"

She lifted her face and looked directly into his eyes. "I want you to . . ." She broke eye contact and pressed her lips together.

"Come on, Kelsey," he coaxed softly. "You can do it."

"I want you to kiss me." She looked up at him. "Right now. And I'm not taking no for an answer."

He reached for her, anticipation heating his blood.

She took a quick step back. "But only if you want to!"

"Kelsey," he said with a groan. "We were so close."

"I don't want a kiss because you feel like you *have* to."

He knew what she was talking about. How many women had he dated who were the gracious hostess and perfect dinner companion not because they wanted to be, but because they knew it was required of their status as his date.

"Kelsey . . ." He slid the crook of his finger under her chin and tipped her face up toward him. "I guarantee that if that ever happens, you'll know."

He claimed her lips with a swift move. Although he braced himself for the jolt, it still took him by surprise. The sparkling sensation fizzed through him, and he delved his tongue into her mouth, wanting more. She tasted sweet, but the way she kissed him was hot and spicy. He promised himself one more, then another, until they melded into one long, wild kiss.

He lifted his mouth away from hers when his lungs protested, leaving her breathless and clinging on to him. "Did that feel like an obligated kiss?" he asked against her swollen lips. He gave a satisfied growl when she shook her head.

"Ah, young love," Shirley's voice floated by them. "Who am I to compete with that?"

"What?" Kelsey croaked the word. She stared at her sorority sisters and blinked. Sure, they were exhausted after the beautiful wedding and extravagant reception, but these women couldn't be serious! "What do you mean there's no shivaree? We have to do it!"

Pinky rolled her eyes and clucked her tongue. "You should have thought about that earlier, Kelsey. If you had organized it instead of"—she gave a long, knowing look at Zack—"goofing off, this wouldn't have happened."

"What is a shivaree?" Zack asked, standing behind her as he placed his hand on her bare shoulder.

"It's a tradition our sorority adopted," Kelsey informed him. "Some time during the night, we gather round the honeymoon suite and serenade the couple."

"—while banging pots and pans—" Hannah added.

"—until the bride and groom open the door and throw coins and sweets at us."

"Okay . . . why?" he asked.

Kelsey tiredly leaned against him, grateful for the warmth and strength he unknowingly provided. "Like I said, it's tradition."

"We used to kidnap the bride and make the groom look for her," Hannah said as she gave a dark look at Honey, the blondest sorority sister, "but we had to stop that after the time the cops were called in."

"Some grooms really can't take a joke," Pinky grumbled.

"Hey," Honey protested, "he was worried."

"You mean horny," Hannah corrected.

"You guys," Kelsey raised her voice, determined to keep the bridesmaids focused. "We have to do the shivaree. Mimi is expecting it."

"Max probably isn't," Margot said as she walked away to rejoin the reception party. "We don't want to give him a heart attack."

"We might," Kelsey called out to her. "Especially if Mimi refuses to have sex because she thinks there're going to be uninvited guests."

"Sorry, Kelsey." Pinky looked anything but repentant as she followed Margot. "You should have thought about this earlier."

She watched the sisters walk away, her mouth hanging

open. Kelsey didn't know what she could do or say to keep them from going back to the reception.

"I don't believe this." She sat down on the stone patio step with a thump, her coffee-colored bridesmaid gown billowing out around her. "The one time I'm not at their beck and call, and they turn their backs on me."

Zack sat down next to her, unconcerned about the state of his exquisitely tailored suit. "Don't let it get to you."

"I used to be able to tell them what needed to be done, and then they did it." She brushed the hair out of her eyes, feeling dazed and off balance. "What happened?"

"You changed the status quo."

"I expected a few bitchy comments. Maybe a lecture or two, but this—this is mutiny!" She sat up straight as a thought occurred to her. "This is because everyone but Hannah is married. I bet that's it. They don't need me anymore."

"You don't know that."

Kelsey wasn't too sure. She was now obsolete, and it showed. She sagged against him and felt her lip wobble when he pulled her closer. "I guess when it comes right down to it, I never really had a say in anything. They just let me think I did so I'd do the work."

"I know how you feel." His words came out choppy, almost hesitant. "You pull away the one thing you offer in a relationship and you find out there was nothing else there to keep supporting it."

"Yep." A lot of good that did her. She stared at the reception, the dancing guests blurring before her. The bridesmaids were kicking off their heels and letting loose. Once again, she was in the shadows and trying to make something work. Only this time she wasn't alone.

"It's going to be okay," Zack promised her softly. "These women aren't who you want to back you up."

"But I'm doing the one thing I swore I'd never do. I'm sabotaging Mimi's wedding."

He gently rubbed his hand along her bare arm. "This isn't your fault."

"I always did the coin and chocolate bags beautifully, and I would make sure there was a boom box with the bride's least favorite song. I used to bring the pots and pans, too." She leaned her head against his shoulder and sighed deeply. "Now that I think about it, that was probably overkill."

"Yeah, probably." Zack's arm shook under her head and she got the feeling he was trying hard not to laugh at the depths of her planning for what should be a spontaneous event.

"I told the other bridesmaids that I wasn't going to do it this time, but did anyone take over? Nope." She shouldn't be surprised. Knowing her sorority sisters, they had no intentions of picking up the slack and had waited for her to jump in like she always did.

"So you and I will do it."

What? Kelsey sat up and gave him an incredulous look. He looked serious. "Thanks, Zack, but you need more than two people to do a shivaree."

"What about Hannah and what's-his-name. Sam? They'd do it for you. And I know Shirley wouldn't need too much convincing."

"No, it's a sorority tradition. If the sisters refused to do it, then it's not going to happen. And I'll get blamed for it. I can see it all now."

"So you're just going to give up?"

"Yes." Kelsey rose from the step and brushed off the dirt

from her gown. "No one is going to listen to me now. Mimi is probably jumpy as a cat wondering when they're going to be interrupted."

"I'll ask the bridesmaids."

"You?" She whirled around and stared at him. "Zack, I think it's really sweet you want to help, but they aren't going to listen to you any more than they will me."

"It's worth a try," he said, watching her closely. "All you need to do is say the word."

She took a step back without realizing it. "Why do you want to help me?"

He lifted one shoulder. "Because I do."

It wasn't that simple. "You're not going to get anything out of it," she warned him. "Except aggravation for trying to coordinate everything."

"I want to help you out because it will make you happy."

His sincerity tugged at her. "You don't need to help me."

She didn't need him to make her happy, but she stopped just short of telling him that. Zack had no idea that his offer meant way too much to her. If he knew that, the balance of power would shift between them.

"Oh, I get it." He leaned back, resting his elbows on a higher stone step. "You don't want to owe me. Don't worry, you won't."

"No," she said through clenched teeth, "that's not it at all. I'm used to taking care of these things on my own."

"I'm sure you do. You probably buy your own birthday present instead of being surprised."

She put her hands on her hips. "So what if I do?"

"Kelsey," he said, exasperation tingeing his voice, "how

can anyone show you how much they love and appreciate you if you won't let them?"

"I'm not stopping anyone." Her voice was almost a whisper. It was embarrassing to admit that. "No one feels the need to show it. At least to me."

"How do you know?"

She wanted to pace. Yell and walk away. "Because," she said very carefully as the emotions pressed against her chest, "whenever I give someone the opportunity, all I wind up with is disappointment."

"Not always."

"Observe Exhibit A." She gestured at the reception, where the sorority sisters were taking over the dance floor.

"They aren't your real friends," Zack said as he rose from the stone steps. "Yeah, they disappointed you, but it's not the end of the world."

"True." If Zack had disappointed her, she would still be reeling.

"If Mimi doesn't get the traditional send-off," he continued, "then it's not a big deal."

"No, I think that's a big deal." She pressed her hand over her heart. "Something went wrong *because* of me."

She looked at where the honeymoon cottage sat. It was quiet and alone in the darkness. Expectant.

Kelsey didn't have a lot in common with Mimi, but she knew how that cottage felt. She closed her eyes. "Zack? Would you he—" —she cleared her throat as the word caught—"help me?"

She gave a start when she felt Zack clasp his hand over hers. Kelsey looked up and her heart did a flip when she saw the understanding in his dark eyes.

"With pleasure."

CHAPTER SEVEN

KELSEY CURLED HER HAND around Zack's arm as they made their way back to the farmhouse. "That was the best shivaree ever!"

"How can you say that?" Zack asked as he rubbed the side of his head. "I was pelted with complimentary bottles of shampoo."

"Yeah, sorry about that. The coin and chocolate bags I made were soft for a reason."

"And conditioner. And mouthwash." He was going to have some interesting bumps and bruises tomorrow.

"Oh, you poor baby," she teased. Kelsey stopped and pressed her hand against the sore spot on his head. "Do you want me to kiss it better?"

"Later." When he wanted Kelsey to kiss him, it wouldn't be a tender peck on his head, and it wouldn't be around the other guests still wandering through the dark grounds.

"Zack, there you are." Shirley tapped his shoulder.

Zack groaned. The older woman's timing was the worst. If she made a scene, all bets were off. He wanted to be with

Kelsey tonight, and he wasn't going to let his flaky godmother stop that.

Zack reluctantly pulled away from Kelsey and faced Shirley, who wore a silver sequined evening gown with elbow length black gloves, a black feather boa, and a long, black peacock feather in her hair. "Yes," he asked, doing his best to be polite. "What is it?"

"Don't wait up for me tonight, okay?"

"I'll try not to." He stared at her, silently communicating with his eyes for her to go away.

Shirley wasn't getting the message. "Unless you want to come play strip poker with us."

Zack kept his face straight, but it felt like his eyes bulged. He was afraid to ask who the other players were going to be. "No, thanks."

"Suit yourself." She shrugged and walked off into the dark. "Good night."

"Good night," Zack said with feeling and relaxed when she disappeared from his sight.

"Hey," Kelsey lightly punched him in the arm. "Maybe I wanted to play poker with them."

He gave her an incredulous look. "Are you kidding me?"

"Yes, I am," she responded with a smile. "But you should have asked me."

"I'll remember that next time."

"Good. By the way, thank you," she whispered before brushing her kiss against his cheek. "How did you manage to get everyone to agree to do the shivaree?"

"It was simple," he said gruffly, wondering why the brief touch made him feel warm. "I could tell who the decision makers were of this group, so I approached them. These guys

always have followers, so it didn't take long to get a group together. I played on a hunch that if the sorority sisters were ter-
ritorial about their traditions, they would want to look like
they started the trend rather than join in."

"Wow." She drew back, her face registering her surprise.
"You sound like some of the CEOs I deal with."

Zack grimaced. It was time to change the subject. "What is
a shivaree for? Other than to make a nuisance out of yourself?"

"I'm not sure," she admitted as they climbed the porch
steps. "Probably to drive away bad spirits. Our ancestors were
always big on the bad spirits."

He opened the front door of the farmhouse and guided
her inside the large entrance. "Nothing short of a miracle is
going to protect that marriage."

"Zack, you are such a cynic."

"Don't tell me you're for marriage after going through all
those weddings." But that would be just like Kelsey.

"I believe in the power of love." A dreamy smile flitted
across her mouth. "Don't you?"

"No."

She made a face. "You're hopeless," she announced and
headed down the hall for her room.

"I believe . . ." He hesitated, not sure if he wanted to tell
how he really felt. "I believe that the only power love has is to
reveal your strengths."

She stopped from searching through her drawstring purse
and looked up. "Aww . . ."

"And your weaknesses," he finished.

She pressed her lips in a firm line. "You should have stopped
while you were ahead." She shook the card key in her hand.
"That almost got you an invitation to my bed."

He looked at her, at her bedroom door, and then back at her. "You mean I'm *not* invited?"

She leaned against the closed door. "Do you want to be?" she asked softly.

He stepped closer until his knee brushed up against her dress. The swish of fabric echoed in his head. "That wasn't the question."

She looked down at her shoes. "I bet Shirley didn't expect to be by herself this weekend."

His mouth sagged open. Why was she worried about Shirley at this moment? Or was she waiting for him to say something? Did she want him to make the decision for her? "What do *you* want?"

Zack watched the muscles in her throat tighten. She opened her mouth, but he sensed what she was going to say and interrupted.

"Don't invite me in because you feel like you have to." He rested his arm against the wall and leaned closer. Her summery scent went straight to his cock. "Or because of the shivaree."

Her eyes flashed angrily. "I don't have sex out of gratitude."

"Good to know." He moved in closer, until his mouth hovered above hers. "Invite me in because you want to." He lowered his voice even more. "Because you want me."

She looked into his eyes. He was trying hard to play it cool, but his chest hurt from waiting. He didn't know where he stood with Kelsey. He wanted her to want him as much as he wanted her.

Kelsey looked away. "Good night, Zack."

He closed his eyes briefly as the disappointment crashed

through him. "Good night, Kelsey." He took a step back as she worked the key. He didn't say anything, didn't move as she slipped into her room and closed the door behind her.

It should have been a good sign that she turned him away. That she didn't feel obligated. But, damn, if he didn't want to kick that door down and let her know that she made the wrong decision.

Kelsey paced her room a half hour later, kicking the folds of her fluffy bathrobe when she turned and marched to the other wall. She felt uptight. Needy.

No. She raised her hands up, stopping that train of thought before it went any further. She was going to get through this night. Kelsey determinedly lay on the bed, snapping the hem of the bathrobe over her legs. She crossed her arms and stared at the ceiling.

She wasn't going to go crazy. She wasn't going to go hunt Zack down. She refused to act that way over something that was just sex.

Kelsey's sigh dragged from her lungs. It wasn't true. She *wished* it was just sex. She could handle that. That was easier to ignore.

She wanted Zack, and he was hers for the taking. But she wanted more. Yeah, she was being greedy, and her only excuse was that she was falling for him.

Kelsey knew it was better that he wasn't emotionally involved with her. Zack Cooper was way out of her league. Once the money was out of the equation, he would take control so fast, and she would hang on for the ride.

But money would never be out of the equation. Zack's

job was to give women pleasure, and he went to the highest bidder. He was probably with Shirley right now.

Jealousy twisted her stomach until she wanted to gag. Kelsey vaulted off the bed and paced some more. She had to get out of here, but once she got out of the room, all bets were off. It was better if she stayed put.

She peeked out of the sliding door, wondering if she should do some laps in the pool. *No! Don't look there!* Kelsey tried to avoid looking, remembering what happened the last time, but she couldn't stop herself.

She did a double take. Zack lay on a lawn chair by the pool. Kelsey squinted and pressed her face against the glass. He really was there, wearing a dark T-shirt and faded jeans.

He wasn't in Shirley's room.

He was hers for the taking.

Kelsey turned away from the sliding door. Was she willing to have one night with Zack, knowing it wouldn't go any further? Would she regret it, or would she regret not going for it?

She was going to go for it. Her nerves fluttered before she turned on the lights. She walked back to the sliding glass door and slowly opened it, her heart pounding in her ears.

Zack's head turned at the sound of the door. It was almost as if he had been waiting. Kelsey clenched the bathrobe tighter to her chest. She felt vulnerable and uncertain. She wished he would make the first move, but he didn't get up from the chair. He didn't say anything. Zack simply waited.

She was going to have to make the first move. Kelsey wasn't going out there. What she wanted to do with him required a bed and lots of privacy. She reached out her hand and beckoned him with the curl of her finger.

She had no idea how liberating and powerful that one move felt. Tension swirled inside her as he unfolded from the chair and rose. As Zack slowly made his way to her room, the pulse in her neck jumped wildly with each step.

Zack stood in front of her, his chest rising and falling. His eyes were hooded, as if he didn't want her to see the lust glittering. His features were sharpened with restraint.

"I changed my mind," she announced softly, but he still didn't move. She stepped away from the door, wishing she was more graceful and sophisticated. "Come in."

Zack stepped into the room and closed the door behind him. Her nervousness beat wildly against her rib cage. When he gathered her close, she sagged against his hard chest.

Zack kissed her. His arms banded around her, pinning her arms to her sides. He teased her lips open and darted his tongue inside her mouth before she knew it. When he lifted his head, she was breathless and hanging on to his T-shirt, her world tilted.

Her bathrobe parted open and he boldly cupped her breast. The silent act was a masculine claim. Kelsey shivered with pleasure and arched deeper in his hand.

"Do you like it when I do this . . ." He rubbed the pad of his thumb against her nipple.

She closed her eyes as the hot sensations rippled through her. "Uh-huh."

"Or when I do this?" He pinched and rolled her other nipple in between his thumb and forefinger.

The sting traveled down to her clit and Kelsey inhaled sharply. "Uh-huh."

"Which do you like?" His voice grew huskier.

"Both," she whispered.

"Which do you like more?"

Did she have to decide? "Both are good."

"If you can't give me an answer," he said gently as he pulled his hands away, "then I leave your breasts alone until you can."

Kelsey blinked her eyes open at his words. He's not going to touch her breasts at all? Her head spun and she grabbed his shoulders as he laid her down on the bed.

Any minute now she was going to take charge. Kelsey nervously licked her lips as she silently watched Zack hover above her. Really, she was going to seize control. Zack was here to do whatever she wanted.

She could be a take-charge kind of woman—but usually when it came to someone else's happiness. She wasn't comfortable with the role reversal, but she was willing to give it a try. She'd start with something simple, like demanding another kiss.

The words evaporated on her tongue as he pulled her belt free and her bathrobe parted open. She instinctively bent her knee to hide from Zack's intent gaze. The shy move didn't seem to worry him. In fact, the way he looked at her made her feel incredibly sexy.

"Put your hands behind your head."

Uh-oh. That sounded a lot like what she asked of him the night before. She reluctantly followed his request, very aware of how her breasts rose from the move.

His hand stroked around her breasts, without touching the curves. Her nipples furled with anticipation as her breasts felt heavy and tight.

Zack explored her body with his hands and mouth. She couldn't predict where he would touch her next. She twisted and turned, chasing his mouth and wishing for him to linger.

Her abdomen clenched as Zack dipped his tongue in her navel. She wanted to pull him back up, stop his pursuit, but that thought vanished the moment he slid his fingers along her wet slit.

Her breath hitched in her throat as she felt the folds of her sex swell. She wasn't sure how she felt about this. All the attention was placed on her. Everything he did was based on her pleasure.

She wasn't sure about this at all.

"Do you like this?" he murmured as he circled her clit with his finger before plucking the stiff nub.

"Mm-hmm." Oh, yes, she most certainly did. "Like" was such a bland word for the ferocious hunger rushing through her blood. Her whole world focused on his fingertip as he dipped into her sex. Kelsey rocked her hips as the need weighed and pressed against her pelvis, threatening to break free.

"Or do you like this?" he asked as he claimed her with his mouth.

Her hips arched off the bed as she groaned. He flicked his tongue rapidly against her clit. She froze, wanting to capture this exquisite feeling and never let it end.

Zack lifted his head. "Which do you want, Kelsey?"

Kelsey grabbed the back of his head and pressed him against her sex. His knowing chuckle vibrated against her and the sensations were almost too much.

He lifted his mouth just a fraction. "Put your hands behind your head," he reminded her, his warm breath teasing her skin.

She wetted her lips with the swipe of her tongue. "I don't want to."

"What do you want to do with them?"

"Touch you."

She felt Zack's hesitation. The iron control he held over his desires slipped for a moment. "Not yet," he answered gruffly.

He lowered his mouth against her, curling his tongue around her clit. Heat swept under her skin as she rolled her hips.

Zack lavished attention on her slit, and she felt the ecstasy coiling deep in her belly. It rippled through her body as he suckled the swollen bud, and when he dipped his tongue in her hot core, her swollen flesh gripped him unmercifully.

A jagged cry ripped from Kelsey's throat as the climax hit hard. Ribbons of lust lashed out, twisting around her womb. Pleasure, thick and fiery, flared from her hips and oozed down her thighs.

Fine tremors wracked her sweat-slicked body. Her legs shook. Breathing hurt. "Zack?"

He rose to whisper in her ear. "Yeah, Kelsey?"

"I want you in me. Now."

She dazedly watched him discard his clothes. The sculpted muscles rippling under his golden skin made her pulse skip with excitement. When he settled between her legs, the sense of rightness overwhelmed her.

"Suck my nipples," she ordered, but she wasn't sure if it sounded more like begging. "Please."

Kelsey saw the satisfaction glow in his dark eyes before he lowered his head. She whimpered the moment his mouth caught her nipple. The pleasure was so intense that she felt the tears forming in the corners of her eyes.

Zack nudged his cock against her entrance. He paused

and she looked at him, their gazes colliding. Kelsey stilled, wondering if he knew that this wasn't just sex for her. It wasn't only one night. This was a life-altering moment, and she knew she was never going to be the same again.

Kelsey slid her hands down her legs and cupped her knees. She parted her legs wide for him. The move might have seemed like surrendering, but she'd never felt so brazen. Even shameless.

The muscles in his shoulders flexed as something dark and primal flashed in his eyes. Zack sank into her with one victorious thrust. Kelsey moaned, arching her back, as he increased his tempo. He drove his cock deeper and harder, stretching and filling her. Kelsey almost felt as if she had been branded and claimed from this one intimate act.

She curled her arms around his shoulders as his thrusts became wild and unrelenting. Hooking her legs onto his hips, the need clawing through her body, Kelsey knew all she could do was hold on tight. Eventually she would have to let go, but not tonight . . .

Kelsey whimpered when the phone rang early the next morning. She flopped a pillow over her head, not ready to start a new day. She wished the night could have gone on and on . . .

The ringing wouldn't stop. Kelsey reached out for the phone, her fingers bumping against something hard and sharp. She groaned and scooted closer to the bedside table, but the sheets tangled around her made it difficult. Her fingertips banged against the phone and she grabbed it.

She brought the phone to her ear under the pillow. "Hello?" Her voice sounded groggy. Can one get a sore throat from panting all night long?

"Kelsey? This is Hannah."

"You lied." Kelsey tossed the pillow off her head.

There was a pause on the other end. "*I* lied?"

"You said no one would bother me if there was a hot guy in my room." She tiredly pushed her long hair from her eyes.

"Oh, my God. Is he there?"

She heard the full blast of the shower in her bathroom. Kelsey smiled, knowing Zack hadn't left sometime in the night. "Yes, he is," she replied smugly.

"Kelsey," Hannah's voice sharpened with urgency. "I want you to remain calm."

"Okay."

"Sam just told me that Zack Cooper *isn't* a gigolo."

"Sure he is." As the night progressed, she became bolder and imaginative. Zack did everything she requested—and some of the stuff she made up, thinking it had been humanly impossible. "This guy is an *expert*."

"Really?" Hannah's voice dipped with interest. "What did he—no! Forget that. Listen to me. Zack Cooper is a multimillionaire. He owns a computer security corporation."

Kelsey blinked her eyes open. "Say what?"

"Zack gets the dubious honor of *not* being listed on the most eligible bachelor list in Seattle *because* of his horrible reputation with women."

Her stomach started to hurt and she pressed her hand, as if it would stop the twisting pain. "You're wrong," she whispered.

"I wish I wasn't! I went to the media room and looked it up on the computer. Zack Cooper is that same Zack Cooper."

Kelsey dragged her knees up to her chest, the tangle of sheets creasing into her skin. "You mean . . ."

"You didn't sleep with a gigolo."

She got that. "Who did I sleep with?" she asked as she curled her shoulders, ready to take the hit of bad news.

"A guy who has a kept woman tucked away in every port. He gets every woman he wants by flashing his money around. Only this time, he got you for free! No, wait. You paid for it, didn't you?"

Chapter Eight

"KELSEY," ZACK SAID AS he stepped out of the bathroom, a towel slung low around his waist. He frowned when he saw she wore a fluffy bathrobe wrapped and belted tightly around her. "Why are you up? I was going to get something for us to eat and stay in bed."

"Oh, I couldn't eat anything." Her gaze traveled down his muscular chest to his flat stomach. She dragged her eyes back to meet his. "Especially after seeing this." She revealed a print-out of his picture that she had held behind her back.

Zack closed his eyes and muttered something harsh. "When did you find out?"

"Hannah just slipped it under the door." She looked at the grainy photo. Zack was smiling proudly over some industry award. Kelsey set the paper down, wishing she hadn't seen it.

"I knew I shouldn't have trusted Sam," Zack said as he ran a hand through his wet hair.

Kelsey squinted at Zack, feeling more confused by the minute. "What does *Sam* have to do with this?"

"Nothing. Now, listen, Kelsey—"

She wasn't going to stick around to hear a slanted version of the truth. She wanted the bare, stark truth. "Why were you pretending to be a gigolo?"

"It wasn't my idea." He shook his head with regret. "Shirley thinks she needs to keep up appearances—"

"Shirley." Kelsey snapped her fingers. "That reminds me. How does Shirley Harrington fit into this? What are you to her?"

"She's my godmother."

Okay, she wasn't expecting that answer. "And you simply agreed to pretend to be her gigolo?"

"I didn't agree," he said with a bite in his tone. "She sprung it on me. The moment I met you, now that I think about it."

"You didn't think that I would have liked to have known the truth?"

Zack folded his arms across his chest. "Actually, no."

Kelsey stared at him. "No?" She felt like she had spluttered out the word. "Did you say no?"

"You wouldn't have approached me—you wouldn't have gotten near me—if you knew who I was."

She didn't appreciate his arrogance radiated from that statement. Nor did she like his reasoning for being dishonest. "I hadn't heard of Zack Cooper, Zillionaire, before."

"That doesn't matter. You thought I was a gigolo. You went after me when you thought all you had to do was throw money in my face."

"No, Zack, that's your method. Don't you throw money at problems to make them disappear? Aren't you known for throwing money at a woman to make her compliant?"

"I didn't throw money at you," he pointed out. "It was the other way around."

"And you make me look like a fool." She felt her cheeks burn with embarrassment. "You could have told me at any time what you really were."

"And you would have acted like this." Zack gestured at her.

"Can you blame me? I think you're one thing and you're quite the opposite!" She'd had enough. She needed to get away from him. Get away from here. "It's time for you to leave."

Zack pressed his fingers against his temples. "Do you hear yourself? You are upset that I'm *not* a gigolo. You are kicking me out *because* I'm a millionaire."

"What's your point?" she asked coldly.

He raised his hands. "Just making it clear."

"I'm kicking you out because you lied to me," she clarified as she watched him pick up his clothes. He headed for the door, but she blocked his exit. "I want to know the truth about something. Why did you do this? Was it for kicks?"

He lowered his head so their eyes were level. "I wanted to know what it felt like to have someone enjoy *being* with me instead of what *came* with me. I wanted something real."

"By *lying* to me."

"Yeah, because that's what it took." He straightened to his full height. "And I'm sorry about it."

"No, you're sorry that you got caught." She stepped away to clear a path for him.

"I would have told you. How else could we have gone on from here?"

She made a face. "You're only fooling yourself if you believe that."

His hand rested on the doorknob. "I mean it."

"You know"—Kelsey leaned against the wall next to the door and crossed her arms—"according to Hannah, you are used to keeping mistresses and lavishing your girlfriends with expensive gifts."

Zack frowned at the change of subject. "So?"

"What makes you think I would have put up with that kind of treatment myself? After all, I had the power in the relationship first."

"Kelsey, who says you wouldn't have had the power? Think about it. You had me panting after you. You had me wrapped around your finger. What makes you think that would have changed?"

"That's what you want me to believe." She would like to think it was true. So much that she was willing to forget about his reputation, thinking that she was different. "Good-bye, Zack. Thanks for *such* a good time."

"You'll be hearing from me," he promised as he opened the door. "Once you calm down, give me a call."

"Don't hold your breath."

One month later

Zack stood before his office windows and stared out at the Cascade mountain range. "She really meant it. She's not interested in having a relationship."

"Is that what you dragged me across the Sound for?" Shirley inspected her nails. "I have better things to do than listen to you whine."

Zack turned to glare at his godmother lounging on the sofa. "Shirley, you got me into this mess by introducing me as your gigolo."

She shrugged, not showing an ounce of remorse. "It piqued her interest, didn't it?"

"And it got me into trouble." Zack walked toward Shirley. "Now you have to get me out of it."

"Forget it. You could have gotten out of it yourself. All you had to do was tell her before the two of you had sex."

Zack halted. "What makes you think—"

"Oh, don't even start with me."

He decided he didn't want to know how Shirley came to the correct conclusion. "Come on, you have to help. Who do you know from that wedding?"

"Just Max." A naughty smile played on her crimson lips. "Although I did meet that cute chef and we met up in the pantry."

"What?" He scrunched up his face. "You didn't."

Shirley tossed her hands up in the air. "Is sex exclusive to the younger crowd?"

"Moving on . . ." Zack tiredly rubbed his hands over his face. "I've tried everything to apologize. Flowers. Chocolate."

"What happened?"

"She returned them." He hadn't been too surprised by her response. "So I went to the next level."

Shirley rolled her eyes. "Why am I sensing diamonds?"

"That's right. I sent her diamonds. In the past, this is when I at least get a nibble. Do you know what I got?"

"Nothing."

"That's right. Nothing!" He couldn't believe it at the time. Hadn't Kelsey realized how much he was groveling? "So I deviated from my pattern."

Shirley's eyes darkened with worry. "What did you do?"

"I had my company approach her boss. We were willing to buy priceless art, but Kelsey had to be in charge of the project. That was the deal breaker."

Shirley winced and shook her head. "Not a good move."

"Yeah," he agreed with a deep sigh. "She was really mad, and refused to take the project. This could have been a great career move for her, but instead I made everything worse for her at work."

Zack was now past the point of feeling offended or confused. He was scared. Nothing he did would help him get what he wanted the most. The fact that he was asking Shirley for advice showed how desperate he was. "Where do I go from here?"

"Sweetie," Shirley rose from the sofa, "I hate to break it to you, but the girl isn't interested in your money."

"I got that, thank you."

"No, sweetie." She patted his cheek. "She doesn't want what you can *do* with your money. It's intimidating her."

He frowned. Women loved his money—usually more than they loved him. His wealth was stronger than any aphrodisiac, and more powerful than a love potion. "I don't understand."

"You might be trying to impress her, but she's looking at it as a threat. You're saying, 'See how sorry I am?' and she sees it as 'See how powerful I am compared to you?'"

Zack hadn't seen it that way. "I'm screwed."

"Pretty much."

He thrust his hands in his hair and groaned. "I don't know what else I can do."

"Don't give up," Shirley said. "But whatever you do, don't push."

Pushing is what he did best. He wouldn't have acquired so much so fast if he stood back and waited. "What other option do I have?"

"You pull." She curled her arms in as if she were lifting imaginary weights.

Push. Pull. Was Shirley speaking in code? "I'm not following."

"Do you love Kelsey?"

"Yeah." He had fallen hard, and the landing was bumpy. He wasn't sure if he would ever recover.

Something close to mischief sparkled in Shirley's eyes. "Enough to beg for her?"

He shifted his lower jaw to the side. "I've already done that." And he wouldn't have done it for anyone else.

"Crawl over broken glass and prostrate before her feet?" Shirley asked, dramatically flinging her arms out wide.

Zack narrowed his eyes. "What if I am?"

Shirley smiled and dropped her arms. "Then I have the perfect plan."

Zack stared at the older woman with open suspicion. "What is it?"

"It's a little risky," she admitted, but disregarded that disclaimer with the flip of her wrist. "There's a possibility that it might blow up in your face."

"Then forget it." Zack already ruined too many chances. He had to find a fail-proof plan or he'd lose any possibility of a future with Kelsey. "It was great seeing you again, Shirley."

She clucked her tongue. "Sweetie, your back is to the wall. You either take a risk or you give up now."

Zack closed his eyes and took a deep breath. His world was definitely off-kilter if Shirley Harrington was making sense. He needed to regain the control he once wielded over his life, and that meant doing whatever necessary to get Kelsey back. "Tell me what I need to do."

CHAPTER NINE

"KELSEY, I HAVE A favor to ask you."

Kelsey gave Hannah a knowing look. "I wondered why you dropped by my office for lunch. You hate dealing with Seattle traffic."

"Well, I'm here to give you the pictures." Hannah nodded at the CD she brought and placed on Kelsey's desk. "You left the wedding so fast . . ."

"Can you blame me?" Kelsey muttered. She had put off looking at the wedding pictures for a month, always finding a reason to "forget" the CD. She hadn't expected her friend would make a point of dropping it off.

She didn't want to think about the wedding, talk about it, or relive it. She wanted to shove the weekend to the deepest, darkest corner of her mind until the memory withered away and disappeared. But first she had to get through this video, finish her wedding montage, and move on.

"What are you doing?" Hannah asked as she watched Kelsey slide the CD in her computer.

"I'm looking at the video so I can complete my wedding

montage." With a couple of keystrokes, the unedited video blared onto the screen.

Hannah rose from her seat and walked over to Kelsey. "Are you sure you want to do that?"

"Yeah, why not?" Kelsey said, but her bravado disintegrated when she saw a close-up of her with Zack at the party barn.

She had been so pathetically hot for him. Kelsey tried not to cringe at how obvious it translated on the video. Zack hadn't seemed to mind. In fact, he had appeared intrigued by her. How had she not seen that before?

"I'm sorry," Hannah said as she rested her hand on Kelsey's shoulder. "I shouldn't have brought this over yet."

She hit the MUTE key, the jovial noise of the wedding festivities grating on her nerves. "Nothing to worry about. I'm over him."

"Are you sure?"

She tried to drag her gaze away from the screen, but couldn't. "Completely. It was just sex." The sight of Zack made her breath hitch in her chest, but her heart crumpled at the way he looked at her. "So," she said brightly as an obvious attempt to change the subject. "What's the favor?"

"Nuh-uh." Hannah took a step back. "No. Forget it."

"It can't be that bad." The last word trailed off as the camera zoomed in on her and Zack. She really missed that smile. She missed him.

No, no, no. She didn't think that. Kelsey automatically grabbed the rubber band on her wrist and gave it a sharp snap. She jerked in response.

"What was that for?" Hannah asked.

Kelsey covered her hand over her stinging wrist. "Anytime

I think that I miss Zack, I snap this band. It's supposed to help break the habit of missing him."

Hannah gingerly lifted Kelsey's hand and pointedly stared at the inflamed, swollen skin under the rubber band. "I can see that it's working."

"I'm getting there," she insisted. She looked at the video again, but it had some shots of the other guests. "Thanks for the CD. There's some great footage."

"No problem. It was fun."

"I can totally use this. Now, what was that favor again?" Kelsey asked as she leaned back on her chair.

"Well," Hannah grimaced, clearly uncomfortable about asking for help. "It's not really for me. It's for Sam."

"Okay." Sam was asking for a favor through Hannah? That was new.

"He wants you to"—Hannah paused and then finished in a rush—"talk to Zack and get an appointment for him."

Kelsey sat up straight. "No way." The words were out of her mouth before she knew it. Hannah wanted her to *talk* to Zack? Was she out of her mind?

"That's what I said, but Sam is getting a lot of pressure from work and he's stressed. And I'm stressed about the wedding and I can't handle that he's stressed."

Kelsey covered her face with her hands. The suggestion of seeing Zack again made her want to hide. "I can't do it, Hannah. Please don't ask me."

"You really can't stand the idea of seeing Zack again, can you?"

"That's not it at all." She wanted to see him again. Longed to, but she knew it would only lead to trouble. If she entered his world, what was going to happen to her? He was wealthy, influential, and had far-reaching power. She was a pushover. She had nothing.

Some power could be considered attractive. What Zack had was scary. Because she had nothing that could stop him from taking over if he wanted to.

She looked at the video again, just in time to see Zack on the screen. It looked like the footage was shot during the impromptu party, and Zack was holding her close like he was about to kiss her. The possessive look on his face made her tingle, but it made her wary as well.

"It's okay, Kelsey. You don't have to. I don't want to make you do something you don't want to do."

"Thanks." Her eyes widened when she saw Zack kiss her on-screen. Tears pricked the back of her eyes and she quickly hit the STOP button. "Maybe I should watch this later."

"Good plan."

Kelsey pushed her hair away from her face and cleared her throat. "So, how are the wedding plans going?"

"Ugh." Hannah made a face. "I got this wedding planner who hates my guts."

"Where'd you find her?"

"Pinky recommended her."

"Well, there you go." She stopped when she saw the office assistant at the door. "Yes, Jane?"

"Sorry to interrupt." The young woman handed an envelope to Kelsey. "This letter came by courier."

"Thanks," Kelsey said and the assistant left. She flipped over the plain envelope, wondering what it was. She hadn't been expecting anything. "Go on, Hannah."

"Well, first of all, the planner acts like I don't know anything. I mean, hello! I've been a bridesmaid a billion times."

"No kidding," Kelsey said as she sliced open the envelope.

"She doesn't seem to understand the word budget, either. I know what I want and what I don't—" Hannah stopped when she heard Kelsey's shocked gasp. "What's wrong?"

"I'm going to kill him." She awkwardly stood up, her legs felt boneless and wobbly.

Hannah's eyebrow rose. "Who?"

"Zack Cooper." It took an effort to say his name.

"That's from Zack? What does he want?"

She held the letter out, her hand trembling as anger coursed through her body. "He is charging me for services rendered to an escort!"

Hannah's jaw dropped. "He is not."

"Read it. Go on." She shook the letter, her fingers crimping the paper, as the bitter, hot emotions roiled inside her. "I am *not* paying him two thousand dollars."

"Two thousand?" Hannah's eyes widened. "Was he really worth that?"

"I'm not paying him." She crossed her arms. "He can forget it."

"Uh, Kelsey?" Hannah glanced up from the letter with a worried expression. "It looks like you're going to have to."

Kelsey scoffed at the idea. "Forget it."

"You see here." She pointed at the letter. "The paragraph that says if you don't pay him in thirty days, he's going to send this matter to a collection agency."

Kelsey stared at Hannah. "What?" The word was barely audible. The love of her life was going to take her to a collection agency? How could he do such a thing?

"You don't want failure to pay for sexual services on your

credit report." Hannah shook her head. "Take my word on it."

"Give me that." Kelsey grabbed the document and quickly scanned the words. "Is he insane?"

She looked at the letter again. It had to be a joke. "This can't be legal!"

"It probably isn't." Hannah paused. "But are you willing to risk it?"

"I am not going to fall for this maneuver. He is out of luck if he thinks I believe this." A thought suddenly occurred to her. "Isn't making me pay for sexual services a crime? I could get him on that."

"And he could get you on making the agreement in the first place," Hannah said. "You did think he was a gigolo, and you were going to pay him."

Kelsey glared at her friend. "Whose side are you on?"

"Yours. Always." She pressed her lips before saying, "But if you do go see him, could you slip in a good word for Sam?"

"Hannah!"

"Okay, forget that." She waved her hands as if discarding the idea. "What do you plan to do?"

Kelsey crunched the letter in her hands and wadded it into a tight ball. "I'm going to find him and throw this back in his face."

The double doors to Zack's office flung open. He slowly stood up as he saw Kelsey march toward him. His heart twisted as he watched her approach. She looked beautiful and elegant in a fitted black jacket and short black skirt. Her heels were as feminine and sexy as she was.

She also looked furious. Anticipation thumped in his veins

as he prepared to take a few calculated risks. "Kelsey. It's good to see you again."

"What is the meaning of *this*?" She held up the letter he sent. It was crumpled and some of the edges were torn. The letter Shirley had suggested he send definitely got a reaction from Kelsey.

He returned to his seat, discreetly waving away his assistant who was ready to drag Kelsey out. He had to play it cool, and that would be easier to do when there was a wide desk between Kelsey and him. "You haven't paid me."

Her eyes went even wider from his cool reply. "I'm not going to pay you. You're crazy if you think I will."

"I fulfilled my part of the bargain."

"While pretending to be a *gigolo*." Her voice rose with each word.

He shrugged. "I never said I was."

"Then you shouldn't have negotiated a price." Her arms lashed out as she gestured wildly at his luxurious office. "You don't need two thousand dollars."

Zack narrowed his eyes as he tried to follow Kelsey's logic. "So, therefore I shouldn't get it?"

She slapped her palm against his desk. "Exactly."

"Kelsey, we made an agreement." He looked at her mouth, his tongue tingling as he remembered how they last sealed the deal. "You need to honor it."

"Honor?" She nearly shouted the word and visibly reined her temper in. "You're telling me about honor?"

"Of course." He rocked back in his chair and steepled his fingers together. "I'm willing to find an alternate way to pay off your debt."

Her jaw tightened. "I am not indebted to you."

"If the money is an issue, you can always pay me back in kind."

Her mouth opened and closed. The muscles in her throat tightened. He saw that his indecent proposal surprised and titillated her. Zack held his breath as his future with Kelsey wobbled uncertainly. He was either going to soar with success or crash and burn.

"Forget it." She grabbed her purse off her shoulder and opened it. "You know what. You can have your two thousand dollars."

Damn, this was not how he wanted it to go. He took the risk and it blew up in his face. But he wasn't going to surrender. He needed to regroup quickly.

"And don't worry," she said as she grabbed and flipped open her checkbook. "It will clear."

He saw her reddened wrist. Zack reached out and grasped it. The heat of her skin nearly undid him. "What happened here?" he asked gruffly.

Her cheeks turned pink. "Nothing." She pulled her arm back.

"Kelsey." He grabbed the checkbook away from her. "I don't want your money."

"No"—she reached for the checkbook but she was going to have to vault over the desk to reach it—"you just want me to be your plaything for the weekend."

"No—although that idea does sound enticing." He couldn't hide his grin as he imagined her lying in his bed and focusing all her love and attention on him. What would it be like if her sole intent was giving him maximum pleasure? His cock stiffened as he considered the endless possibilities.

Kelsey exhaled sharply. "Zack, you just don't get it."

"I do. It's not that I have money and influence, and it's not that you think I can use it against you. You don't like the fact that I have so much power over you."

"Well, that sounded arrogant."

"But you don't realize how much power you have over me." And it took him time to come to terms with it. He tried to fight it and ignore it, but he couldn't.

"If I do, it's not much." She dropped the pen onto his desk. "That's the problem."

"You do have power over me." He set her checkbook down and rose from his seat. Zack walked around his desk, grateful that Kelsey wasn't trying to keep her distance. "You have no idea how much I'd give to see you smile at me. Or watch you defend me. You have my stomach tied up in knots."

"I'm sorry about that," she whispered and dipped her head. "I never meant to."

"I'm not complaining." Zack reached out and curled his finger under her chin. He gently lifted her face so she would meet his gaze. "I want to do things for you. I don't feel obligated or manipulated. I get pleasure from your pleasure."

"That doesn't change anything."

"I won't abuse the power I have over you," he promised. "You've got to trust me on this."

She looked away and didn't say anything.

"And I have to believe"—Zack swallowed roughly as he realized he was taking a leap of faith—"you won't misuse the power you have over me."

She gasped in outrage over the suggestion. "I wouldn't!"

"You already have me jumping through hoops."

"You're just upset that I didn't fall for your usual spiel." She took a step back and rested her hip against his desk. "For all I know, you're simply fascinated by the novelty of *not* having a woman at your beck and call."

He knew that wasn't the case at all. "Shall we try it out? This weekend in exchange for two thousand dollars."

Kelsey pursed her lips and Zack's chest tightened. "I'm not going to be your call girl."

She didn't reject his suggestion out of hand. That was promising, but he could barely breathe as he waited for her reply. "I don't know," he answered slyly. "That could be fun."

"Here are the rules."

She was going for it! He wanted to grab her and hold her tight, but he had to be careful. He wasn't home free. Not by a long shot. "Hey, there were no rules when I spent the weekend with you."

"You should have thought about that beforehand." She turned and started to pace as she considered the parameters. "Number one: I am not having sex with you this weekend."

What? She is refusing to have sex? "Why not?" He couldn't stop himself from asking. "Wait, what's your definition of sex?"

Kelsey didn't seem to hear his questions as she continued to pace. "Number two: Don't even try to shower me with gifts because I'm not going to put up with it."

No gifts? He wanted to show her how much she meant to him, and what better way than with presents? "Not even flowers?"

"Not even flowers." She stood still and held out three fingers. "And number three: the minute you start taking me for granted, I am out of there."

That would never happen. "Deal." He held his hand out.

She grasped her hands with his and pulled him toward her. "I thought we always seal it with a kiss."

She brushed her mouth against his. Her sweet and spicy taste went straight to his head and to his cock. Just one kiss and he was ready to lay her down on his desk and strip her naked. It took all of his restraint to pull back.

"I'm going to be on my best behavior," he promised in a soft growl, "but you're going to break rule number one before the night is over. You do know that, right?"

She drew her head back. "The weekend starts tonight?"

"Yes, and"—he looked at his watch—"if we don't hurry, we will be late."

"Late? Late for what?"

"My cousin's wedding." He scooped up her checkbook and purse and gave them to her.

"Aw, man." She almost stomped her foot. "You're taking me to a wedding? We're not even going to have the weekend to ourselves?"

"You'll have to wait for that next weekend." He draped his arm around her waist and escorted her out of his office.

"You're getting ahead of yourself," she pointed out with a smile. "I didn't agree to a next weekend."

"You will."

Chapter Ten

Six months later

"LET ME LOOK AT that ring." Pinky didn't wait for Kelsey's reply and grabbed her hand.

Kelsey was amazed that these women were excited over yet another engagement ring. They were still at Hannah's wedding in their bridesmaid gowns. Did these women never overdose on wedding cake and champagne?

"You guys," Kelsey groaned. She cast a quick look around the wedding reception, hoping that no one noticed the bridesmaids huddled in a circle at the far corner. "This is Hannah's day. We should be focusing on the happy couple."

"Oh, my God." Pinky tilted Kelsey's hand and the emerald cut diamond caught the lights. "Is that a Harry Winston?"

Kelsey disentangled her fingers from Pinky's. She had a gut feeling the woman was about ready to test the diamond with the sharp edge of her teeth. "You don't think it's too big?"

"No!" they answered in unison. Kelsey jumped back in surprise.

Honey frowned. "How can a gigolo afford a ring like this?" She looked at her other sorority sisters for answers.

Mimi rolled her eyes. "He's not a gigolo," she replied impatiently. "He's a freaking gazillionaire. How did you figure it out, Kelsey?"

Kelsey could tell Mimi was not happy that she managed to find the wealthiest husband of the group without even trying. She knew the other bridesmaids wouldn't believe she wasn't marrying Zack for his money, so she wasn't going to explain. "I hadn't. Hannah found out and told me the day after your wedding." She looked over the women's bowed heads and searched for Zack in the crowded ballroom. Kelsey felt the zip in her veins when she spotted him.

Zack was surrounded by men clamoring for his attention. No doubt wanting some of his Midas touch to rub off on them. He admirably hid his annoyance as he lifted a champagne glass to his mouth. Their eyes met and she felt the coil of desire winding tight against her pelvis.

As magnificent as he looked, she wondered how long it would take to get him out of that tuxedo. Tonight, she was willing to beat her personal best time. The wicked flame in his dark eyes goaded her.

"So when's the wedding?" Margot asked, hunched over Kelsey's ring hand as she inspected the diamond closely.

She dragged her gaze away from Zack. "I don't know." Kelsey struggled to break free from Margot's tight grasp and grunted the moment she escaped. "Soon."

"Where is it going to be?" Honey asked.

"We're looking into Fiji."

"Oooh." From the looks on her sorority sisters' faces,

they were already planning out wardrobes for the destination wedding.

"Everyone is invited. All expenses paid." Kelsey winced at the high squeals of excitement. "I want you all to be brides-maids."

"Yes!" Margot said instantly.

"Absolutely!" Mimi agreed. "What are your colors going to be?"

"That's not important right now," Pinky decided as she stepped directly in front of Kelsey. "First we need to know who will do the bridesmaid dresses. I heard Vera Wang's collection this season was to die for."

"Oh, you guys don't have to worry about that." Kelsey patted Pinky's arm. "I saved all of my bridesmaid dresses and we'll just alter them to fit you."

The sisters stopped jumping. The shouts of joy died instantly. The women's expressions ranged from confusion to horror. Kelsey did her best to keep a straight face, but she felt the edges of her lips twitch.

"Why would you want to do that?" Mimi asked, the first to recover. "You are marrying a rich man. You don't need to skimp on the wedding."

"It's not about the money. I know each of you put a lot of thought in what your bridesmaids wore"—she clasped her hands to her heart—"and I feel that the dresses would be a wonderful reflection of who you are."

"I don't know if that's a good idea," Pinky said, her eyes wide as her cheeks flushed with color. "My bridesmaid dresses had a hoop skirt, and those are out of fashion."

"They were never in fashion," Kelsey replied with a smile. "So don't worry about it."

"This won't do." Margot shook her finger. "The brides-maid dresses in my wedding were daffodil yellow and that doesn't go with my coloring."

Kelsey narrowed her eyes. "We are the same coloring."

"No, I don't think—" Margot's frown magically trans-formed into a bright smile. "Hi, Zack!"

"Ladies." Zack nodded as the women fluttered around him like exotic birds. He wrapped his arm around Kelsey's waist, and rested his hand possessively on her hip. "I'm sorry to interrupt, but Kelsey, this is our song."

Kelsey listened to the music the DJ played and raised an eyebrow. Since when was Tina Turner's "Private Dancer" their song? She didn't question him as he led her to the dance floor.

When he found a spot, Zack turned around and gathered her close. Once she was in his arms, he sighed with male sat-isfaction. "I overheard your conversation and you are wicked," he whispered in her ear.

"You're just now figuring that out?" she murmured as she inhaled the faint scent of his cologne.

His hands drifted down her back and rested provocatively low. "When are you going to tell those women that we've already eloped?"

She shrugged a shoulder. "Oh, let them sweat it out a little longer."

"So I can't announce to the world that you're my wife?"

"Tomorrow," she promised. She hadn't expected Zack's impatience to publicly claim her. She knew he loved her, but she now sensed that he was deeply honored that she'd stood by his side and had taken his name. That knowledge fizzed happily inside her.

"Tell the truth." Zack drew his head back. "You're keeping

quiet about our marriage because you didn't want anyone to call you matron of honor."

"No," she replied haughtily. "But don't use that word when describing me."

"Matron?"

She wrinkled her nose. "I hate that word. Matron. Matronly." She shuddered.

"You don't look matronly in that dress."

Her sex clenched when she saw the hunger in his eyes. The bridesmaid dress was short, sassy and strapless, but the way Zack looked at her made her feel sensual and brazen enough to act on it.

Kelsey twined her arms behind his neck. Her breasts pressed against his chest, and she wondered if he could feel her tight nipples through the thin silk. "This song is inspiring me," she confessed.

"'Private Dancer'?"

She stepped out of his embrace and crooked her finger. "Let's go back to our room."

"Uh-oh." Zack's lopsided smile tugged at her heart. "Does your idea have anything to do with me giving you a lap dance?"

She liked the suggestion. A lot. She could easily imagine Zack crouched before her, his muscles flexing, and the sweat beading on his skin. She could see herself asking him to remove the crisp dollar bill from between her thighs without using his hands . . .

"No." She drew the word out. "This time *I'm* doing the dancing for money."

His mouth sagged open. "Seriously?" His voice went hoarse.

"Mmm-hmm." It still amazed Kelsey that she could make him blush and make him sweat. She could easily bring a smile to his face, or a sigh to his lips. She had the same power over Zack that he had over her. They both knew it, and that made for a wild ride.

Zack suddenly patted his hands along his jacket. "I don't think I have any ones on me."

"That's okay," Kelsey said as she took his hand and led him off the dance floor. "I'll take whatever you have to offer."

CHAPTER ELEVEN

KELSEY WALKED OUT OF the ballroom with Zack, confidence crackling under her skin. She didn't know why she felt this way. She had never stripped for a man. Never danced for money. Hadn't tried anything this brazen.

But the idea of doing it for Zack made it sound . . . fun. She looked over her shoulder and smiled when she saw the lust sharpening Zack's features. *Real* fun.

She strutted into the elevator and pressed the floor button. Kelsey felt Zack's gaze on her. It was hot and carnal, but she didn't blush. When the door closed, he reached for her.

"No, no, no." She dodged his hands. "No touching the merchandise."

A mix of amusement and frustration flitted across his face. "At all?"

Hmm. He had a point. No touching put a damper on the fun. "Not yet."

He took a step toward her, but she didn't budge. "Doesn't the client get to decide that?"

"No, I do," she said as she watched the floor numbers change, ignoring his appraising look.

The elevator bell dinged and the door parted open. She sashayed into the hallway and walked to their suite with bold strides. She raised her hand next to the door and posed as she waited for Zack to find the key card.

Kelsey rested her hand on her jutted hip, enjoying the freedom of pretending. She would never have swaggered or thrust her hip out. Never allowed herself to enjoy taking charge.

She watched Zack's hand shake as he tried to swipe the key card in the door. "Need help?"

"I got it." It took a few more swipes until the light turned green. With a look of triumph, Zack wrenched the door handle and held it open for her.

Kelsey purposely brushed against Zack, enjoying the way he tensed before she strode into the room. "Make yourself comfortable," she offered as she headed straight for the entertainment set. Kelsey turned on the radio and hunted for the classic rock station. She was going to need something hard, fast to match the way her blood was pumping.

After she found the music she was looking for, Kelsey grabbed a chair and put it in the middle of the room. "Sit here." She turned and saw that Zack had already discarded his jacket, tie and cummerbund.

The guy moved fast. She needed to remember that before he took control of this little fantasy.

Zack pulled out the bills from his wallet—all large de-nominations. "You are an expensive dancer," he teased.

"I'm worth it," she promised with a purr.

Hmm. She should pull back on the confidence. She didn't

want to promise more than she could deliver. She didn't want to disappoint him.

Kelsey's chest tightened at the gleam in Zack's eyes. No, he wouldn't be disappointed. He was getting hot simply watching her play pretend. Everything else would be bonus.

"I don't have a lot of bills," he said as he sat down on the chair she offered.

"Use them wisely."

"Do you take credit cards?" he asked hopefully.

"No." She wasn't going to make this too easy for him. "Anything else?"

"Yeah." He looped his arm over the back of the chair and stretched his legs out. "Dance for me."

Kelsey closed her eyes as she listened to the music. The heavy beat of the drum pulled at her. She parted her legs as far as her dress would allow and swayed to the beat.

She laid her hands on her hips until the music caught in her blood. Kelsey gave a throaty hum to the music as one of her hands drifted down past her hips. She bunched up her skirt, slid her hand up and down her leg, before splaying her fingers over her sex.

Kelsey raised her other hand, fanning her fingers along her breasts before skimming up her neck and face. She thrust her hand in her hair, imagining Zack pulling at the pins, until the soft brown tresses swung against her face.

"Take off your dress," Zack ordered with a growl.

"Impatient, aren't you?" Kelsey murmured as she opened her eyes.

His legs were sprawled in front of him, his fists resting against his knees. From where she stood, Kelsey could see the hard bulge in his trousers. Zack looked ready to pounce.

And she hadn't even taken off an article of clothing. *Hmm* . . . She couldn't wait to see him go wild when she was buck naked and riding him.

She reached for the zipper at the center of her back. She arched and thrust her pelvis more than was necessary. She felt Zack's tension rise as she pulled the zipper down. Her dress shifted, threatening to fall.

Kelsey held on to it, wanting to watch Zack's expression as *he* watched her. She oh-so-slowly wiggled and shimmied out of the dress with every drum roll and cymbal crash of the song. She felt incredibly sexy and wanted each moment to linger for as long as possible.

Zack's eyes widened appreciatively when she revealed the black satin bustier. A muscle bunched in his cheek when he saw the black thong, but his face flushed with desire when he spotted the black garter belt.

The dress fell to her feet. She stepped out of it and slid the pointed toe of her shoe under the fine fabric. Kicking it in the air, she watched Zack catch her discarded dress. He didn't seem to realize, his dazed attention still on the aggressive curves of her lingerie. "Holy . . ."

Kelsey put her hands on her hips and posed. His rapt attention made her hot and wet. Never before had she been so thankful for buying an expensive, confining bra to go under a bridesmaid dress.

She was vaguely aware of the new song on the radio, and belatedly remembered she was supposed to be dancing. She deepened her knees with every move and rotated her hips to the beat. Kelsey turned around, giving Zack a good view of bare bottom. The rounded curves of her buttocks tingled, knowing he was looking at every inch of her.

And she would give him even more to look at. Taking a calming breath as her stomach jittered with nerves, Kelsey parted her legs wide before reaching down to unbuckle her strappy heel. Zack's low groan made her fingers tremble. She always loved that sound.

Kelsey swung to the other foot and unbuckled the shoe. She straightened, kicking off both heels. Thrusting her bottom out, letting him see how the thong clung to her wet slit, she looked over her shoulder. "Did you say something?"

"Come here." His voice sounded gravelly as he tossed her dress to the side.

She swiveled on the balls of her feet and approached him, her hips rolling with every step. Her stomach tightened as he unbuttoned his shirt with swift, powerful moves. The folds of her sex grew slick as he shed the sophisticated image layer by layer, revealing the primitive man.

Kelsey clasped her hands behind her back, her girlish pose at odds with the daring black lingerie. "Yes, Zack?"

"Give me a lap dance." The frank need blurred his words.

She shook her head. "Show me the money."

Zack's eyebrow rose but he didn't reply. He reached inside his shirt pocket and pulled out a crumpled bill. He held it between his fingers, silently offering her to take the money.

"Now, now, Zack," Kelsey said in a low, seductive voice as she raised her leg and set her foot between his legs. "You need to give the cash. Put the money on me."

Zack's eyes narrowed. "How do you know that?"

"I read." She moved her leg and rubbed the sole of her foot against his hard cock. He lurched under her touch. "A lot."

Zack lowered his hand and stuffed the crisp bill underneath the lace edge of her stocking. The money felt rough and scratchy along the soft skin of her inner thigh. It made her role feel more real.

He cupped the back of her leg with his hands. She couldn't predict his next move. Would he move his hand up to squeeze and knead her bottom? Or would he slide his fingers along her damp panties before dipping into her sex?

"Men aren't allowed to touch me." She tried to sound firm, but it didn't come out that way. The fact that she didn't pull her leg away didn't help her claim.

Zack's eyes darkened. "Says who?"

"House rules," she improvised.

"Make an exception."

The way he said it made her wonder if she was enjoying her power a little too much. She wanted to tease him, but she wanted him to have as much fun as she was having. "You can take off my stockings," she offered.

He slid one hand down her thigh and roughly snapped the silk free from the garter belt. Hooking his fingers beneath the lace top, he dragged the stocking down the length of her leg. She lifted her foot as he threw the stocking next to the dress. "Now the other leg."

She didn't refuse. The stockings were suddenly too confining, trapping her body heat and becoming an unnecessary barrier to Zack's touch. Kelsey placed her foot between his legs and he pulled the stocking free from the garter. She heard the rip and felt the silk give as he glided it down her leg. He paused long enough to press a kiss on an old scar at her knee.

"Uh-uh," she said huskily, wanting to regain control. "That's against the house rules."

Zack tossed the stocking over his shoulder and Kelsey watched it float to the floor. He reached inside his shirt pocket and extracted another bill. She frowned as she watched him carefully fold the money. "Come closer."

The two words made her stomach flutter. So promising . . . and so dangerous. She stepped between his knees, her breath hitching in her throat as he reached for her. Zack tucked the money in her panties. Not at the waistband like she had expected, but between her thighs.

His fingers brushed her wiry curls. Kelsey's womb clenched when his thumb grazed against her stiff clit. She shuddered and stepped back. Her legs wobbled and she wasn't sure how she was going to dance to the music, but she was going to go for it.

"Are you ready for your lap dance?" she asked, her voice low and uneven.

"Yeah." He leaned back in his chair. His eyes glittered as he waited and watched. Her nipples furled tight and rubbed painfully against the bustier.

Kelsey boldly straddled his legs and crouched down. She shivered as Zack rubbed his hands up and down her bare legs. He kneaded her flesh, tickled the sensitive area behind her knees, and teased the crease where her legs met her bottom.

Her pulse skipped a beat as she crouched low. She rubbed her wet slit against his cock, hard and fast to the frenetic beat of the music. Desire knotted inside her, tighter and tighter, until she gasped for breath.

Kelsey straightened her legs and reached for the hooks hidden in the back of the bustier. She froze when she felt Zack's hands cover hers.

"Let me."

Kelsey hesitated. She was letting him get his way with everything. She should make him pay for the privilege.

Zack must have known what she was going to say. He

reached in his shirt pocket and pulled out another bill. He waved it under her nose.

She looked at the money and then at his shirt pocket. "How many more do you have left?"

"One more," he admitted.

She still had her panties on and he wanted to waste his money on something she would do herself? He must really want to help her strip naked. "Okay," Kelsey agreed softly and set her hands on his shoulders.

Zack lowered his hand on her hip and slid the bill under the low waistband of her panties. He then reached around her back. Kelsey sucked in her breath as he parted the first hook.

She looked down at him as he silently focused on his task. Her breasts were level with his mouth, but he was watching her face. Did he see every emotion racing across? The pink blush creeping from her chest, up her neck, and flooding her cheeks? The excitement glittering in her eyes?

Her fingers dug into Zack's shoulders as he slowly peeled the black satin from her body. She exhaled as the boning of the bustier stopped pressing against her ribs. As it stopped separating her breasts and pushing them higher.

She watched Zack stare at her breasts. Her skin flushed and tightened as he licked his lips. He leaned back in his chair and she followed as if there were an invisible connection. To her surprise, he tilted his head up and looked at her.

"Dance for me, Kelsey," he said with a sly smile.

Her mouth dropped open and she snapped it shut. What a tease! Her breasts felt heavy and full, her nipples stung, and his mouth almost brushed the tips before he pulled away.

Well, two could play at this game. By the end of this song, Zack would be begging for a taste.

She watched Zack's eyes turn dark and smoky as she drew small circles around her nipples. She fondled her breasts, tweaking her nipples between her fingertips. The bite felt good, but she needed more. She pinched hard and cried out as the sensations forked through her like lightning.

Zack's jaw tightened as her groan echoed in the hotel suite. Her gaze collided with his. A naughty idea flitted through her mind. She didn't know if she could do it, but she wanted to give it a try. She lifted one breast high and lowered her head. Holding Zack's gaze, she darted her tongue toward her nipple.

She hadn't reached her nipple. Not even close. But the fact seemed to escape Zack. He was no longer leaning back and enjoying the show. He leaned forward, ready to draw her swollen nipple in his mouth.

"Zack," she said lightly as she cupped the underside of her curves. "Are you sure you want to use the last of your money to touch my breasts?"

He looked up at her, momentarily confused as she unhooked her leg from his and stood in front of him.

"What do you want, Zack?" She pressed her breasts together and swiveled her hips to the beat. "Your last dollar. How do you want to spend your money?"

His jaw twitched, and Kelsey knew she was pushing her luck. But did that stop her? No, she was enjoying it all too much. It wasn't often that Zack was denied. This would do him good.

"Make it worth your while," she added, unable to hide her smile.

The look in Zack's face shifted. His eyes glittered with victory. As if he got her.

Kelsey felt her forehead crinkle. But that couldn't be. She had *him*.

He reached for his last bill. He waved it around in lazy, sweeping circles. The anticipation built inside her. There was just one place he could tuck in the bill.

He lowered his hand against his hard cock. She frowned as he unzipped his trousers. Was he ending the game?

Kelsey's eyes widened when he placed the bill in his zipper.

"Remember, Kelsey," Zack said as he stretched his legs out wider. "You can't use your hands."

She stared at the bill. How did he expect her to get that? Sure, she had heard of strippers who had amazing muscle control and could pick up the money just by sitting on it. Not only did Kelsey think that was an urban legend, but even if she had religiously practiced her Kegel exercises, there was no way she was going to acquire that trick in the next minute.

She could bend at the waist, catch the money between her breasts and lift it away. Then again, no one said she couldn't pick it up with her mouth. She glanced at his cock that seemed to swell under her gaze. Kelsey swallowed roughly as the pleasure bloomed deep inside her.

Kneeling before Zack and watching his eyes glow with lust, Kelsey was never more aware of his masculine strength. He seemed more intimidating and powerful. She placed her hands on his legs and felt his muscular thighs bunch under her gentle touch. That telltale sign gave her an added boost of confidence.

She lowered her head and inhaled the musky, hot, male scent. Kelsey was tempted to drag the zipper down and take him in her mouth, but she wasn't going to give up just yet. Placing her lips against the fly of his pants, she slowly made her way up his hard, thick cock to the cash. She liked teasing him and pressing down against his twitching cock. She felt the power roll through her when Zack shifted abruptly. Her heart raced when she heard his muffled groan.

Kelsey captured the money between her teeth. The smooth paper slid easily so she bit down harder until she heard it crinkle. The bill grazed her bottom lip as she slowly dragged it from Zack's zipper, praying that it wouldn't get caught.

When she pulled the cash free from his pants, she spat out the money, not caring where it landed. Kelsey looked up to her husband. She liked his mussed, rumpled appearance, but it was the passion in his eyes that made her catch her breath. "Aw, Zack," she said as she pouted playfully. "I guess the game is over."

"Come on, Kelsey." His voice came out in a rasp. "Don't tease me. Finish the game."

She shook her head. "You have no more money."

He squeezed his eyes tight. "Kelsey."

The tortured look pulled at her heart. She couldn't refuse him, even if she wanted to. She reached for his zipper and dragged it down gently. "Take off your pants," she requested.

He shucked off his shoes and pushed his clothes off his hips and down his legs. Zack kicked them to the side and watched her with hooded eyes.

His cock rose from his body, thick and proud. The tip was swollen and wet. She grasped the length from the base, his dark hair cushioning her hand before she began to pump. Zack leaned his head back, his breath hissing between his clenched teeth.

She leaned forward and swirled her tongue along the swollen, wet head of his cock. She loved the taste of him and couldn't get enough. She laved and stroked him, feeling the heavy pulse against her tongue. Kelsey covered the tip with her lips and sucked, listening to his low, guttural groans.

Kelsey slid her mouth down his cock when a loud clatter in the hallway startled her. She reeled back, balancing on her heels when she heard the shouts and banging.

"What the hell is that?" Zack growled, glaring at the door. The way his muscles bunched, she wouldn't be surprised if he marched to the door and confronted the problem in all his naked glory.

The metallic vibration down the hall sounded familiar. "The shivaree." She had forgotten all about it.

"What?" he glowered at her.

"For Hannah and Sam," she told him, placing her hands on his knees. "Their room must be on this floor."

He grimaced as he heard the banging pots. "We should have killed that tradition when we had the chance," he muttered darkly.

"Are you kidding?" she asked as she slid her hands up his legs and grasped his cock. She slowly pumped his cock, one hand over the other. "I fell in love with you during that shivaree."

His expression softened, but suddenly cringed when he heard the off-key singing. "You're kidding, right?"

"Not at all." Kelsey rose to her feet and dragged her panties off her legs. The money scattered onto the floor. Zack watched, almost as if he were spellbound, as she hooked her legs around his hips.

"I don't have any cash," he reminded her, his chest rising and falling as he tried to contain his excitement.

"That's okay, Zack. Consider this a freebie," she said with a wink. "After all, you are my favorite customer."

"I'm your *only* customer," he said as he clamped his hands on her hips and guided her down the length of his cock. She felt his possession with every breath she took.

The clanging metal and noisemakers sounded far away as Zack stretched and filled her. Heat zipped through her blood and reddened her skin. The promised pleasure teased her senses and she strove to reach it. Kelsey grabbed the collar of Zack's open shirt as she arched back.

Zack groaned and closed his eyes as she swiveled and rotated her hips. "Kelsey . . ."

She rocked against him as the music and voices washed over her. The white-hot orgasm caught her by surprise. Her inner walls squeezed Zack as the pleasure rippled through her.

The crash of lids punctuated the roll of her hips. It flowed and ebbed as she rode Zack. Harder, faster, as sweat dripped from her skin until suddenly Zack jerked and thrashed underneath her. The cheers down the hall drowned out his hoarse roar, but Kelsey felt the vibrations to the soles of her feet.

She collapsed against Zack's shoulder, gasping for air, as her blood pounded in her ears. She had no idea how long she stayed curled against him when she noticed all was silent. Kelsey lifted her head and listened. "It's quiet. Hannah and Sam got rid of them fast."

"Thank God." He frowned as Kelsey disentangled herself from him. "Don't go," he muttered sleepily.

"I'm not," she assured him as she stood up. Kelsey weaved, feeling slightly light-headed and woozy. "I'm moving this party to the bathtub."

Zack slowly rose from his chair and shrugged off his

shirt, now creased and damp with sweat. A tired smile tugged at his mouth as he watched Kelsey pick up the bills she earned. "What are you going to do with all that money?" he asked as he stretched.

The muscles rippling under his skin distracted her for a moment. "I'm not sure," she said, "but by check-out time, I will have blown it all."

He froze in midstretch. "On what?"

"My private dancer." She crooked her finger at him. "Come closer, Zack. It's time to show me all your moves."

THE BRIDESMAID'S DIARIES

CHAPTER ONE

July 2

Yesterday was the worst day of my life. It was worse than the day I failed my driver's test. Worse than when I got fired from my first job and came home to find my student loan payments kicked in. Worse than the day the Novocain wore off while I was getting my wisdom teeth removed. I could have sworn nothing would top that. Guess I was wrong.

The day started out normally. I was getting ready for the wedding I organized. (I'm the events coordinator for my family's winery. Might sound glamorous, but trust me, there's nothing oo-la-la about counting broken wineglasses and mediating between parking valets.)

Anyway, I was heading for my office at the winery when Brad showed up. Brad and I have been dating for a while. Actually, it seemed like forever, but I guess it would feel that way since my parents and his parents are neighbors who set us up. They had dreams of connecting our struggling wineries and creating a, well, struggling dynasty.

Brad didn't even have the courtesy to greet me, now that I think about it. Rather, he dropped the bombshell and got it over with. "This isn't working. I'm breaking up with you."

This was a complete surprise since three months ago he made strong hints about wanting to get married. I had even turned down a job offer across the country because our life together meant staying here. Couldn't he have made this announcement last week, before our last boring attempt at sex? At this rate I was perfecting the art of faking an orgasm.

But it seems like Brad has been faking it, too. In a manner of speaking. He thought he could eventually love me—but it turned out he didn't want me after all. Didn't want to marry me, sleep with me, or have anything to do with me.

This time I got the point. I also noticed that he didn't care what I wanted. (Big surprise there.) I sure didn't want to get stuck telling our parents that we're through.

But before I could watch my parents' hopes shatter into a million pieces, I had a wedding to take care of. Weddings are the most stressful events, but this bride was a real pain in the butt. She always had been. Believe me, I know because I went to school with her for twelve years. She didn't grow on you. Ever.

It goes without saying that she didn't have a lot of bridesmaids. Sure, she had the money for a large wedding that could support an army of attendants, but she knew only two women who would put up with her. (And I bet one of them was getting bribed to play nice.) So when the maid of honor came down with the flu the day of the wedding—and I seriously question if the woman really was sick—guess who was the same size as that absent bridesmaid?

Yep. Yours truly. At this point, I'd suggested taking away one groomsman but the bride wanted the party to look symmetrical. The truth was that she needed to make it look like she had friends.

So there I was, dumped by my boyfriend on that day and dressed in this burgundy monstrosity that was not meant for me. I tried to look happy for the bride—because the video recorder was on—but I was dying inside. As in wilted, curled up, shriveled and blown away dying.

It didn't help that I was surrounded by people celebrating love and marriage, cheering on two people who want each other and couldn't imagine life apart. All I could think of was that no one wanted me. Not as a bride. Or as a bridesmaid. Or as a wedding guest. Or as a woman.

It was that last thought that got me into big trouble. That and several glasses of our award-winning champagne. The next thing I knew, I was hitting on the best man.

This guy was hot. As in drool-worthy, knee-melting sexy. And fascinating. And attentive. He had those crinkly laugh lines fanning around his blue eyes.

I'm a sucker for crinkly lines.

He was so gorgeous so I . . . slept with him. Though no sleeping occurred. How could I when I had the wildest, most imaginative sex ever. That night I learned that I had been faking it ALL WRONG!!

I still can't believe some of the stuff I did with him. To him. I'm suffering from a full-body blush, tingling and achy and . . .

I can't believe I slept with a guy I barely knew, which is not like me. So what if I had the worst day of my life? Finishing it with the ultimate mistake is not the way to go!

This morning when The Best Man gave me the obligatory speech about how he wanted

to see me again, I had to say no. I didn't
want to draw out the mistake, but it was
more than that. I was feeling unsettled.

I have to admit, it was really difficult
to say no, especially when he kissed me
good-bye. It was so sweet and gentle that it
made me tear up.

But it didn't make me change my mind. I
don't care if The Best Man made me feel de-
sirable or cherished for the first time.
What I did was wrong, unprofessional, and
stupid. I hope no one will find out, but
most of all, I hope, wish, and beg to the
gods that I will never see him again. ~

Tara Watkins read her words, the dull pain twisting in her
gut. It was hard to believe two years had passed since she had
been dumped, drunk, and dressed in someone else's bridesmaid dress. Sometimes it felt like it just happened, but usually
it felt like it was a lifetime ago.

She glanced over the comments visitors had left over the
years. Most commiserated and shared their horror stories,
which made her realize she was not alone. She wasn't sure if
that knowledge made her feel better or worse.

Are you sure The Best Man gave an "obligatory" speech? I bet he meant it.

She paused when she saw the comment from Nomad, a
guy who popped up on her feedback section one day and
played the devil's advocate ever since. He might feel the need

to give the male perspective, but his pointed questions always gave her a burst of hope that she couldn't afford.

Anyway, could she really trust relationship advice from a guy who named himself Nomad?

"Tara?"

She jumped, knocking her knee on her desk. "Yes?" Her heart raced as she pushed on the button to hide the computer screen. She glanced at her office door and saw her assistant.

"I'm heading for the rehearsal," Jazmin told her, clasping her clipboard against her chest. The young woman vibrated with excitement.

"I'll be right there. I have to change first." She glanced at the adjoining filing room that she also used as a makeshift dressing area. Her sundress was hanging up on the edge of a shelf, her black sling-back heels on top of a metal cabinet. "Do you have everything?"

"I've got my checklist, my cell phone, and my emergency kit." She ticked the list off on her fingers.

"Emergency kit? Jazmin—"

The assistant pulled out the small plastic container from her blazer pocket. "It has aspirin, Band-Aids, duct tape."

Tara frowned. "Duct tape?"

"Moist towelettes, sewing kit, and smelling salts."

"Um . . . wow. All that for a rehearsal dinner?"

"It's best to be prepared." The assistant dropped the box back in her pocket and gave it a loving tap.

"O-kay." Tara knew her eyes were wide, but nothing she did could get them half-mast. "Sounds like you have every-thing under control."

"I do." Jazmin nodded her head so fast it reminded Tara of a windup toy. "This is going to be fun!"

"Uh-huh." Tara barely muttered her response as she watched the assistant hurry away, enthusiasm crackling with each step. Tara couldn't remember ever feeling like that while on the job.

Maybe she shouldn't compare. This was Jazmin's first chance at being in charge of an event, and the woman just happened to love weddings. Maybe with a little more fervor than what would be considered healthy, but Tara bet that after a year of coordinating weddings, she'd get back to normal.

On the other hand, Tara had never liked weddings, and after that event two years ago, she'd developed an acute allergy to them. Too bad her job required her to handle weddings every week!

It was surprising that no one had figured out her true feelings about weddings. She must be really good at hiding what she thought. Either that, or no one was looking at her to begin with. Tara smiled wryly. That was probably the case.

She propped her jaw with her palm and, with one hand, tapped on her keyboard to reveal what was on her computer screen. Scanning the blog entry again, she wasn't sure why that horrible day made her start a diary on the Web. She was private. Reserved. It was comfortable being invisible.

So why did she share the most humiliating, depressing event of her life to the world? Anonymous or not, it wasn't something she would have normally done voluntarily. Yet she needed to tell someone. She needed to throw her story out into the world and let it be known that she had been hurting.

It turned out a lot of people heard her. Tara glanced at the long list of comments people left for her. These days her blog was frequented by thousands of visitors. They wanted to hear her troubles and triumphs. They asked and heard what she had to say regarding antiquated wedding rituals, about suffering through bridesmaid duties, or what she really thought about reining in demanding Mothers of the Bride.

This is where she got to tell how she truly felt, uncensored. About love, sex, being single, being alone. Writing it all down on the blog is probably what allowed her to keep sane when she dealt with one wedding after another.

She was going to need that kind of support this weekend. Tara sat up straight in her chair, entered her blog program with a few keystrokes, and wrote:

Everyone, I have to make a confession. I've been holding out on you. I don't know why. I think it's because I kept hoping it would go away. But it didn't, and now I'm stuck.

You know that awful day that started this blog? Guess what? I get to go repeat the wedding. Today. As in a few minutes.

You read that right. I'm required to hit REWIND and experience the worst day of my life all over again. I get to reenact the wedding right down to dealing with the same bridesmaids and groomsmen. The only difference is the bridesmaid dresses are uglier.

Damn those renewed vows ceremonies. What moron started this trend? I'd like to get my hands on him.

I'll keep you posted. ~

She heard the knock on her door. "Just a minute," she said as she clicked on PUBLISH.

"Sure."

That voice! She'd remember the low, husky timbre no matter what. Tara's eyes widened as hot flashes rolled through her. The screen looked blurry all of a sudden and her hand shook on the computer mouse. What was he doing *here*?

Tara reluctantly glanced up and saw him leaning against the doorway. Her gaze locked on his blue eyes. Her heart turned and landed with a thud against the wall of her chest.

He still had those crinkles. They were a little deeper. A little sexier, too, damn it!

His dark blond hair was longer these days. It was slightly curly and streaked from the sun. His smile was like a slash of lightning against his weather-beaten face.

Tara abruptly stood up, her chair skidding back. She didn't know why she did that, other than he was much taller than she remembered. The dark suit and darker dress shirt accentuated his lean, muscular build.

Panic shot through her limbs, leaving her jittery and graceless. She didn't plan on seeing him here. Not when she was alone and unprepared. She had hoped to avoid him throughout the party or, better yet, that he would not show up.

Should she act like she didn't recognize him? Do a disinterested, "Can I help you?" No, she didn't think she could pull that off. Not with the way she was blushing.

"Hello, Tara." His voice rumbled from his chest.

"Luke," she said with a fixed smile. The name felt unfamiliar on her tongue. That was a surprise considering how much she thought about him. Luke Sullivan. Or what her blog readership would know as The Best Man.

And there he was, in the flesh.

She winced as she remembered his sweat-slicked, naked flesh pressing against hers as he settled between her legs before he—

Tara blinked hard, pushing the memories aside. She might not want to think about him in those terms. Not if she wanted to get through the weekend.

Luke slid his hands into the front pockets of his trousers. He hoped the move hid the way his hand trembled. Now if only he could hide the nervous twitch in his upper lip.

It was important he didn't make a mess of this reunion. It had been two years since he'd seen Tara, and he had only the weekend to catch up. First he had to stop staring at her.

She looked different. The wavy blond hair that fell to her shoulders was now pulled tightly back into a high ponytail. Her high, angular cheekbones were more pronounced, but what he noticed the most were her eyes. They were the same dark and mysterious blue as the Pacific Ocean after a storm.

But he noticed other things too. Her collarbone protruded from her simple ivory blouse, indicating that she had lost weight, but she still stood tall and proud. The regal tilt of her long jaw let him know she felt stronger. It looked like Tara Watkins had taken a few blows and was just about ready to kick back at the world.

The corner of his mouth tugged with a knowing smile. He'd arrived just in time.

"Um, so"—she rested her knuckles on the desk, but showed no interest in stepping away from her corner—"what are you doing here?"

"I'm the best man," he reminded her. "You are the maid of honor. We're going to the same wedding rehearsal."

"The wedding tent is that way." She pointed out the window. "You can't miss it."

He shrugged one shoulder. "Since I'm here, we might as well go together."

She gestured at her clothes. "I'm not dressed yet."

His gaze lingered on her blouse. His hands tingled as he remembered what it was like to palm her breasts. "I can wait," he said, his voice unexpectedly rough.

"I'll meet you there," Tara said, her tone careful and controlled through her polite smile.

"No, thanks." He shifted and rested his back comfortably on the doorframe. Luke crossed one ankle over the other, as if he had all the time in the world.

Her lips compressed for a moment. It was as if she couldn't decide whether to argue or not, and just decided it wasn't worth the effort. "Okay." She walked toward the side door. "I'll be right back."

"Where are you going?" She didn't seem the type to sneak out and leave him.

"I'm going to change."

"Don't you live on the grounds?" He had already stopped by the renovated carriage house on the vineyards, assuming she still lived there. The building was so tiny it would make a lot of people feel claustrophobic.

"I do," Tara said as she opened the door, "but I bring my clothes in here because it saves time."

He craned his head and looked into what appeared to be a filing room. Above the metal cabinets were shelves for paper and office supplies. The only personal item he saw was a mirror propped up against the wall. She probably changed in there because it was bigger than her bedroom, but he wasn't going to mention that.

"Why are you surprised to see me?" he asked as she closed the door.

The door swung open and she peeked around, her eyebrows dipping as she frowned. "Excuse me?"

He stepped into the office. "I said, why are you surprised to see me? I have to be here. The groom is my brother."

"I'm not surprised. I'm . . . I'm . . ." She rotated her hand, as if she were trying to come up with the word.

"You're . . . ?" He mimicked her.

Tara stilled her hands and pursed her lips, but Luke could see the reluctant amusement gleaming in her eyes. She motioned at the chair in front of her desk. "Why don't you sit down? I'll only be a minute."

"Here?" Luke sat on the chair and leaned back, but only because he realized he was making her edgy. Edgy wasn't good for his plans. He could compromise, if it meant he would eventually get his way.

She stepped back into the filing room and closed the door. The lock didn't click shut and the door opened slightly to reveal a sliver of a beige filing cabinet.

Luke took the opportunity to survey her desk. There were no knickknacks. Not even a colorful pen holder or a bright pink notepad. Nothing to show what kind of person Tara Watkins was. Just a laptop, a phone, and lots of papers. "You didn't answer my question," he called out.

The rustling sound from the filing room stopped. "What question was that?"

"Didn't you know I would be here?" He looked around the

room. Once again, nothing but a few calendars and dry boards. Even her handwriting was in block letters and black ink.

"I really didn't give it much thought."

Luke turned his attention to the door. He didn't have to hide his smile this time. She was lying and—

Whoa. Luke's smile tilted and disappeared.

The door to the filing room had yawned open. Not so much to cause alarm, if it hadn't been for the mirror tilted against the wall. He saw the back of Tara's head, her ponytail swaying.

Look away. Look away. Luke put his elbow on the chair and leaned closer to the desk, and was rewarded to see Tara slip off her blouse.

Look the other way!

But he couldn't. Luke shifted in his seat as he stared at her back. He never thought of the spine or shoulder blades as sexy until now. He'd love to trace his fingertips over the planes and curves.

"Anyway, aren't you some reporter?" she asked and her image disappeared from the mirror.

Luke jerked upright in his seat. "Travel writer," he corrected, finding it difficult to speak.

"Right, that's what Joy said."

Satisfaction purred deep in his chest. He wasn't going to ask why she and his sister-in-law were talking about him. It was enough for him to know that she did.

"Wouldn't you rather take your time off somewhere exotic?" she asked, her voice sounding as if it were coming deeper from the room.

"There's nowhere else I'd rather be." He found the lure of the mirror too irresistible and leaned to the side again. The mirror showed her at an odd angle, but he'd take what he could get.

Tara's head dipped down as she unhooked the back of the bra. The lingerie was nothing more than a scrap of white lace. Fragile and delicate. "I grew very fond of this place," he added as heat seeped in his skin.

She paused and lifted her head. "Excuse me? I didn't catch that."

Take off the bra. Don't stop now. Don't leave me hanging. Just do it! "Don't you like this area?"

"I haven't really thought about it." She shrugged and the white slender straps slid down her arms.

Her breasts were a breath away from spilling out of the cups. Luke's tongue seemed to swell and stick to the roof of his mouth as he waited.

Tara turned and faced her dress as she removed her bra.

Damn it! Luke reared back in his seat, shoving his hands in his hair. Why did she have to do that? He slowly dragged his fingers down his face as the tension and frustration swirled inside him. The woman was a natural-born tease!

"I don't have much to compare it with," she continued.

What? Luke splayed his hands in the air. What was she talking about? She was perfect. Explorers would have named mountains after her. Pioneers would have—

Oh, right. She was talking about *traveling.*

He almost blew it, right at the start. He had to keep his senses. "You don't like to travel?" he asked, looking back into the mirror.

"Never had the chance," she said as she reached for her dress. She slowly faced the mirror as she remembered something, clasping the black-and-white fabric to her breasts. "Well, except for college. My friends were going to go backpacking through Europe. I wanted to do that so badly, but I didn't have two pennies to rub together."

He had almost missed her look of yearning and regret. He'd seen that look before. Sympathy twanged inside him, because he knew what it was like to wrestle with wanderlust. He didn't know how she could stay in one place without going stir crazy. "What about now?"

"Now I don't have the time," she said, straightening her shoulders. It looked as if she'd given herself a mental shake. "There are events every day at the winery."

Luke didn't say anything. He lost all train of thought as Tara held the dress away from her to step into it. The front of his pants tented as she bent from the waist.

Her breasts swung freely and Luke curled his hands into fists. He remembered when she made a similar move two years before. Only she had been straddling his hips, and his mouth was directly underneath her pale pink nipple.

She had teased him even then. Holding his wrists down on to her bed, she had let the tip of her breast graze his lips. Every time he had lifted his head to take her into his mouth, she had moved out of reach. He could have easily broken from her hold and flipped her onto her back, but he had enjoyed watching her take charge and have fun with it.

He had teased her hard nipples with the dart of his tongue. Swirling, licking, pressing his tongue flat, until she couldn't stand it anymore. She had to let go of his wrists. He remembered how his victorious laugh had been muffled as she grabbed the back of his head and pressed him against her breast.

"I'm almost ready," she called out.

"I know," he said hoarsely and swallowed hard. There

was a noticeable tremor in his hand as he pulled at his shirt collar, which suddenly felt too tight.

"What?" she asked as she tied the halter top at the back of her neck.

"Do you plan a lot of these vows renewal ceremonies?"

"This is our first one." Her hands smoothed down the fabric against her hips and disappeared from the reflection.

"Is that right? Are you going to be maid of honor and coordinator again?"

"My assistant is in charge this time." She froze as if she unintentionally gave something away. She looked at the door that separated them. "Although I will probably be called out a great deal to help."

Luke rolled his eyes. "Of course." He got the message, loud and clear. She was not available for his every whim. Or so she thought. He was willing to adapt to her schedule.

"I've never been to one of these ceremonies," he said. "What's expected of me?"

"Treat it like it's a regular wedding," she suggested. She grabbed something from the shelf.

"That's it?" The two words were strangled in his throat as she pouted her lips. She made that exact move against the tip of his cock the last time they were together.

"Pretty much," she said as she applied gloss.

"So it's a repeat of what happened the first time around."

Her fingertip rested against the edge of her lips as she froze like an animal scenting danger. "Not everything."

We'll see about that.

Tara glided her palms against her smoothed-back hair before turning away from the mirror. Luke stood up and

buttoned his jacket over his hard cock as Tara pushed the interconnecting door open.

"Ready?" he asked, watching her bend down to adjust the
shoe strap around her heel. The halter top had a wide slit in
the middle, offering him a bold look at her cleavage.

"Yes, let's go." She closed the filing room door and hurried past him. Luke hadn't made a move before she stopped
and snapped her fingers. "Forgot my purse."

Luke silently waited as Tara walked around her desk. He
watched the gentle sway of her hips. The dress pulled tightly
against her bottom as she bent down to retrieve a black clutch
purse from a drawer.

She tucked the purse under her arm and hurried past the
desk. Tara stopped in front of him and tapped her forehead.
"Oh, and the lights."

She took a step to the filing room and froze. He heard her
sharp intake of breath. Luke glanced at the connecting door,
which wasn't fully shut. Again.

Dread slammed through his chest as he saw the strip of
mirror. From where they stood, they could see the dry clean-
ing hanger dangling from the edge of a shelf in the reflection.

Luke squeezed his eyes shut.

Busted.

CHAPTER TWO

TARA WANTED TO DIE. Just lie down on the floor and die. Cold stone dead.

But life never went the way she wanted it to, Tara reminded herself as she silently went to the file room and fumbled for the light switch. Pulling the interconnecting door shut, she walked stiffly across her office and headed for the door. "Ready?" she asked tightly, refusing to look Luke in the eye. She hit the light switch off with more force than needed.

She wasn't going to say anything. She was sure her cheeks were bright red, and the way she was hurrying away from her office might be a telltale sign of her embarrassment, but if he wouldn't say anything, neither would she.

Maybe she was jumping to conclusions. She was assuming he saw her taking her clothes off. He might not have seen a thing. Or just a flash of leg, at the most. Luke would have said something. Teased her. Wouldn't he?

Had she stripped in front of Luke? Did she bare her body for him? Wiggle and roll her hips as she put the dress on? Cupped her breasts as she adjusted the halter top?

Her skin burned at the thought. She was never changing in the filing room again.

Did he see her? Tara stepped outside with Luke and headed for the tent, unaware of her surroundings. She didn't feel the warm summer breeze or hear the gravel crunching under her heels. Embarrassment and something a little more dangerous, a little more mysterious tugged at her.

She slid a glance at Luke's face. He quickly looked away. His skin was pulled tight across his features. A ruddy color streaked high on his slanted cheekbones.

Oh, he did. Luke saw every inch of her.

Her knees felt like they were going to buckle and yet, a naughty thrill zipped through her. He saw her undress and he liked the show!

What would it have been like if she knew he was watching her? Tara didn't know the answer to that. She shuffled to a stop as she turned the question around in her mind. What would she have done, knowing she could pretend ignorance once she stepped out of the room?

"Oh. My. God." The bride said in a loud voice, her hands held up high. Everyone stopped and turned.

The woman always knew how to grab attention, Tara silently decided. Every movement and outfit choice was designed so she would be noticed in a crowd. That is, if the large jewelry and big, unnaturally red hair didn't do the trick.

"Tara Watkins," Joy screeched, startling the birds in a nearby tree, "are you wearing *white*?"

Tara looked down at her print sundress. Well, yes, Joy had her there. Her dress did have a white background, but there was a prominent black floral design on it as well.

Joy clasped her palms to her cheeks and stared at Tara in horror. "I can't believe you would do that to me!"

"It's the rehearsal," Tara reminded her, in a tone she mastered to soothe even the most irrational of brides. She wasn't sure why Joy pointed out her dress to everyone. White or not, it was certain to be eclipsed by the bride's bright green strapless dress.

"It doesn't matter. This is my wedding!"

Renewing of vows ceremony, Tara wanted to clarify, but she bit back the words and watched Joy bring the other bridesmaid into the discussion. The bride grabbed the woman's elbow and hauled her away from flirting with one of the ushers.

She felt Luke step behind her. Tara inhaled his warm, spicy aftershave as he bent his head close to hers. The scent was exotic and forbidden. "I think you look beautiful," he whispered, his mouth brushing against her earlobe.

Heat flared in her belly. "Ssh." She cast a quick glance at Joy and the bridesmaid as they whispered, stared and pointed. No doubt complaining about every aspect of her dress. The color, the style, the wearer, and her shoes while they were at it.

"Why?" Amusement threaded through his husky voice. "I can't think you look beautiful?"

She hunched her shoulders as her skin prickled with awareness. "Not in front of the bride," she said in a low tone through her fixed smile.

"Ah, gotcha." He straightened to his full height. "I'll tell you all about it later."

Yeah, you wish. She'd deal with Luke and his ideas, but first things first. Tara took a step closer to the bride, who immediately stopped gossiping and pushed the other brides-maid away. "Joy, I don't want to cause you any distress," Tara said as sweetly as possible. "Would you like me to go change?" It was not a big deal to change outfits, but this time she'd do it at home and without an audience!

"Wear the dress," Joy said with a loud sigh. "But only because we're behind schedule already."

Tara spared a glance at Jazmin, who gave a small don't-believe-a-word-of-it shake to her head. Tara wasn't sure how her assistant would feel about that comment, but it was clear that she didn't let Joy fluster her.

It seemed Jazmin took it *all* in stride. She actually appeared to be enjoying the entire process, even during this baptism of fire. The woman was thriving in her element, blooming with confidence and leadership as she approached the bride to dis-cuss something on the ever-present clipboard.

Tara couldn't remember feeling like that before. She was more efficient these days, to the point of being on autopilot, but thriving? Not so much.

She jumped when she heard her name and felt Luke's hand on her arm. "I'm sorry?"

"What do you enjoy doing around here when you're not working?" Luke asked as he guided her to a row of elegant straight-backed chairs.

"I'm always working." She looked over her shoulder at Jazmin. It felt strange not being in the middle of executing and troubleshooting.

"Okay, what do you do when you leave the winery?"

She rarely did. She could go days—weeks—without pass-ing the main gates. But she didn't want him to know that! It would sound like he's the only exciting thing that happened to her for quite some time. Which was not the case at all. "I prefer staying on the grounds."

Luke took a long look around them. He shielded his eyes from the blazing sun as he surveyed the orderly vineyards and quiet small buildings. Tara wondered what he thought of her home. For some reason it mattered.

"You should show me around," he finally said. "After the dinner."

She gripped the back of the chair. "Why?" He wouldn't get to see anything. Night would have fallen, and everyone would have gone home by then.

Luke's slow, lazy smile gave an extra zing to her pulse. It skipped through her veins as her heart pumped hard.

Ah. She was slow on the uptake. It was *because* it would be dark and everyone would have gone home! Tara tilted her face and looked Luke in the eye. "Maybe I haven't made myself clear. Renewing the vows doesn't mean everything that happened on the wedding day will reoccur."

He arched one eyebrow. "Your point?"

She stepped closer and looked around to make sure no one could hear. "Just because I slept with you once," she whispered fiercely, "doesn't mean I'm going to repeat the experience."

His eyes darkened. "I know there's no guarantee."

She frowned at his choice of words. "You mean chance."

"There's a chance." His finger skimmed her bare arm, the tender touch igniting a firework of sensations just under her skin. "Don't you think about us? About that night?"

"Nope." She moved her arm and rubbed it briskly.

"Not at all?" Luke lowered his voice, and the rasp of his words made it sound even more seductive. "Not even once?"

She pursed her lips as if she considered his question. "Can't say that I have."

"I remember."

Well, good for you. Give the boy a gold star. "I don't. It's all very hazy." She waved her hands around her eyes. "I had so much to drink."

"I remember every detail, and you weren't drunk." His voice was still above a whisper, but it held an underlying hint of steel. "You were enjoying a buzz. Maybe a little tipsy, but you were not drunk."

She knew it was useless to argue the point. Especially when he was correct. Tara turned to face Joy, who was calling for one of the groomsmen in her usual brash manner. "Hush, I'm sure we're supposed to be listening to directions."

Luke gently grasped her right elbow. "I remember what it felt like having you underneath me. You were wild."

Tara felt a blush zooming up her neck. "I don't recall that." She stared unseeingly in front of her, warding off the image of him hovering above her. Or how she bucked and twisted against him, her legs tangling with his.

Luke's other hand rested against her left hip, startling her back into the present. She felt caged. His heat and scent surrounded her.

"Or when you trapped my cock between your breasts. You squeezed them tight and let me ride you." The tension shimmered off of him as he spoke. "I hope I didn't leave any interesting marks on your sides."

The blush was spreading into her face and down her chest. She had no idea what possessed her to do that. Her breasts weren't anything to showcase. "You must have me confused with someone else."

"And when you sixty-nine'd me . . ." Luke spoke in reverent awe. "That was the most unbelievable experience ever."

"What?" Tara whipped her attention on Luke. What was he talking about?

"I felt my scalp rising when I—"

She jerked her arm away as raw, hot emotions stormed through her. "I did not do that!"

"I know." He grinned. "Gotcha."

Tara batted his hand off her hip and looked away. She pursed her lips even though she felt the need to breathe deeply. The idea that he couldn't recall what they shared—or confused her with another lover—burned like acid. She should have been able to laugh it off, but for some reason she couldn't.

"You remember every detail just like I do," Luke said with great pride.

She crossed her arms and took a step away from him. She'd have moved farther but the chairs were blocking her. "I'm not listening to you anymore."

"That will only make me try harder."

Tara rolled her eyes. He had a point. The more she ignored him, the more audacious he would become. Yet she couldn't change tactics. She wanted to see how far she could go before he gave up. How long it would take before his attention wavered. She knew better than to believe Luke's interest would last.

"Although, I might be on my best behavior if . . ." He gently trailed his knuckle down the length of her spine, and she shivered with pleasure. "No, you wouldn't agree to that."

What wouldn't she agree to? She had done more with Luke than she had with any other man. He should know that she was very open-minded, so it must be something really wicked. Excitement bubbled inside her.

She shouldn't ask, but she was dying to know. She swallowed, but her curiosity was too strong. "If what?"

His hand rested against the small of her back. The anticipation fizzed in her blood as she felt the heat of him through her skirt. Her stomach clenched, wondering what his indecent terms would be. Not that she would take him up on it, of course.

"If you give me a guided tour of the winery after the dinner," Luke suggested.

"Huh?" They were back to that? There had to be more. He did not want to go on a simple nighttime walk with her. She'd rather he just say right out what he wanted to do. The possibilities were teasing her, almost too much to bear.

"Luke!" Joy called out. Tara turned to see the bride marching over. She wanted to groan from the interruption, but kept her expression blank.

"So how about it?" Luke's hand skimmed up her back. His fingers flirted with the knot of her halter top.

She knew the knot was secure, but that didn't stop her nipples from tightening. It didn't keep her from imagining Luke unfastening her dress and allowing the halter to fall, unveiling her to the world.

The fabric against her breasts suddenly felt too heavy and itchy. "I should ask if others would like to go," Tara responded as coolly as she could.

"No, this is an exclusive tour."

The possessiveness in his voice pleased her. "Fine," she said, doing her best to sound indifferent. "I'll show you around."

"Luke?" Joy stopped in front of him and tsked, shaking her head. "Oh, Luke you're so tanned."

"I've come back from the Greek islands," he said.

Envy shot through Tara. She'd like to visit there. At this point in her life, she'd take any island.

"No, no. This is all wrong," Joy said in a shrill voice.

Make that a deserted island, Tara decided.

"I told you to get a facial."

Facial? Tara stared at Joy. Was she kidding? Luke Sullivan was not the kind of guy who could sit through a facial.

"Look at these lines." Joy reached out and rubbed her fingers at the edges of his eyes. "And these crow's-feet."

"Women love those lines," Luke teased his sister-in-law. He smiled and the lines deepened. "I'm told they're sexy."

Joy was not impressed. "They lied."

Luke tilted his head. "What do you think, Tara?"

"I haven't noticed them much."

His eyes twinkled, but Joy stopped him from saying anything as she grabbed the front of his hair. "Didn't I tell you to get a haircut?"

Luke firmly pulled Joy's hand away. "This *is* the hair cut."

"It needs to be shorter." She did a double take as a man walked by. "At least you didn't get bangs. Excuse me," she said and ran after the man.

"She's very lucky that she's married to my brother," Luke said as they watched her leave.

"Is that right?"

"Otherwise I'd dunk her in the first vat I could find. I still might do it. Care to help me?"

"We can make it look like an accident." She widened her

eyes at the slip of her tongue. What is wrong with her? She'd never done that before. "I didn't say that."

"Yes, you did."

"Okay"—she placed her hands on her hips—"pretend I didn't say that."

"What's the fun in that?"

Tara dropped her stance. "Please, Luke? It wasn't professional of me."

His eyes flickered like blue flames. "I like how you said my name," he said softly. "Say it again."

Tara shifted her bottom jaw. "Luke," she warned.

He shook his head. "No, that wasn't it. Try again."

A startled yelp pierced the air. Tara turned quickly and saw one of the men standing by Joy and Jazmin. He held a hand at the front of his hair.

Tara's mouth dropped open when she saw the bride holding a clump of hair in one hand. "I won't tolerate bangs in my wedding party!" Joy said before handing the scissors back to Jazmin, who stood frozen with shock.

"I don't believe she did that," Tara said in a horrified whisper.

Luke's sigh was long and heavy. "I can. I've heard enough stories about the Christmas family photo incident."

"I don't want to know. Now if you will excuse me, I need to talk to Jazmin. Obviously I never taught her the warning signs to look for when the bride asks for a sharp metal object."

"Are you sure you want a guided tour of the winery?" Tara asked him as they watched the last of the bridal party get in their cars and head to the bed and breakfast down the road.

"I'm sure." He had Tara all to himself and he wasn't going to squander the gift.

"Why do you want to?" she asked as she strolled down the main path. "You've been to the top wine areas of the world. The Loire Valley, Tuscany . . ."

Luke raised his eyebrows but kept silent. It appeared that someone had been keeping track of him. He did those articles about a year ago, and hadn't mentioned them to Tara during the dinner. He hadn't expected Tara to follow his travels, and he shouldn't feel so pleased about the revelation.

"Those wineries are grander than my family's." She gestured with a wide sweep of her arm.

"Have you been to those wine countries?"

"No." She gave a sigh. "I hope to see them one day."

"I haven't seen much of this place." And it didn't look like he would tonight. Small garden lights dotted the pathways, and a few plants and shrubs were artistically backlit, guiding them in the dark.

The buildings were nothing more than shadows. Silence and darkness cocooned them. Her world felt very safe and cozy. He could almost understand why she didn't venture far.

"This can't compare," Tara insisted.

"Is this how you start your tour?" he asked lightly. "You might want to work on it."

"That remark is going to cost you," she said. "You don't get any free samples."

He slid a look at her.

"Of wine." Tara clucked her tongue. "Free samples of *wine*."

"I'll live."

"Okay, the Watkins started this winery in 19—"

"No"—he raised his hand to stop her—"I don't want the tour that everyone else gets."

She stopped and crossed her arms. "Well, aren't you picky? You're already getting a private tour."

"I want to see the winery through your eyes." Guilt weighed briefly on his shoulders but he shrugged it off. He knew what she thought of the place, but he'd act like it was the first time he'd heard it.

Tara frowned. "I don't understand."

"Where's your favorite place?"

She shook her head. "I don't look at the winery that way. There's no one place I'd rather be over the others."

He knew that wasn't true. She loved the cramped carriage house where she lived. But it was possible that she saw her home as hers, and not a part of the family business. "Then show me where you've made your mark."

Tara looked even more confused. "My mark?"

"Yeah, where did you make your stamp that says 'Tara Watkins was here'?" He held his arms out wide as if it were written on a banner.

"I don't . . ." She drifted off as a look of sadness flitted across her face. "I haven't made one."

"There's nothing here that you added to the vineyard?" he prompted. "After all the time you've been here? No improvements, nothing?"

"Oh, that." She disregarded the idea with the wave of her hand. "Most of the things I've done are safety measures and mechanical upgrades. The effects aren't really seen."

"And the other stuff?"

She looked off into the distance. "I guess there's the fountain."

"Fountain?" That didn't sound like something Tara would do. Did she have a frivolous side she kept well hidden? "I haven't seen it."

"It's this way." She nodded toward a tree-lined area past the cluster of buildings. "Follow me."

"Why did you put it all the way back here instead of in the front where everyone could see it?"

"This isn't for decoration. I put it back here to guide cars around this intersection."

Luke laughed. Now that was the Tara he knew.

She glanced up at him. "What's so funny?"

"Nothing," he replied as his mouth twitched with amusement. They turned the corner of the last building and he saw the fountain. It sat in the middle where the dirt trails and gravel pathways knotted.

Artistically arranged lights glowed on the bronze and brass fountain. Water sprayed and streamed from the statue at the center. It appeared to be a frozen moment of a Bacchanalian feast. The god of wine was in the center of seminude maidens.

Tara's choice surprised him. Sure, she would pick something that had to do with wine, but Luke had expected something quiet and refined. Artwork that blended in.

He walked along the wide rim of the fountain and peered at the clear water. Only a few pennies and dimes dotted the floor. "Not many wishes."

"It's not a wishing fountain. It's to direct traffic."

"We need to change that." He pulled out a coin from his pocket and handed it to her. "Make a wish."

She looked at the money in her palm and slowly looked back at him. "Are you kidding me?"

"You've made wishes before, haven't you?" Tara couldn't be that far gone. If she was, he had his work cut out for him.

"Of course, before I knew that I should save every penny. If I took this money and put it in the bank, especially one that offers a compound interest—"

Luke rolled his eyes. He tapped her hand and watched the coin arc in the air and plop into the water. Cold droplets sprayed Tara and she took a hasty step back.

"You wasted my wish," she accused.

He shrugged, not feeling a hint of remorse. "You weren't going to wish anything."

"I didn't say that." She perched on the damp edge of the fountain and reached for the coin in the water. "I get a do-over."

"You don't get to do over wishes."

"My fountain, my rules."

The skirt stretched tautly along her hips and legs, leaving nothing to the imagination. "Go for it," he said, his voice rough and low.

Tara glanced over her shoulder. There must have been something about his look because she cupped her hand and splashed him hard. The move dislodged her and she squealed as she slid off the side of the fountain and into the water.

Luke propped his foot on the fountain and studied the way she was sprawled before him. "I think that's called karma."

Tara growled in the back of her throat and splashed him again. The water hit him like a wall. He didn't say anything as his jacket clung to his body. He didn't wipe away the water dripping from his face. Instead he silently toed off his shoes and determinedly stepped in.

"What are you doing?" She scurried back on her hands

and heels. She watched, almost mesmerized, when the water drenched him from the knee down.

"Helping you out." He shrugged off his jacket and tossed it next to the shoes. His hands went for the knot in his tie.

"By coming in and getting me?" She struggled to get up, her heels sliding on the slick floor. "And taking off your clothes? I don't think so."

"But it's my pleasure." He tossed his tie onto his jacket and placed his hands on his hips. Lust kicked him so hard he saw stars. "You know what? I don't care what Joy says. I'm glad you wore white."

She hurriedly glanced down and saw that the white fabric was transparent. Tara gasped and crossed her arms over her breasts, her hands clasping her shoulders.

"Come on, Tara. I've seen it before." He smiled as he felt the flash of wickedness. "Recently, in fact."

Tara gasped louder. "You did see me!" She kicked the water at him and lost traction.

When she wobbled, Luke reached out and grabbed her wrists. As Tara found her balance, he slowly parted her arms. If it weren't for the black floral print, the dress might as well have been invisible. "There's no reason to hide."

"No reason to stare, either." She tried to twist from his view, but he wouldn't let her.

Luke felt his cock stir as he watched her dark pink nipples tighten and furl. "You like it."

"I do not!" Her hands bunched into fists as she fought to break free from his grasp. "I don't like being stared at."

He had to admit that Tara had become a pro at hiding. Nestled deep in her family's winery, she'd gotten too comfortable. He was more than willing to rattle her cage.

He drew her closer until her nipples poked against his wet shirt. Luke leaned down and gently pressed his mouth against hers. She was as sweet as he remembered.

She turned her head. "What was that for?"

He looked into her eyes and his heart clenched. "I'm making my wish come true."

She frowned. "You didn't make a wish."

"Not today." He tilted his head and kissed her before she got away again.

Releasing her wrists, he wrapped his arm around her waist and drew her flush against him. Luke cupped the back of her head, threading his fingers into her wet hair as he continued the kiss.

He slowly traced the outline of her lips with a teasing, seductive touch. He wanted to claim her mouth. Claim *her* until she mewled and purred, but her tentative response sent a chill down his spine. His pulse skipped and stuttered when she flattened her hands against his chest. Was she going to push him away?

Her fingertips dug as she bunched his shirt into her hands. Tara roughly pulled him closer and opened her mouth wider for his kiss.

His heart galloped as he slanted his mouth over hers and drove his tongue inside. He slid his hands down her back before clutching her bottom. Tara's moan hummed inside his mouth as he kneaded her buttocks.

Luke skimmed his hands over her bare wet skin and reached for the knot behind her neck. Tara broke the kiss and shied away. His hands slid down to her waist as she took a step back. "Luke, we shouldn't."

Need roared through Luke. He was panting hard and his

skin felt too hot, too tight. The sound of the fountain splash-
ing echoed in his ears.

He didn't want to go too fast. The last thing he wanted to
do was scare her off.

Luke took a step toward her and erased the distance between them. Tara stood still, her chest rising and falling. He
dipped his head and licked the drops from her cheeks and
down her chin before trailing his lips down her slick throat.

Leaning her back on his arm around her waist, he slid his
mouth along the halter top until he reached the tip of her
breast. His warm breath wafted over the cold, damp fabric.
Luke took the tight crest into his mouth and sucked hard.

A keening cry ripped from Tara's throat. She grabbed the
back of his head, twisting his hair around her tense fingertips.
He sucked harder, grazing her nipple with his teeth, as she
swayed wildly.

Tara arched farther and yelped as her heel slipped. Luke
caught her before she fell back with a splash and he laid her
down on the brass edge. She watched him with a sexy, mysterious smile and a sparkle in her eye that drew him like a siren's
call.

The lights cast shadows upon them. Tara's dress teased his
senses unmercifully. The fountain lights and the floral pattern
of her outfit played hide-and-seek with her body. He rubbed
his hands down her sides and watched her shiver with pleasure.
She splayed her legs and stretched her arms above her head.

The craving inside him was like a violent ache. She was
open for him, ready for him to explore. He wanted to taste
her, drive into her, and make Tara his. But most of all, he
wanted to watch her face as the pleasure took over.

He slid his hands along her damp legs, bunching the

soaked dress up her past her hips. When he finally revealed the satin panties, Luke cupped her sex and was rewarded by her groan.

He wanted to peel her panties off and roll the wet satin down her legs. Then he would settle between her thighs and thrust into her until he made every one of her fantasies come true.

If he wanted a one-night stand, he could let that happen. But he wanted more.

For a second he felt guilt but he swept it aside. He watched Tara as he rubbed her clit with the pad of his thumb. His cock hardened with each pant she made. She bucked against his hand, the friction between satin and flesh driving her wild.

Sliding his fingers along the lace edge of her panties, he dipped his fingers into her core. Her greedy flesh gripped his fingers and sucked him deeper. Luke groaned, his cock beating against its confinement.

He pumped his finger while rubbing her swollen clit. Luke watched the expressions flit across her face as she chased the pleasure. He knew the moment she caught it.

Tara's mouth parted as her lips darkened and her skin flushed. Her breath hitched in her throat as tension shimmered from her body. Her flesh clamped around him as she came in rolling waves, the first crashing into the next.

Tara moaned softly before she sagged against the brass, her muscles limp. She closed her eyes as she tried to catch her breath. "Luke," she said in a husky voice as she reached for him.

Luke's guilt returned with a vengeance, almost as fiercely as the throb of his cock. He couldn't go through with this. He knew what she wanted and what she craved. He knew how she felt about him. About them.

He knew almost everything, but not because she told him. He wished he could say it was because he noticed every detail about her, but that wasn't true. It was because he read her Web diary.

Luke reluctantly withdrew his hand and splayed his fingers along the damp silk. The heat under his palm made it more difficult for him to stop.

Tara shifted under his touch, her muscles twitching from the aftershocks. "What's wrong?"

He was giving her what she wanted. Fulfilling her every desire. So why did he feel guilty?

"Nothing. I thought I saw something," he lied as he stroked her. "It could have been someone."

Tara's sharp intake of breath warned him. Luke watched her skin flush. He cupped her sex as she arched her back. Tara stunned him when she closed her eyes and moaned as the orgasm rippled through her.

CHAPTER THREE

LUKE STARED AT THE ceiling over his bed at the quaint bed-and-breakfast. He felt edgy, his body hard and restless. The first streak of dawn had pierced the darkness, but he had given up on the idea of sleep hours ago.

He closed his eyes and remembered Tara splayed out on the fountain, wet and almost naked. He loved how hot and uncontrolled she became under his touch. Luke had felt powerful and humbled at the same time, and was rewarded by the euphoric look on her face when she came.

Luke groaned at the memory and cupped his semihard cock. He had wanted to drive into Tara and feel her flesh squeezing him with every thrust. But then he had to do something stupid and get noble.

Big mistake. He should have grabbed the opportunity with both hands. Tara probably wouldn't let him get near her once she found out the truth. And that was the problem. She was going to be upset when she found out that he read her blog.

Nothing wrong with that, right? It's out there on the Web, for anyone to come across. Except for the fact that she discussed him and how conflicted she felt about that night they had shared.

Then there was the fact that he was using the information Tara put on the blog to get closer to her. Luke grimaced. If he put it like that, it did sound bad. But was it wrong to use the information when he knew it gave Tara pleasure?

The memory of Tara's responses at the fountain made him groan. Luke rubbed the heel of his hand against his erection, willing it to go down. She had looked at him with desire and trust.

It was the trust that got him. He knew it was wrong of him, Luke admitted with a sigh. He would regret reading the blog. He remembered when he stumbled upon it almost a year and a half ago while researching a tribal wedding ritual. All of a sudden he started reading a Web diary by some events planner who had a strange, secret pet peeve about wedding veils.

There had been something about that blog that made him read more and more. Then he had read the first entry and it all had made sense. Everything clicked. Tara Watkins was the voice behind the bridesmaid's blog.

It had been love at first sight for him. He didn't believe in that kind of stuff, and when it hit him, he thought it was instant attraction. Lust. Anything but an elemental connection that tilted his world.

But as the wedding continued, he saw her hurting. He understood the proud tilt of chin and the pain in her eyes. Something inside him felt the need to protect her.

He hadn't planned on sleeping with her. Sure, he had wanted it. Wished it, but he wanted Tara to want him. He didn't want to be her rebound or revenge sex. He had wanted it to be about the two of them enjoying each other.

Luke circled his fingers around the base of his cock as he remembered that first night. She had been wild and incredibly sexy. Tara had not been drunk. Not by a long shot.

He had walked her to her carriage house and they stepped inside her tiny home. After Tara closed the door, she had surprised him by grabbing his tuxedo jacket and kissing him hard.

The kiss had sizzled a path down to his toes and threatened to curl them backward. His body had gone hot as she had speared her tongue in his eager mouth and had sensuously rubbed her body against his.

He squeezed his eyes shut, his breathing rough and hard. That had been only the start of their night together. Tara had been insatiable, and he had been more than willing.

Her feelings had to do with more than attraction, he was sure of it. The only reason she opened up to him, took him to her bed, and showed her wild streak was because she instinctively trusted him.

He knew that he needed to earn that trust. He had to tell her about the blog. He didn't want to, but it was the right thing to do. Even if it meant she'd never trust him again.

Luke stared up at the ceiling, his breathing slowing down. Maybe he could tell her after the weekend, after one more night together . . .

This ceremony is not turning out like I expected. I still can't believe what that bride-turned-barber did. What a psychotic beyotch! And I really can't believe what I did with The Best Man. Again!

I'm so mad at myself for repeating my mistake. I could blame my first night with

The Best Man on my breakup. Rebound sex therapy, that kind of thing.

But I don't have that excuse this time. I fell—literally—for The Best Man again. Probably a lot quicker than the first time, which makes it more embarrassing.

Nothing is stopping me from having a sexual relationship with this guy. I want him; he wants me. So why am I holding back?

Simple: He makes me want to break free from this safe little place that I have carefully structured for myself. A place where I can't get fired, or dumped, or hurt.

He makes me feel alive and curious. I feel strong and powerful, but I know that's just an illusion. He also makes me feel like the center of his world. It's a little scary having that kind of attention, but I like it.

Why is it scary? Because it's temporary. It would disappear if we tried to make it last more than a night. I don't think I could handle that. It's one thing to know it won't last, quite another to watch it happen.

Now that I think about it, the best man is the WORST man to start anything with. A groomsman usually sees a bridesmaid as his wedding favor. And, let's face it, you can't start a relationship with someone you first viewed as a goodie bag. Bridesmaids can be just as guilty. I've seen some fight over the best man the same way they tussle for the tossed bouquet. Do they really think anything is going to come out of it?

I might have slept with The Best Man for all the wrong reasons, but it isn't just about sex anymore. I don't think it ever was. At least, not on my part.

He's going to be gone by the end of the weekend, and I'm going to be trapped here, my senses half dead, my dreams stunted, and knowing what I'm missing.

Maybe I should tell The Best Man that we can't do this. Then again, this is the last night. Why take a stand now? Should I go for it while he's still here? What do you guys think? ~

Tara leaned back in her chair and read her words on the computer screen. Terrific. She was trying to base an important decision on the advice of people she'd never met. People whose names were Bashful_Bride07 and MacBaby. It was official: she had lost her mind.

She could already figure out what Nomad, the most vocal male visitor, would suggest. He would say GO FOR IT in big bold letters and use every emoticon he could find. Nomad had made no secret that he was cheering for The Best Man. He thought Tara didn't take Luke's feelings into consideration. As much as she would like to argue, she knew Nomad had a valid point.

Her visitors' opinions, even Nomad's, would probably be better than anything she could come up with. They could probably see her situation very clearly. They never melted under Luke's sexy smile or knew what it was like to be in his arms.

Tara tiredly rubbed her eyes and slumped deeper into her chair. The morning light was now streaming in her office window, but she was no closer to coming up with a solution.

No one would understand that she liked who she was when she was with Luke. She was impetuous and daring. She wanted to try everything and live for the moment. With Luke, her humdrum existence shattered, revealing a wondrous place just under the surface. Her wishes were out there, simply waiting for her to claim them.

But was that a new vision, or simply an illusion? Tara thought she could see it more clearly when she wasn't dazzled by the starlit night, but her body and heart still clung to the dreams Luke had inspired.

She heard footsteps in the corridor outside her office. Tara quickly exited out of the program, her pulse pounding fast. Was that Luke searching for her? Her stomach gave a funny little flip at the possibility.

Tara glanced up at the door, an expectant smile on her face, her heart lurching in her throat and getting stuck there when she realized it wasn't Luke.

She blinked when she saw her father pass her office. "Hi, Dad."

He backed up and looked through her door. "Are you working today?"

That gave her a moment's pause. "I work every day," she reminded him. All family members did. Her mother was probably opening their wine store like she did each morning.

It was a way of life they had chosen. Well, her parents chose it. Nothing was wrong with it, Tara thought, but it wouldn't have been her first pick.

"I thought you were a bridesmaid this weekend," he said as he stepped into her office.

"Yes, but that's a different kind of work." And she would never have agreed to it if Joy's ability to throw money around hadn't made up for the inconvenience. "I'm checking my e-mail before I have to get my hair done."

"Why?" He glanced at her hair. "What's wrong with it?"

"Nothing, but Joy wants the bridesmaids to have a very specific hairstyle." Not to mention expensive, Tara thought with the roll of her eyes. At least she was able to talk Joy out of requiring the bridesmaids to get their hair dyed a matching shade. "I'll be back in the office tomorrow."

"Sounds good." He turned to leave. "I saw the events calendar for this month. I like seeing it that full."

"Thanks." She smiled at her hard work being recognized. Her days and nights were filled with cooking and wine appreciation classes, wine tasting club meetings, and corporate dinners. Saturdays and Sundays were just as busy. It had taken a great deal of hard, consistent work to get their events calendar to look like that.

"Tara . . ." Her father rested his hand on the doorjamb, like he wanted to go, but felt as if something had to be said.

Something about his manner pricked at her. Oh, no! Her eyes widened until they stung. Someone *did* see her with Luke at the fountain last night.

Her stomach jerked violently and she wanted to double over from the pain. She had been spotted. The rumors had already started. This wasn't going to be good.

Tara hunched her shoulders. "Yeah, Dad?" Her voice barely carried. She wanted to sink under the desk and curl up in a tight ball.

"When you created this job"—her father looked everywhere but directly at her—"I thought it was something for you to pad your resume."

"Oh?" Why was he talking about that? Uh-oh. Tara closed her eyes and took a deep breath. She was getting fired. By her own father. It didn't get much worse than that.

She couldn't let that happen. That flutter in her chest wasn't relief; it was panic. If she couldn't keep a job in the family business that she had developed herself, then she was going to suffer out there in the real world.

"Uh, yeah," Tara said, thinking fast. She had to point out her best qualities. "I know you felt that way, but I wanted to *help out*. It was the least I could do since you guys gave me the carriage house and a chance to *work hard*."

Her father didn't seem to catch her hints. "And then when . . ." He paused and gave a long sigh.

Tara knew what that sigh meant. Thanks to working in a family business, communication was comprised of a lot of shortcuts and codes. She was just given the Brad sigh.

"I know," she said softly. Her parents were still disappointed about Brad's desertion and the end of their expansion plans. They didn't need to say anything; she felt it all the time. Now she managed to heap another disappointment on top of that.

"I thought this"—he gestured at her office—"was something you could use to get your mind off of him."

She sure had. Tara threw herself into her job. It didn't matter that she hated being an events coordinator. She made it her duty to do it well and keep quiet about her true feelings.

"But I never thought I would see the day when . . ."

She knew her father wasn't much of a talker, but he was slowly driving her insane. He was looking at his feet now. The tips of his ears were beet red. Tara wished he'd spill it and end the agony for them both.

He finally looked up and gave one of his rare, shy smiles. "When your events brought in more money than anything else this vineyard produces."

Tara stared at him, her jaw slowly dropping. "Huh?" This had nothing to do with Luke? Her dad didn't know anything about the fountain?

"And most of our labels are selling well as a direct result of your events. Your mother showed me the numbers last night."

"Really?" The tension seeped out of her body and she sagged against her chair.

"Yep." He tapped his hand on the wood jamb. "Good job. Keep it up."

"Thanks." She watched him walk away, and mulled over what her father had said. She was a success.

Huh, and she helped save the family business. A heavy, suffocating weight lifted from her shoulders that she didn't even know was there. She helped out and she did it without marrying the neighboring prince. That was a bonus!

This was a sign. She probably received other signs, but hadn't been looking. Tara knew she should stop fighting the inevitable and accept that this was where she belonged.

She shifted in her seat as a curl of apprehension wrapped around her. Tara shook it off. Life-altering decisions were not meant to be comfortable.

This was what she was going to do. She didn't need the

opinions of her blog visitors to tell her she was beginning to bloom and thrive here. She would stop thinking of other choices. Those possibilities were never up for grabs and she wasn't going to kid herself anymore.

She was staying. Nothing and no one—especially Luke— would make her regret that decision.

Pleasure zinged through Luke when he finally spotted Tara heading for the tent. Her beauty always made him stop and stare. He didn't how he'd managed to run into her, but he prayed that his good fortune would hold out.

Time to take a gamble and test his luck. It was a half an hour before the wedding, and he had been looking for her all day. If he didn't get to talk to her now, it would be too late.

Had she been avoiding him? Knowing Tara, she was probably shy about what happened the night before. Luke had a feeling that her untamed responses surprised her. Maybe that was wishful thinking on his part. He'd like to think he was what brought out the wanton in her.

Luke was having feelings for her that he never felt with anyone else. He was protective of Tara, but encouraged her to be reckless. Her lusty responses gave him just as much enjoyment as her quiet displays of tenderness and affection.

He wanted it all, and he was willing to take a big risk to get what he treasured most.

"Tara!" He strode toward her and her expression brightened when she saw him. Her smile packed a punch and Luke paused in midstep. He finally made progress with Tara and now he had to risk it all. He didn't want to jeopardize what they could have, but he knew it was necessary. "I've been looking for you."

"Really? I'm sorry." She pressed her hands against the intricate knot of blond hair piled on top of her head. "I've been dealing with bridesmaid stuff."

He had to admit that the strapless, knee-length dress was a strange color. Joy had called it sage or thistle. Some weed name. He thought it looked more like the color of mud. It wasn't a color at all, but that didn't diminish Tara's beauty.

"You look gorgeous," he finally said when he realized he had been staring.

"Thank you." Heat flared in her eyes as she studied how he wore the black tuxedo. "So do you."

"Listen, Tara." He grasped her elbow and guided her to the edge of the pathway. "We need to talk."

Her shoulders went rigid. A shadow of misery darkened her eyes, but when she blinked, it was replaced by a cool look. "About what?"

"I need to tell you in private."

"You know, Luke"—she pulled out of his grasp—"I really don't have time. Even though I'm not the events coordinator for this particular day, I still need to check in on Jazmin."

Luke braced himself and took the leap. "I read your Web diary." Her look of incomprehension spurred him on. "The Bridesmaid's Blog. I visit it every day."

"You. Do. *What*?" She struggled to speak, each word getting louder.

"I didn't know it was your blog at first," he said in a rush. "I stumbled on it when I was researching."

She slowly pressed her hand against her forehead. Luke's heart twisted when he saw how her fingers shook.

"How long have you been reading it?" she whispered.

"Uh . . . a while." He rubbed the back of his neck. "I've also read the archived entries."

She pressed her lips together and then flinched as if she thought of something. "Do you comment?"

Luke hesitated, knowing he was in some seriously dangerous territory.

"Luke." Her voice sharpened. "Do you participate in the comment section?"

It was too late to backtrack. "Sometimes."

Tara winced and dipped her head. "I don't believe this is happening. Which one are you?"

He bid for some time as one of the florists walked past them. "Nomad," he said in a mumble.

She jerked her head up and stared at him. She looked uncertain if she heard him correctly. "You're *Nomad*?"

He nodded.

An angry red mottled her cheeks. "You're one of the guys I've been talking to all this time—especially about The Best Man?" The need to lash out shimmered from her. "You rat!"

He held his hand up in protest. "Hey, I didn't tell you what to do about The Best Man. I told you what The Best Man *might be feeling*."

Tara looked at him as if he were speaking a foreign language. "It doesn't matter," she informed him. "You are still a rat!"

He didn't need her to keep telling him what he already knew. "That's why I stopped last night."

Tara's stricken expression nearly undid him. "How gentlemanly of you." Sarcasm sliced through her words as she glared at him.

How could he explain that he understood what she wanted

because she freely discussed it in that diary? She had no idea what she revealed by what she said, what she didn't say, and how she chose her words.

Tara Watkins wanted to be noticed. Not by the world, or a group of strangers, but by someone who would appreciate the risk she was taking. She needed someone who encouraged and protected her as she spread her damaged wings.

But it was more than wanting to be noticed. The cocoon she had spun was beginning to feel tight. She wanted to find a life that nurtured her dreams of exploring. Luke wanted to be there when she broke free to take her on one adventure after another.

Luke knew that moment was not going to happen any time soon, if the way Tara was glaring at him was any indication. She couldn't get far away enough from him.

"You should be ashamed of yourself for reading my diary," she whispered fiercely.

"It's on the Internet," he pointed out, growing impatient. "It's not private. Thousands of people read it."

"Thousands of people that I don't know," she countered, "and who don't know it's me."

"Are you sure?" She worked with a lot of people, but Tara believed she resided in a bubble where her actions didn't ripple into other people's lives. "For all you know, Joy could be reading it."

She reared back. The red flush of anger retreated. "Did you show it to her?" she asked in a horrified whisper.

"No!" Did she think that poorly of him?

Tara's complexion took on a sickly pale shade. Her features looked pinched. "Who have you told?"

"I wouldn't tell anyone. You know that." Anger slowly simmered inside him.

She crossed her arms. "No, I don't."

"Yeah, you do." He wouldn't let anything happen to her when they were together or apart. The idea that he wouldn't take good care of her offended him.

He leaned closer and whispered in her ear. "We are hot for each other, and we both know you wouldn't do half of these things with another man. But you do it for *me*. Because you trust *me*, and you feel safe with *me*."

"Wow, you don't read my blog very carefully." She tilted her head and looked into his eyes. "Do you skim over it, hoping to find the juicy parts?"

"What are you talking about?" He felt a creeping sense of dread. He bet there was a new entry on her Web diary today. One he hadn't read because he had been too busy looking for her.

"Whatever we have is"—she arched her hand through the air—"over."

"Over?" he repeated dully. "It just started."

"It's over. And do you know why?" She poked her finger against his chest. "Because I *don't* feel safe with you."

Luke watched her walk away. Her words echoed inside his head. They were like a kick in the gut, and he staggered back. The woman he wanted to love with wild abandon didn't feel safe around him.

He had to change her mind. Luke watched her turn the corner. Not once did she look back. He didn't have much time to convince her. Maybe twelve hours at the most.

How was he going to convince the skittish woman that the safest place to be was in his arms?

CHAPTER FOUR

IT WAS DÉJÀ VU all over again.

Tara dully watched the bride and groom renew their vows. Her cheeks hurt from the happy expression she was trying to project. She felt like her fake smile was going to crack and fall off in pieces.

How did she manage to get into the same position from two years ago? Okay, so it wasn't exactly the same, but her heart felt like it had been ripped from her chest and stomped on.

What's the big deal? Tara thought as the string quartet began yet another classical piece. She hadn't planned to keep up a relationship with Luke. It was a wedding fling, a maid of honor hooking up with the best man cliché. She had already made the decision to end what they had.

But why did he have to read her blog? Tara closed her eyes as embarrassment prickled her skin. Why did Luke Sullivan, of all people, have to find her online diary?

That page she had on the Web was her safe place. Safer than the winery because it was free from expectations and family judgment. On her blog, she hadn't used names, no specific location names, nor did she display any pictures.

With those parameters set, she had let loose on her feelings and opinions. She had put down her ideas and dreams. Tara cringed, knowing she also included her regrets and mistakes.

She put herself out there, totally in the open. She had been virtually naked and loved every minute. Tara sighed and opened her eyes. Just as her luck would have it, she wasn't as free as she had thought. She had been recognized.

Tara's gaze automatically went to Luke. He was standing behind the groom, towering over him. Luke's blue eyes caught hers and held them. She wanted to look away, but found it too difficult.

She could almost feel Luke willing her to give up. To stop ignoring and avoiding him. It couldn't be any more obvious that he wanted her to talk to him. Forgive him.

Not in a million years.

Tara tore her gaze away as the minister announced the bride and groom as man and wife. She joined in the applause, noticing that Joy beamed with sheer happiness. At that very moment, the bride appeared sweet and loving as she watched her adoring husband.

I'll give it five minutes. Joy's tender feeling would pass by the time the couple reached the end of the white carpet. The bride would inevitably find something to complain about.

It was Tara's turn to leave with Luke. They shared a knowing look before Luke winked. He knew exactly what Tara was thinking.

She suddenly felt exposed. And not in the same way she felt when he saw her naked.

Revealing her body didn't offer the same risk as showing her innermost thoughts. Having someone see her—really see her—tossed her emotions in a jumble. It scared her, made her want to put up the shields, and even hit back.

But that didn't explain the warm energy that also radiated inside her chest. It was light and had the power to push back the dark confusion. She didn't know why she felt so conflicted. It almost had her running for cover.

"You can't ignore me for the rest of the night," Luke murmured as they made the short distance to the end of the aisle.

"Oh, really? Watch me." She grimaced at the slip of the tongue.

Luke chuckled as he guided her to the receiving line. "I plan to."

She didn't think she could handle being with him for the remainder of the night. Especially when she would be required to dance with him. She had to put her foot down now.

"You can cut the gentlemanly act," she said in a low voice that only he could hear. "I know exactly what kind of man you are."

"Yes, you do." Luke shrugged. "And I know exactly what kind of woman you are."

She flinched before she could stop it. Luke had seen her, warts and all. She was far from any man's dream girl. "So why are you still here talking to me?" she asked lightly.

He looked down at her. His eyes darkened as the world around them blurred. "Because I like what I see."

Tara leaned closer to him and heard Joy's screech of laughter. She jumped back and blinked, the world back in focus. "Yeah, right," she said and transferred her attention to the line of guests making their way through the receiving line.

She might have scoffed at Luke's answer, but it shook her to the core. He'd seen her when she wasn't on her best behavior. When she had been snarky and inconsiderate and—she hated to admit it—rude.

Sure, she wasn't like that all the time on her blog, but there were moments when she was. Worse, she didn't apologize for those entries. The anonymity made her feel like there would be no consequences.

And he had liked that? Please. She had been on her best behavior with Brad, and he was still revolted at the prospect of spending the rest of his life with her.

Luke really believed he liked what he saw. Maybe it was to assuage his guilt for continuing to read her blog. Maybe he liked the ladylike version of her and was conveniently ignoring the rest. Or he liked the idea of knowing her secrets.

Whatever the reason, it didn't change a thing. She wasn't going to have another wedding fling with The Best Man. He could compliment her as much as he liked—and even mean it at that time—but if she wanted to protect her heart, she'd do the smart thing and avoid him.

But she couldn't shake the feeling that it was too late. She wasn't going to escape unscathed once this weekend was over.

Night had fallen and the small garden lights were ablaze. The festive music from the reception reached Tara, and she hummed along as she grabbed the metallic garland and draped it along the edge of the groom's car.

Tara couldn't believe she was thinking this, but she was never so grateful for catering to an unreasonable bride as she was today. The decision to avoid Luke had been easier than she expected thanks to Joy's unending list of demands.

She didn't have a chance to sit down or visit with others as she kept running to and fro. Joy was really making the most of "her" day. The groom didn't seem to notice or worry. Maybe he considered this his day *off* from meeting Joy's every whim.

Tara needed this break from the wedding. She inhaled the scent of the roses that mingled with the summer breeze and the winery's garden. She could use the quiet time to pull her thoughts together.

It felt good to slow down and let her mind wander. She felt like a mischievous fairy as she decorated the car that would whisk the happy couple to their honeymoon. The sight of the rich red roses and gold swags made her smile.

Great, now she was acting like Jazmin, she thought with a wry grin. She wondered if Jazmin would look at weddings in the same way again. Tara would feel bad if her assistant developed a jaded view of this ceremony. Already the young woman had met with more situations that her emergency kit couldn't cover.

"So this is where you're hiding."

Tara froze when she heard Luke's smug voice right behind her. The peaceful night shattered as her pulse quickened.

"I'm not hiding," she replied. Although she had jumped at the chance to escape when the opportunity presented itself. "I'm helping out Jazmin."

She didn't look at him but she knew Luke was studying the decorations on the luxury car. "Nice," he finally said.

"Thank you." Her tone indicated that he could leave, but Luke didn't get the hint.

He slid his hands in his pockets and rocked back on his feet. "Kind of a step up from the shaving cream and tin cans."

"I saw this in a movie about an Indian wedding," she said, preoccupied with the symmetry of the design, "and we've been doing it ever since."

Luke leaned against the car. "Is India one of the places you want to visit?"

She stepped back and viewed her handiwork. "I'm sure I mentioned it on my blog."

"Huh." He propped his head with his hand. "Talking is no longer necessary since I've read your diary."

"That sounds right to me." She took a few steps to the side. It wasn't necessary, but it allowed her to keep some distance.

"Interesting." He grabbed one of the small rosebuds and twirled it between his fingers. "So, tell me, Tara. What sign was I born under?"

She glanced up and looked at him. "Your sign?"

"That's right. My sign." He stuck the rosebud sideways in her design. "What do you know about me?"

"Enough." She plucked the rose off.

"But you don't know. You are centered on your life and your feelings. You don't venture far from your blog to see what others say or feel."

She stepped back, hurt by his accusation. "That isn't true!"

He grabbed another tiny furled flower. "Prove it."

"I don't have to." She knew it wasn't true, although it rankled her that Luke would think so.

"You're so concerned about protecting yourself that—"

"You make a living writing about your adventures," Tara interrupted. "You've been interested in traveling ever since you were a kid who was often sick in bed. You read books about far-off lands and you were determined to see those places."

The rosebud bent between his fingertips. "How do you—"

"You concentrate mostly on the Mediterranean countries because you found mythology fascinating in college." She rested her hip against the car door. This might take a while.

"I'm sure that had something to do with the fact that you had a May-December romance with your professor."

His jaw dropped. "Who told you about—"

"You are addicted to Italian food"—she started to tick the list off her fingers—"can't speak French without accidentally offending someone, and you have a fear of snakes after that incident on the island of Rhodes."

He closed his mouth with a snap. "Anything else?"

"I was cheering for the snake."

The crinkly lines deepened around his eyes. "I bet. When did you learn all this?"

"We're both in the travel and recreation business," she said, wondering if her excuse sounded legitimate. "I've read your articles and essays through the years."

He arched an eyebrow. "You went far back."

She shrugged one shoulder. "Some of your stuff is archived on the Web. So see, I do venture out, thank you very much."

Luke crossed his arms. "And why is that different from what I did by reading your blog?"

Oooh. Tara glared at him for setting the trap. She had tried to prove something and didn't see that coming until it was too late. Worse, Luke had a point she hadn't considered.

"You can't compare the two," she announced as she swung open the back passenger door.

Luke grabbed hold of the door before it hit him square in the chest. "Sounds like we're very similar."

"There is something very different about my reading an article you published," she explained as she needlessly fluffed the garland, "and you reading my diary without my permission."

"You read my work without permission."

Tara rolled her eyes. "True, but that is different. I wrote about stuff that had to do about us."

"Also without my permission," Luke was quick to point out.

"Stuff," she said through clenched teeth, "that I didn't want you to know."

His eyes brightened as if he finally understood. "And you feel at a disadvantage because you don't know what I've been holding back."

"If you put it that way, okay, yes," she admitted grudgingly. "That's how I feel."

"Then what do you want to know?"

She tossed her hands in the air. "Luke, it can't be forced like a game of twenty questions."

"I don't have the luxury of time," he said with a hard edge to his voice. "What do you want to know?"

She held her hand out to stop him. "I'm not playing this game."

"Do you want to know," he started slowly, "that when I visit a place, I skim the surface?"

She narrowed her eyes with incomprehension. "What does that have to do with anything?"

"But I couldn't wait to come back here," he admitted. He looked earnest. "I want to know everything about you."

He was already getting too open for Tara's comfort. "You're comparing me to a place?"

"There's no comparison. When I close my eyes, I don't dream about the places I've been, or the places I want to be. Not anymore. I dream about you."

Tara's stomach flipped as her cheeks grew hot. "I don't

believe you." She tried to hide how his words flustered her. "Nice line, but I'm not buying. Now please move. You're crushing the garland."

"Then . . ." He paused and rubbed the back of his neck. A dull red crept up to his face.

Tara rested her hand on her hip. "Oh, this should be good."

"You should know that I"—he looked down at his shoes— "convinced my brother to do this ceremony."

Tara's eyes widened. "What? *You* thought of the renewing vows?"

"No way," he said with a laugh. "It was all Joy's idea, but when my brother was waffling, I egged him on to do it." He shifted his bottom jaw, as if he wasn't sure if he should keep going. "Because I knew I had an excuse to come back."

Tara sat down on the backseat, her legs dangling out of the car, as she considered his words. "That's not very nice of you."

"He'll live."

She gave a long sigh and looked in the direction where the music played. "It would have been so much easier if you'd told me from the start that you'd read my blog."

"You would have stopped writing it," he said as he rounded the car door. "You would have backed away. Like you're doing now."

Luke knew her too well. "Maybe."

"And then we would have both lost out."

She looked up at him and held up a warning finger. "I still haven't forgiven you."

"That's okay," he said with a sexy smile. "I haven't started to grovel."

Tara gave a startled laugh. "Oh? Are you going to kiss my foot?" She raised a foot and rotated her ankle.

The twinkle in Luke's eye was her only warning. Her breath caught in her throat when he dropped to his knees. "I was kidding!" She jerked back her foot, but Luke proved faster and firmly grabbed her ankle. "Honest!"

"All part of the groveling package," he said as he slid the delicate strappy sandal off her bare foot and set the shoe down on the floor of the car.

Nerve endings tingled from her fingers to her toes as he cupped her heel. Her foot appeared fragile against his large hand. "Seriously, I forgive you." She tried to wrestle away. "You can let go now."

Luke's eyebrow lifted at the rise in her voice. "Hmm . . ." He brushed the tip of the rosebud along the bottom of her foot. Tara screeched and jerked her knee up.

"Are you ticklish?" he asked, devilment lighting his eyes. "I don't think you mentioned that on your blog." He grazed the flower lightly against the arch of her foot.

"Luke!" She tried to fend him off with a kick. Luke tossed the rose over his shoulder and grabbed her other foot. He pulled sharply and she slid forward.

Tara yelped and grasped for the backseat, her fingers sliding against the leather. Her words of protest dissolved in her throat as Luke's hand traveled up her thigh. His skin felt rough and hot as her flesh prickled with anticipation.

Her startled gaze met his knowing eyes. Her heart skipped a beat as he lowered his firm lips against her ankle. Warmth flooded her sex just as his blunt fingertips spanned her panties.

"Luke"—her voice sounded weak even to her ears—"don't even think—"

He rose and stepped into the car. Tara started backing away as he closed the door behind him. Her pulse skyrocketed as he crawled over her with a masculine grace. She lay sprawled underneath him, her heartbeat dancing against her ribs.

She licked her lips. "We can't do—"

"Everyone is at the party. Now kiss me." He brushed his lips along her jaw. "Please."

She tipped her head and met his mouth. Tara closed her eyes as she inhaled his scent mingling with the leather. His warmth surrounded her, exciting and comforting at the same time. His firm lips opened as she moved her tongue inside his mouth. He tasted of champagne and wedding cake.

He tasted of fun and adventure. And she wanted more.

His kisses teased her until her mind spun. Long and leisurely, Luke explored her mouth while he caressed her body with his hands. By the time Tara pulled at his jacket, wanting him closer, she no longer cared where they were.

Luke nudged her legs open with his knee and bunched up her skirt with his hands. Tara grabbed at his tie, her moves frantic as she struggled with the knot. When she finally unraveled the tie, she tugged at his shirt. She couldn't pull it free thanks to their position. "Sit up," she ordered breathlessly.

"Not yet." He slid her panties down her legs and tossed them on the floor before he sat up, taking her with him.

Tara straddled his legs and only then remembered she still wore one shoe. The thought fled her mind as Luke pushed down her strapless top. A shudder swept through her as he cupped her breasts. Her hands shook as she unbuckled his belt and slowly unzipped him, pausing while his hands played and teased with her tight nipples.

She couldn't wait another moment as the need coiled

painfully tight, low in her belly. Tara yanked at his pants and Luke assisted her by lifting his hips. She slid his clothes down his legs, revealing his hard cock.

"Wait." Luke grabbed for the back pocket and searched for a condom. Tara wiggled with unconcealed impatience, her core clenching, as she watched him glide on the latex. By the time Luke grasped her hips and guided her down, Tara wanted nothing more than to claim him.

Tara slowly sheathed him, her wet, swollen channel clinging to his cock. She moaned, heat flashing through her, when Luke filled her to the hilt. Tara arched back, the movement allowing Luke to hit a spot that robbed her of her next breath.

Luke cupped the underside of her breasts and sucked her nipples. She felt the tug to her sex. The pleasure intensified as she rolled and bucked against him.

Digging her knees in the leather, she rode him hard and fast. Her hair escaped from the expensive up-do and tumbled against her face in waves. Luke grabbed her hips and grinded her against him. The rhythm took her breath away. The pleasure built inside her, coiling tighter and tighter until Luke thrust sharply and groaned his release.

He slid his hand between them and pressed his finger against her swollen clit. He rubbed little circles and she swiveled against him. She rocked wildly as the coil sprung free and her release pulsed through her body.

Tara collapsed against him, her face tucked against his shoulders. Her choppy breaths wafted against his neck and she could see his pulse twitching under his skin.

Everything seemed sharper, brighter to her. The scent of sweat and musk mingled with the leather. Her organza dress and his fine tuxedo scratched her skin. Their gasps for air and the sound of crunching gravel—

Crunching gravel! She froze as a sickening dread hit her full force. That could only mean one thing.

"What?" He murmured, rubbing his hand against her back in a soothing, affectionate gesture.

"Ssh." She pressed her fingertips against her mouth, hoping she was wrong. "I think someone is outside."

Luke tensed underneath her. He tilted his head slightly as he listened. "They're coming this way."

"Oh, crap!" she whispered fiercely and lunged for the closest door. "Quick, lock the car!"

"No." He stopped her and pressed her body tightly against him. "The automatic locks would be heard."

"What are we going to do?"

"No sudden moves," he said, already sliding to the edge of the seat, the leather squeaking under their moves.

"What are you doing?" she asked, her voice high.

"Trust me," Luke said against her ear and rolled off the seat. Tara squeezed her eyes shut and grabbed onto his shoulders. She swallowed back a yelp when her spine hit the floor. Luke covered her, making it a tight, uncomfortable fit.

"This is your bright idea?" They were definitely going to get caught and might as well surrender now.

"Ssh."

The sound of footsteps grew closer and seemed to be moving around the car. Panic struck her chest. Her shoe! Where was her shoe Luke took off? Wait . . . didn't he put it in the car? Tara investigated by stretching her bare foot.

"Don't move," Luke said very softly against her.

She flinched when she heard the static of a walkie-talkie. "Hey, Frank, this is Jazmin."

Oooh . . . could this get any worse? Tara wanted to whimper. Her two employees were talking next to her while she was half naked—and in a very compromising position—in the back seat of a car.

"Have you seen Tara?"

Don't open the car door . . . Do not open the car door . . .

"Nope," Frank replied, his voice metallic from the electronic device. "Try her office."

Jazmin signed off. There was no sound. No movement. The silence dragged endlessly, tearing at her nerves. Tara could picture Jazmin staring at her decorating paraphernalia. It would be unlike Tara to leave that lying around.

Luke didn't seem to share Tara's panic. Wedged firmly between the seats, he hadn't made a move. She felt the tension rolling from him, but his breathing was quiet and controlled.

Tara pressed her lips as she heard Jazmin making a small turn. Was she looking at the car? In the car? For the life of her, Tara couldn't remember if the windows were tinted.

She tried very hard not to imagine Jazmin pressing her face against the window. Luke's black tux could only hide so much!

Jazmin walked away, the sounds of her footsteps fading. Tara sagged against the floor. Relief flooded her bones, making her feel tired and limp.

"That was a close one," she whispered to Luke.

"What?" He lifted his head. "You don't get off on being an exhibitionist?"

"Are you crazy?" Where did he get an idea like that? "The only person I want to see me is *you*."

His smile was possessive and sexy. Tara didn't move as she felt her heart turn over and tumble. She was very close to falling in love with him, and she wasn't sure if she was ready for that kind of adventure.

His eyes lit up. "I have an idea. A travel magazine is sending me to Morocco. You should come with me."

Yes! Sheer joy filled her and it was as if her body couldn't contain the force of it. She wanted to go more than anything. It was more than living out a dream; it was about getting a chance to explore what she started with Luke.

But something deep inside her tugged her back. Instinct? Fear? Common sense? It didn't matter. "I don't think so," Tara said, dropping her gaze.

"It'll be fun," he insisted as he carefully disentangled himself from the car seats. "I leave tomorrow."

Her head jerked back and she stared at Luke. "Tomorrow! That's not enough time!" It would have been impossible had she planned to go, but now it wasn't enough time to be with Luke before he left her again.

"Sure it is." He reached out and grabbed her hands. "Come with me."

With one smooth move, she was sitting against Luke on the back seat. "I can't," she said and scooted away.

"Tara."

She let go and yanked up her dress before tucking her hair behind her ears. "The only place I'm going with you is back to the carriage house." She opened the car door and quickly stepped outside. "Come on."

Chapter Five

Two weeks later

I made a mistake. I should have said yes to
The Best Man.

Tara stared at the words she just added to her blog. It was one thing to think it, another to see it written. And quite another to know that Luke would see those words.

She wanted to go back into the computer program and delete her entry. Her hand hovered over the mouse, but she didn't press a button. Indecision had swirled around her for weeks.

It had even been a while since she posted. Other than a brief and censored recap of Joy's wedding, Tara hadn't added a new entry to her Web diary. Breaking the habit had been hard. She had no idea how much she relied on the blog to discuss her feelings. But she couldn't discuss her innermost thoughts on her little corner of the Internet. It felt odd and awkward saying anything of importance because she knew Luke was reading.

She couldn't reveal that she missed him so much. She didn't want to appear too vulnerable and needy. She didn't want him to know that she willed the phone to ring, or that she had searched for his name on the Internet the other day. Tara cringed as she remembered that low moment. Googling was probably not a good sign on her part.

She should be able to tell him how she felt in her e-mails and phone calls. That she wanted him by her side, in her bed, and in her life. Instead she kept all communication on the surface, asking about what he'd been up to, recounting anec-dotes about her day.

Tara knew she was being greedy, but she couldn't contain it any longer. True, she had received more than what she ex-pected, but it wasn't enough. She wanted much more. She wanted it all.

"I'm going now."

Tara gave a start and looked at her office door to see her assistant peeking in. "Bye, Jazmin."

"Are you all right?"

"Yes, of course." She closed the screen showing her blog and turned away from the computer. "Why do you ask?"

"I don't know." Jazmin stepped into the office. "You've seemed kind of down for the past few weeks."

"I haven't noticed," she lied breezily and suffered a pang of guilt. She hadn't been very efficient since Luke left, and her hours at the office had increased. Not that the extra overtime had done much good. Tara had developed a tendency to stare off into space. The world sped before her, but her reactions were sluggish.

Worse, she was starting to hate every minute on the job. Being an events coordinator had never been her passion, but these days it was a burden she couldn't escape. She wanted to drop everything and run away. The feeling to leave everything she worked hard on for two years was so fierce that it scared her.

"It's me, isn't it?" Jazmin pressed her hand against her chest. "I've done something wrong."

"You?" Tara wasn't sure if she had zoned out in the conversation again. She had been doing that lately.

"The Sullivan wedding," Jazmin clarified. "Someone complained, right? It's okay. Break it to me."

"Jazmin"—Tara leaned back in her chair—"I know I passed on the compliments we received because of that wedding. And I told you that we have a few more leads from guests who are interested in having their wedding here."

"But not the complaints," Jazmin pointed out.

"I haven't heard any," Tara promised. She paused, knowing it was time to let go, but almost too nervous to do it. "In fact, at this rate, you'll be handling all of the weddings."

"Really?" Her eyes widened and an ecstatic glow infused her face. She took a step back, a little wary. "Are you sure? What about you?"

Tara cast a glance at the stack of files on her desk. "I'm sure I'll find something to keep me busy."

Jazmin looked at the files and shuddered. "There's such a thing as too busy. You know, Tara, you might want to consider a vacation one of these days."

She wanted to. The yearning twisted inside her until she thought she would snap. But leaving, even for a brief time, would be a bad idea. It would give her a sample of something she couldn't have. She wasn't strong when it came to Luke, but she would put her foot down on that.

"Not that I'm trying to get rid of you," Jazmin hastily assured her, obviously misinterpreting Tara's silence.

"I know, but it's been a while since I've gone on a vacation."

"Take baby steps and try a day off," Jazmin suggested.

Tara wouldn't know what to do with herself if she wasn't working. She would miss Luke even more, but she worried she might find something more troubling. If the busyness of her schedule didn't distract her, Tara might have to look deeper into herself and discover nothing there.

Tara didn't want to be all work and no play. She wanted to go to interesting places and do fun things. She wanted to enjoy life. She wanted to start now.

She glanced at the clock, which showed it was seven in the evening. She should work for another hour or two, but she couldn't handle coordinating another couple's happy day. "I think I'll start by leaving early."

"You're a wild woman, Tara," her assistant said with a smile as she left.

Tara turned off her computer and tiredly rose from her chair. She slowly made her way out of the building, not sure what to do. She felt a little bit lost.

Tara headed for her carriage house with determined strides. She had to do something to get out of this funk. The restlessness was growing stronger every day.

Her cell phone rang. She groaned but grabbed it out of her pocket. Work habits were hard to break. Looking at the display screen, Tara's heart skipped a beat. She flipped the phone open and was already smiling before she answered. "Luke?"

"Hey, Tara." He said her name like a caress. Her skin tingled. Her breasts felt full and heavy—and he was half a world away. It wasn't fair that he had so much power over her.

She dipped her head, allowing her hair to veil her face, creating an intimacy that the phone didn't allow. "Where are you?"

"My favorite place in the world." Satisfaction permeated his husky voice.

Regret pinched her heart. She would have loved to see it with him. She wanted to share the important and special moments. "Where is that?" she asked, forcing a lilt in her voice.

"Guess."

"Rome?" Luke would love that place. The food, the art, and the culture. She wondered if she would love it just as much.

"Guess again."

"Paris?" Those amazing landmarks would be a draw for him. As a bedridden child, he would have read about Notre Dame or one of the opera houses. He was probably on the Eiffel Tower at this very moment.

"No, not even close."

"I give up. Where are you?"

"I'm right in front of you."

She stumbled to a stop and looked up. Luke was leaning against her door as he pocketed his cell phone in his faded blue jeans. Tara ran to him, the gravel spraying under her feet. *Luke was here. He came back.* She jumped into his arms and held him tight as he swung her around.

"You should have told me you were coming back," Tara said as she rested her head against his chest. His warmth and steady heartbeat made her want to snuggle deeper into him.

"I need to tell you something."

She lifted her head. "What?"

"I made a mistake," he said with a lazy grin.

It couldn't be that bad if it made him smile, Tara decided, but his words still made her heart jump. She slid down his body and slowly set her feet on the ground before looking in the direction of her office and then back at him. "Have you been reading my blog?"

"Huh?"

She waved away the question when she saw the confusion flicker in his eyes. "Never mind. What mistake are you talking about?"

"I left without promising you that I would come back." Luke cupped his hand against her cheek. "I won't make that mistake again."

She sighed. Maybe this is why she had been holding back, or why she hadn't felt completely safe to let go. Luke could be as gentle and as daring and as loving as possible. It didn't matter if she knew he was going to leave.

She needed to hear this promise, and she hadn't realized how much. It was more than about missing him. It had more to do with the fact that Luke would always leave her behind.

She didn't want to think about that. Not now. Not when Luke stood before her.

It was time to seize the day, Tara decided as she firmly pushed her worries to the side. She needed to make the most of the time they had together. Live in the moment and worry about the rest later. Much, much later.

"Come inside," Tara urged him as she opened her front door and ushered him in. "How long have you been waiting? You should have called me the moment you landed. I could have gotten you from the airport."

She pressed her lips together when she realized she was babbling. She couldn't contain herself.

Luke kicked the door closed behind him and leaned against it, cradling her against his chest. She nestled against him, inhaling his scent and reveling in his body heat. She wanted to burrow deep into him and cling.

Ooh. Cling. Not a good sign. She lifted her head from his chest and looked up at Luke. No clinging, she ordered herself firmly.

Luke gently held her face between his hands. Tara closed her eyes, concealing the tears. She shivered as he brushed his fingers along her cheeks.

"I just got here," he said as he grazed her mouth with his own and then pulled away. "But it feels like it's been too long since I got a chance to do this."

He kissed her deeply. He tasted of danger and excitement. She held on to him tight, longing for him to take her on the wildest adventure.

Her fingers flexed and bunched against his T-shirt, and Tara realized what she was doing. She was clinging again. *No clinging! Understood?*

Tara quickly stepped out of his embrace, her movements jerky and graceless. From the darkening of Luke's eyes, she could tell she surprised him.

"Are you hungry?" she asked with a distracted smile. "Thirsty?" She turned and glanced at her kitchen. She spent more time at the office than at home and wouldn't have enough to feed a large, hungry man.

But Luke didn't respond. Instead he gently pulled the ends of her hair. Her pulse skipped a beat as he wrapped the blond length tightly around his hand. Her scalp tingled as he cupped the base of her skull with his palm.

Luke took a step even closer with his hand still in her thick hair. He had caught her and she felt like she could finally let herself go.

She looked into his eyes. Luke appeared exhausted. World-weary. She wanted to take care of him, to fuss and spoil him, but she instinctively knew that he would hate that kind of treatment.

Tara saw the hot flame in his eyes, but didn't know what to predict until he claimed her mouth with his. She wanted to slow him down and savor every moment, but a part of her knew she had to pack in a lifetime during this short reunion.

Luke pulled his mouth away, his lips swollen and red. "Tara," he said in a groan. "Take me to bed."

Whoa. Her knees wobbled. There was something about the way he said that. It was a primal growl as if his civilized veneer was about to slip and reveal the untamed animal underneath.

"You'll have to release me," she said. She liked the husky, sure sound of her voice, but she really enjoyed the look of regret in Luke's eyes before he slowly spun her around, unraveling her hair from his hand.

A carefree laugh pressed against her throat as she turned and turned. She felt dizzy, but she kept turning. Her world was colorful and topsy-turvy when Luke was around. It was unpredictable and messy as the chaotic emotions swirled and caught in her chest.

She wouldn't have it any other way.

Tara opened her eyes as she turned and bumped into something warm and solid. Luke. He caught her before she collided with the ladder. She smiled and turned away, grasping one rung with her hand.

"Wait," Luke murmured against her ear. She shivered as his warm breath caressed her skin. Tara almost let go of the rung to face him when he grasped her waist, preventing her from turning.

"What are you up to, Luke?" Tara asked. She wasn't worried or scared. More like curious.

"Stay where you are."

She looked up at her loft bedroom. "I thought you wanted—"

"I do. And we'll get there. Eventually," he promised with lust in his quiet voice.

Tara opened her mouth, but the question died on her tongue as he dipped his hand along the V-neck of her blouse. He cupped her breast, humming with pleasure against the side of her neck.

She arched her throat to give him better access. Excitement surged inside her just from the feel of his mouth against the delicate skin. She sunk the edge of her teeth in her bottom lip as he found her nipple at the same time.

Tara murmured, not quite sure what she said, as he rolled her nipple between his fingers. She knew the pink crest darkened and furled under his touch, as her other breast ached for his attention.

"I missed you," Luke whispered in her ear. His voice was rough and low.

She closed her eyes as his admission ricocheted in her heart. "I missed you, too."

"I missed everything about you," Luke continued. "The way you feel. The way you fit next to me."

She was wedged against him, his chest pressed against her back. He felt strong and powerful. His pelvis cushioned her bottom. She was wet with arousal as she felt his hard, eager cock, pressing against her cleft.

"I miss the way your breath catches in your throat when I do this." He pinched her nipple and she gasped as the hot pleasure darted through her.

"Luke . . ."

"I miss the way you call out my name. Especially when I'm driving deep inside you."

Her sex clenched at the memory. She pressed her legs together as he bunched her skirt up her thighs.

Right this very moment she wished she wore something sexier to work. Not the pencil-slim skirt or the boring blouse. She wished she had worn something other than the functional bra and panties.

Luke didn't allow her poor clothing choice to get in the way. He slid his hand along the seam of her skirt until he hooked his fingers along the low waistband of her panties. He yanked the silky lingerie down her leg with flattering insistence. As he crouched behind her, she kicked off her shoes and the scrap of damp silk.

Tara tightly gripped the rung above her. She wanted to race up the ladder and throw Luke onto her bed before the fire burned her inside out.

Luke let her skirt fall back in place. "Stay still."

Wasn't he in a rush to get her to the bedroom? "What are you doing?"

"I'm going to take you here."

She looked around and realized he meant *here*, here. As in *on the ladder*. The rickety, old ladder that probably couldn't handle two people at a time, let alone allow anyone to hang on to it while making love.

He was crazy. No, she was, because she stood still, hanging on to the rung for dear life as he dragged the side zipper down her skirt. She didn't think to help as he pulled the fabric off her legs. She hadn't considered moving a muscle as he wrenched the buttons free and removed her blouse.

Luke reached around to unfasten the front closure of her bra. She liked the feeling of him surrounding her. Tara leaned back against him as her bra opened. She felt the groan in his chest as he peeled the white silk from her curves, letting it fall from his hands before he cupped her breasts with a possessiveness that left her breathless.

He fondled her breasts with bold strokes that went straight to her core. She felt every touch deeply. One audacious move from him and she would melt.

Luke seemed to know this. It was like he was in tune with her. His hands roamed her curves and she was all too aware of the contrast between her nudity and his fully clothed body. But all self-consciousness fled the moment he cupped her sex and speared his fingers through the hair shielding her clit.

She could feel her swollen clitoris stirring from the hooded protection, desperate for Luke's touch. But this time, he ignored what her body was clamoring for and swept fingertips along her wet slit.

Tara whimpered as her knees buckled. She tilted her bottom as he rubbed his fingers against the puffy folds of her sex.

Her flesh was slick, coating him, as the tremors of excitement zinged in her veins.

"Climb the ladder," Luke told Tara. The words sounded disjointed, almost foreign.

She frowned as she tried to focus on the ladder in front of her. She was hot, bothered, wet, and aching and *now* he wanted her to climb the ladder?

She didn't want to. She didn't think she had the strength, but she felt Luke's hands on her hips as he guided her. His touch almost felt too hot for her skin.

Tara had climbed a rung, one foot higher than the other, when he told her to stop. She wasn't too far off the ground, but if her foot slipped, it was going to be a clumsy fall.

When she heard Luke unzip his jeans, Tara grabbed the rungs as tight as she could. She wished she could curl her feet against the ladder.

The anticipation danced under her skin when she felt Luke pressing the tip of his cock against the wet folds of her sex. She was at the perfect height and angle for him to drive into her. Her womb twitched with dark pleasure as Luke clamped his hands on her hips and surged forward.

Luke groaned against her neck. Tara's hold slipped as her mouth sagged open from the sudden, fierce invasion. Her slick and puffy sex drew him in, sucking his length in deeper.

He slowly withdrew and thrust again. Short, long, choppy, smooth. She couldn't follow Luke's tempo and abandoned all attempts to meet his thrusts. She moved when he guided her, and stayed perfectly still when his fingers dug into her hips. She bucked and rode, or swayed and arched, her flesh clinging to his cock.

Luke's thrusts suddenly grew short and uncontrolled. His hand slid down to her clit, capturing the stiff bud between his fingers. He squeezed her swollen clit and Tara's world splintered. Her mind spun, the stars sweeping behind her closed eyes. She felt Luke come, wild and rough as her sweat-slick hands slid from the rungs.

She was free-falling. Spinning. Tara hunched her shoulders, preparing for the crash, but it didn't come. She opened her eyes and stared at Luke's flushed face.

He had caught her. Somehow she knew to cling to him, even when she swore she wouldn't.

She just wouldn't make it a habit.

"You need to get a bigger place," Luke complained later that evening. He bumped his arm against the glass shower door and cursed again.

"This place suits me just fine," Tara declared and twined her arms around his shoulders. They were fitted snugly against each other and his cock prodded her.

"That's only because you haven't tried to fit two people in this shower." He paused from washing her back. "Have you?"

Tara laughed and it echoed in her tiny bathroom. The shower stall barely fit one person, and it made for some interesting positions washing with Luke.

Luke took one step forward and she was pressed against the slippery shower wall. "Tara?"

"No, I haven't," she admitted with a smile and hooked her legs around his hips.

Luke dropped the soap and clasped her waist. Something tender flickered in his eyes. "I'm going to Egypt next."

She sighed with envy. "You lucky bum."

His hands slid up her sides. "Come with me."

"Luke, we've been through this before." She splayed her fingers along his wet chest. "I can't get away."

"Tell the truth," he said as he cupped the undersides of her breasts. "You don't want to."

She clucked her tongue. "That's not true."

"You can have other people take care of your work for a couple of weeks," he suggested as he stroked her breasts. "Hell, you could quit your job and find a replacement."

Tara tilted her head back in pleasure. "This is where I belong," she said in a whisper. "I made this winery very successful and I need to be here to maintain that level of success."

"Just because you're good at something doesn't mean you're required to make it your life's work." He trailed his soapy hand down her stomach. "You need to follow your passion."

"This isn't about passion." She grabbed for his hand before he went any lower. "I have responsibilities."

"You mean you have a debt to pay."

She unhooked one leg from him. "You don't know what you're talking about."

"You feel that you let your family down when you didn't get married to Brad. They were counting on that marriage."

"I know it's not my fault," she said, unhooking her other leg. She reached for the shower door, but Luke blocked her.

"Then why did you try to make up for it?" he asked. "Working nonstop, sacrificing your dreams and doing whatever you could to bring in the money."

His comments were too close to the bone. When her father had praised her, she wasn't quite basking in the glow of achievement. She was suddenly unburdened.

"Come with me to Alexandria," he insisted.

She wanted to go to Egypt, she wanted to fulfill her dreams of travel, and more importantly, she knew she should make the compromise. "I might be able to take a week or two off, but I can't do it right away."

"No, you'll find an excuse and stay."

Luke had no idea how much it took out of her to offer that. "Then what do you want from me?"

"I want you to leave here and live with me."

"What?" She wasn't expecting that. Not this soon. She wasn't ready! "Live where? I can't do that."

He placed his hand on her shoulder. "Tara, I love you, and I want to be with you."

Her eyes stung with tears. She had wanted to hear those words, but now they required action from her. "We are together."

"The phone calls and e-mails aren't enough," he said with a touch of exasperation. "I don't want to be the occasional weekend fling who only shares your bed."

"You know," she said with a wry smile, "most guys wouldn't complain about that setup."

"I want to share the world with you."

She closed her eyes, her only form of protection against the words she wanted to hear. "On your terms."

"You're not happy here," Luke said softly, his voice barely heard over the shower spray. "You've denied yourself for so long, that you don't know what it's like to be passionate about something."

He could see it too, huh? She was happy with him. But that didn't mean she was going to throw away everything to follow him to the ends of the Earth. "I put my blood, sweat and tears in this place. Isn't that a form of passion? I sacrificed everything and now I'm enjoying the results."

"You weren't guaranteed it would be a success," he pointed out. "What is stopping you from putting that same kind of effort into us?"

"Why do I have to choose?" She pushed down his arm. "Why can't I have both?"

"We can't continue to build a relationship so far from each other and it's too important to give up," he said.

Fear pierced her heart. "So you're going to leave me if I don't agree?"

He shook his head and water sprayed from his hair like a crown. "No, I won't. But I'm going to make a wish in that fountain of yours when I leave. And I'm hoping that one day you're going to love me enough to take a leap of faith."

THREE WEEKS LATER

Tara stopped and looked around, trying to get her bearings. *Toto, we're not in Kansas anymore.*

Alexandria's exotic beauty overwhelmed her. Everything was so different from what she knew. Egypt didn't look anything like her lush vineyard in the Pacific Northwest. The scent of spices in the air was as mysterious as the snippets of conversations she overheard.

She was in a land where she didn't know a soul. She had no command of the language or the customs, and there was a strong possibility that she was lost.

No need to panic, she told herself as she looked for the

hotel, desperate to latch on to something familiar. This was supposed to be fun and exciting. A taste of adventure should kick in at any time.

Oh, God, how does Luke do this? He must have nerves of steel. She knew now that she didn't.

I should have told him that I was coming, Tara thought for the umpteenth time since leaving the airport. She wasn't ready for this and she couldn't predict what was going to happen next. Her heart was pounding a million miles a minute and she would have burst into tears if she wasn't suffering the first level of dehydration.

Her gaze scanned and grabbed on to a name she recognized. It was the hotel. Tara wanted to crumple to the ground and kiss the sidewalk with relief. But she didn't want to add dysentery to her list of woes, so she held her bag more securely on her shoulder and made her way through the street. She didn't stop until she stepped into the air-conditioned splendor of the building.

Her choppy sigh hurt her parched throat. She shivered as the cold air wafted over her heated skin. Tara swiped the sweat from her brow and walked to the registration desk.

Her back still felt damp with perspiration. She had dressed all wrong for the trip. She was itchy, creased, and had a stain on her shirt of questionable origin. A blister was forming on the back of her heel.

And she had once dreamt of traveling the world. Tara shook her head at that fanciful idea. What a joke.

A wave of fatigue hit her as she watched a guest argue with the hotel employee at the desk. Maybe this was a bad idea. Traveling was supposed to be a life-affirming experience, not a test of mettle. Yet, she couldn't turn back now.

"Tara?"

Great. She thought she heard her name. Now she was hallucinating. She was pretty sure that was a sign of severe dehydration. She should probably get something to drink, but she wasn't sure what would be safe for her untried and queasy stomach.

Tara felt a hand drop on her shoulder. She tensed, her fingers clenching her purse. She didn't know what the laws were here regarding self-defense, but no one was going to mess with her.

She swung around, her gaze clashing with blue eyes and crinkly lines. Tara's knees threatened to buckle as she stared at Luke. He looked gorgeous, as if he had just stepped out of a vacation magazine. Tanned and fit, he wore a crisp white shirt and pressed khakis.

"Tara?" Luke whispered her name as his eyes shone with amazement.

She belatedly splayed her arms. "Surprise!"

Okay, this wasn't the reunion she had planned. She envisioned waltzing into the hotel looking like a well-seasoned world traveler. She would have wowed Luke with her grace and easygoing nature.

Instead she looked like she had been chewed up by some travel demon, regurgitated, and spat out. And probably smelled like it, too.

Although the way Luke was looking at her, he didn't seem to mind. It looked like he wanted to sweep her into his arms and do her right there on the floor. A jolt of excitement forked through her exhausted body.

He grabbed her hand and Tara clung to him. "Come with me," he said, tugging her to the bank of elevators.

"No, thanks. I came all this way to stand in line." She frowned as the words seemed louder in her head.

"Yeah, you said that out loud," he told her, the grooves in his face deepening with a smile as he whisked her into the crowded elevator.

"What are you doing here?" he asked, disregarding the other passengers in the elevator who were listening.

"I took a leap of faith." Tara winced when she saw her reflection in the elevator door. "And I went splat."

His gaze met hers. "No, you didn't. You took the plunge." Luke shook his head with wonder. "I can't believe it."

"Neither can I." It all felt surreal. She had quit her job, found a replacement, packed her things and headed off to find Luke. No one told her that following her gut instincts would be a wild, terrifying ride.

He lowered his head and pressed his mouth against her ear. She tilted her head and leaned back on his shoulder. "You don't know what this means to me," Luke said.

"It better mean a lot." She jumped when she heard Luke's chuckle. Oops. There went that talking out loud thing again. She pressed her mouth closed and didn't even utter a sound when Luke dragged her out of the elevator.

She watched silently as he opened the door to his hotel room. She stepped in and looked around, dropping her shoulder bag on the floor.

"Where's your luggage?" he asked.

"Copenhagen, the last I heard." She peeked into the bathroom and was secretly thrilled to find a normal looking toilet and shower stall. "My suitcase is better traveled than me." Another wave of fatigue hit her and she wobbled.

Luke was right behind her and grabbed her by the shoulders. "Are you okay?"

"I need to lie down." So much for their reunion. She didn't have the energy to get undressed, let alone undress him.

"Not a good idea. It will make the jet lag worse."

She shuffled straight to the bed. "I've been upright for thirty-six hours."

"Thirty-six hours? But it only takes—"

"Don't ask." She wasn't going to get into it. Tara lay down on the bed. Her sigh was close to orgasmic.

"Tara"—he crouched down next to the bed and tenderly brushed her hair away from her face—"I'm glad you're here."

"Me, too." She cracked an eye open. "But at the risk of sounding negative . . ."

"You? Never," he teased.

She opened both eyes. "What if I'm not cut out for this kind of life?"

"You are." The mattress dipped as he lay down next to her. She sighed with pleasure as he gathered her into his arms. "I'll take care of you," he promised. "I'll show you the shortcuts. You'll be able to handle anything that will come your way."

She believed him. With Luke at her side, she'd be okay. "But what if I'm wrong and this is one big mistake?"

"We'll figure it out. Together." She curled up snugly against him. "And we'll use your carriage house as base when you're feeling homesick."

Tara yawned and closed her eyes. "Got it all figured out, huh?"

"I'm making it up as I go along," he confessed. "That's part of the fun."

"Oh, has the fun started?" Her voice was muffled against his chest. "Why didn't you tell me?"

Luke's soft chuckle jostled her. "Tara, I promise, the best is yet to come."

WEDDING WRECKER

CHAPTER ONE

SHE LOOKED LIKE A Jane Austen movie reject.

Amber Hughes stared at her reflection as the noise in Tilly's Wedding Shoppe faded. She tried to mask her growing horror, but she couldn't drag her attention away from the tangerine taffeta. Maybe it was the watermark design in the fabric that had the mesmerizing effect.

No, it was the empire waist. Amber stared at where it was supposed to be, but her bustline blocked the view. This was why she never wore a high-waist dress, or a low-cut square neckline, for that matter. Her breasts looked bigger than ever, ready to burst through the taffeta.

She should have seen this coming.

Amber could pinpoint exactly where she made her mistake. It was when she unexpectedly received a Christmas card from her old friend Madison, and felt obligated to respond in kind.

That was always a no-no. Everyone knew that random Christmas cards from single women in their twenties were suspect. It meant they were testing out their address book.

There was only one reason why a woman would do such a thing. She was engaged and needed an estimated head count for her wedding. Or worse, she needed to know how many best-friends-forever would be willing to sacrifice their paltry savings for the honor of wearing questionable pastels.

Amber stared at the neckline again, wondering if that was a hint of nipple she saw peeking from underneath the fabric. Maybe her first mistake was thinking she would be exempt from all this. Guess not. From now on she would not send Christmas cards to women of marriageable age.

Great. Amber rolled her eyes. Now she was *sounding* like a Jane Austen reject. She sighed, her breath stuttering out of her throat as the dress seams pinched.

Madison's face popped into the mirror's reflection. The slender blonde leaned close to Amber's ear. "Try not to exhale," she whispered the unhelpful tip, "or you might suddenly go topless."

Her flat-chested friend might not be speaking from experience, but she unfortunately had a point. Amber looked at Tilly, who was kneeling beside her, pinning the hem. The older woman had a reputation for artistic temperament, but considering how much she charged for creating dresses that would be worn only once, the luxury of breathing should have been included in the price.

"It's too low in the chest," Amber told the seamstress. "And too tight."

Tilly didn't look up from her task. "No, it isn't."

Amber blinked hard and stared at the woman. Was Tilly blind? "Yes, it is." She frowned when she saw Madison from the corner of her eye. Her friend was frantically waving her hands, motioning her to be silent.

What was her problem? Amber knew she was in the right. It was obvious that the dress didn't fit properly. She needed it fixed before the wedding.

"Nothing can be done about it now," Tilly replied, pulling another pin from her mouth. She looked up long enough to glare at her. "Had you gotten measured along with the other bridesmaids . . ."

"I e-mailed my measurements just as you had requested." She jumped when a wayward straight pin pricked her ankle. Amber refrained from kicking back, but it was a close call.

"I don't know why you're being so picky," the seamstress said as she stabbed another pin in the fabric.

"Because I'm addicted to oxygen."

"You aren't the main attraction," Tilly muttered. "No one will even be looking at you."

Amber and Madison shared a look in the mirror. *Wanna bet?* The unspoken comeback hung between them until Amber looked away.

It was obvious that people were already looking at Amber. She heard the whispers behind her back and felt the glares aimed at her head. The disapproval hit her in crashing waves, trying to drag her down until she surrendered.

It didn't used to be this way. She had once been the most coveted bridesmaid. Amber once hated that label. It chafed at her like an old-fashioned girdle. Yet, no matter how she tried, she couldn't get rid of the image.

Until the one time she did what any good bridesmaid—any good friend—would have done. When the clergyman had asked, "If anyone objects to the union between this man and this woman, speak now or forever hold your peace," she spoke up.

The shocked gasp rippling through the congregation still rang in her ears, as did the way her voice wobbled when she accused the groom of having sex with one of the bridesmaids in the choir room just moments before the ceremony. But what she remembered most of all was the bride's expression. Her friend Bailey's face had been pale and tight, just like the three-thousand-dollar bridal gown she had been stuffed into.

At the time, Amber thought she was saving Bailey from a disastrous decision. Instead she had done the unthinkable. The unforgivable.

The wedding went on. The events had been set into motion. Nothing and no one could stop it. After all, Bailey and her parents spent thirty thousand dollars on the ceremony and reception, right down to the paper napkins with the names and date imprinted. It wasn't as if you could use those again.

Even though her words were determinedly ignored at the wedding, no one would let her forget what she had done. Theories were bandied about Acorn Grove. Mrs. Adams down the street decided Amber had been secretly jealous of Bailey for years and simply lost it. Jeff at the auto shop wondered if alcohol had been involved. The old Fillmore sisters told everyone who listened that her behavior was the result of sparing the rod and spoiling the child.

It didn't matter if she had spoken the truth. Amber was now the town pariah and her years of good behavior were no longer applicable. She missed the benefits of being a good girl and wanted them back, but that wasn't going to happen in a million years.

The disapproval scraped at her for months until it became unbearable. Amber had gratefully taken a job across state, but it couldn't erase what happened. And when Bailey's marriage lasted less than a year, Amber didn't need to live nearby to know what was being said. She was being blamed for planting the seed of doubt.

All this because she had spoken up when she thought it was important. She had tried to prevent heartbreak, but only caused it. She lost Bailey as her friend, and her status in the community while she was at it. The only good that came out of it was that no one would ask Amber to be a bridesmaid, or even invite her to another wedding.

Then Madison had to remember their childhood promise and take away that benefit. But that's okay, Amber decided. She was willing to do whatever it took to make the wedding successful. Blending in was the name of the game. If the ceremony went without a hitch, then her last wedding appearance would soon be forgotten.

Yeah, right. What was she thinking? She was going to stick out like a sore thumb at Madison's wedding.

She tried to take a deep, calming breath, but the dress wouldn't let her. There was no way she could survive a whole wedding day in this getup. The stitching wouldn't last through one move of the obligatory Chicken Dance at the reception. "We need to fix the neckline," Amber said firmly.

Tilly held up her hands in defense. "It's not my fault if you gained weight."

"Just in my breasts?" Amber asked, not trying to hide her sarcasm. "How is that possible?"

She shrugged. "You are a Hughes."

Acorn Grove's answer for the perpetually stumped: Blame it on DNA. "Tilly"—Amber clenched her back teeth—"we both know you didn't follow the measurements I gave you."

Madison sucked in air, the hiss echoing in the suddenly quiet shop.

"That's it." Tilly stood up, and her bones creaked and popped. "I'm done."

"Done?" Amber looked at the lopsided hem and then at the older woman's retreating back.

Madison ran after the seamstress. "She didn't mean it, Tilly."

"Yes I did." Tilly and Madison turned the corner and disappeared, her friend's voice trailing behind them. Amber looked at the other women in the shop. "Where are they going?"

The customers judiciously avoided eye contact, grabbed the pattern book they were leafing through, and went to the other side of the shop.

She tossed up her hands, but the tight sleeves held back her arms. "Okay, can anyone help me out of this dress?"

"Hey, Wedding Wrecker."

Her heart jumped as the seductive voice washed over her. Amber pressed her legs together as the wicked heat tingled from the tips of her breasts to the center of her sex. "Anyone but you, Josh."

"Aw, you don't mean that." Joshua Griffin hooked the rented tuxedo with his fingers and held it over his shoulders. He had heard Amber's voice from the other room and had to investigate. He'd probably regret following the impulse, but for now he was glad he took the time to look in. The sight of Amber Hughes in a tight dress was worth it.

Josh walked leisurely toward her, the sound of his boots echoing with each step against the scarred wooden floor. He watched her posture go rigid as he got closer. Her jaw jutted out defiantly by the time he stood in front of her.

He couldn't take his eyes off of Amber. She was like a riot of color splashed on a white wall. A disruptive force in a sea of calm. She looked just as out of place in Tilly's Wedding Shoppe as he felt.

She'd changed, and the pastel gown wasn't going to hide that fact. Amber's sweet feminine look was long gone, replaced with an edge. Her brown eyes were no longer wide with innocence, but had a sexy slant as she watched him cautiously approach.

He wasn't sure if the changes were a good thing, because his gut instinct said it was only skin deep.

Her black hair was long, the waves wild and free. It was the kind of style any man would want to see fanned across his pillow or caressing a path down his stomach. Josh flinched as his diaphragm tightened at the image.

Dragging his gaze down, he noticed that she was still voluptuous the way a woman should be. Her hips had enough curve for a man to hold on to. Her breasts, high and rounded, were ready to break free from their taffeta prison.

He stared at the neckline that plunged dangerously low. The sight gave a kick of heat to his bloodstream. "You've grown."

Amber's glare sizzled. "You haven't changed a bit." She turned her back on him and tapped her foot impatiently.

He looked at the back of the gown. The zipper was slowly making its descent, unable to hold the shiny fabric together. "You're kind of stuck in there, huh?"

She whirled around, keeping an eye on where his hands were. "Don't worry about me. I'll be fine."

Josh held his free hand up in mock surrender. She didn't have anything to worry about. He always kept his distance, which hadn't been easy since they had the same circle of friends and once shared the small world of Acorn Grove.

"It was good seeing you again, Josh," she said, taking another step back.

Okay, there had been that *one* time he touched her. The only time his restraint slipped was on the day that she had left town. Something close to fear and loss had gripped his chest. He knew it was his last chance with Amber and he had taken it without a second thought.

He had been at the gas station when she stopped by to fill up her car. Amber had paid and waved good-bye to him without a pause in her step. The tight binds that had held him back suddenly broke free, and he had followed her to the car.

She had opened the driver's door and stopped when she'd seen him. Amber had backed up against the car as he leaned into her. She hadn't said anything, which made him wonder if it was all a dream, but the feel of her finally against him had warned him it wasn't and not to blow it. He remembered he had gently cradled her chin with his hands. His fingers had shaken as he bent down for a kiss.

The moment his mouth had brushed against hers, all those years of restraint evaporated in a puff of smoke. Josh knew the kiss had been hard and rough, but Amber hadn't complained. She had grabbed the back of his head and pulled him closer, her nails digging into his hair.

The kiss hadn't lasted long, but it had packed a punch that knocked his world sideways. Years of wanting had fueled the moment, and he couldn't keep up.

Amber had parted her legs for him and before he knew it he had held her wrists against the car.

And then she had bit his bottom lip. Not a nip. Not a love bite. She had sunk her teeth so hard that he reared his head and jumped back. Josh had pressed his hand to his mouth to check for blood when she had jumped into her car. He had stood there, stunned, as she drove off.

He absently swiped his tongue along his bottom lip as he recalled the sting. Amber's eyes darkened as she watched his movement. Satisfaction filled him. He knew then that she remembered, too.

Amber tossed her hair back and tilted her chin. "What brings you here?" she asked with a hint of frost as her cheeks blushed.

"I'm getting my tux." He lifted his hand that rested on his shoulder, gesturing at the black tuxedo encased in its protective wrap. "For the wedding."

Her eyes narrowed with suspicion. "Which wedding?"

Huh, she didn't know. Josh smiled, only too happy to inform her. "Carl and Madison's."

She closed her eyes for a brief moment. "I didn't know you were a groomsman." Her shoulders stiffened and she took a quick look down at her dress.

"I'm one of the ushers," Josh said, his eyes intent on her hand slowly reaching for her neckline. "Good thing, too, because then I have plenty of time to keep you out of trouble."

She scoffed at the suggestion as she yanked up the bodice. "You are the one who kept finding trouble. I was the class monitor who always told on you."

"True." But that didn't mean Amber was an example of good behavior, no matter what she thought. She used to cause havoc and get away with it. She was the good girl variety of trouble, which was the worst kind.

He never had much use for good girls. They were always trying to redeem him. They wanted him tamed and domesticated. Instead of accepting him, the good girls wanted to change him into a trained beast.

Those women never understood that he did the taming in the relationship. They couldn't wrap the concept around their minds. Good girls always believed in fairness and equality and rules. They lived by, hid behind, and worshipped rules.

He did, too, Josh thought with a sly grin. Especially when it was in the bedroom. That was when he was in charge and he made the rules.

Amber would never be one to follow those rules. She had been the know-it-all at school and the teacher's pet in every class. Her parents spoiled her rotten. Maybe not with material things, but that home revolved around Amber's life.

She wouldn't last one minute in his bedroom, Josh thought with a pang of regret. She couldn't take instruction, or be denied, or wait for pleasure. It would open her to a whole new sensual world, not to mention do her some good, but she'd kill him first.

In the past, he was very selective about whom he slept with. They were sophisticated women who understood the rules. So why did he continue to fantasize about Amber?

What was it about her that made him want to break his rules about good girls? It wasn't the challenge. It was more than the promise her body offered. He liked her, understood and reluctantly admired her, but that didn't explain this long-standing attraction.

He could list all the reasons why he *shouldn't* be interested. Amber Hughes couldn't keep out of other people's business. She made up her code of conduct and expected others to follow, and on her schedule. She had a set idea of what was right and wrong, and was intolerant when it didn't suit her ideas.

His silence seemed to make Amber jumpy. "What?" she asked, sounding exasperated. Cornered.

He wasn't going to tell her. Not now, probably not ever. His train of thought would have her running for cover.

But there was something *he* wanted to know. Josh shifted his stance and looked directly into her eyes. "Why'd you agree to be a bridesmaid?"

Amber hid her look of surprise by making an exaggerated face. "I want to add orange to my growing collection of bridesmaid dresses. What's it to you?"

Josh shrugged. "You managed to ruin another of my friend's weddings, and I'm not putting it past you to try again."

She drew in a sharp breath and clutched the dress to her chest before marching toward him. "I ruined? Why does everyone blame me for that?"

"You objected to the wedding in front of everyone. That puts a damper on the ceremony."

"Excuse me," she said in a voice that could wither a lesser man, "but I wasn't the one doing Isabel against the wall right before promising to forsake all others."

She had a good point, but Josh felt obligated to emphasize the obvious. "Your timing for the announcement sucked."

Amber clenched her teeth. "I didn't have much choice in the matter."

"If you say so, but a word of warning." He stepped close and said in a low, firm voice, "Don't mess with *this* wedding."

She didn't step back or duck her head. Amber glared back at him. "I don't plan to."

"Good." He turned and headed for the exit.

"I didn't plan anything happening at Bailey's wedding, either!" she called after him.

Josh kept walking. "I'm keeping an eye on you this time, Amber. One false move and you'll have to answer to me."

His warning held infinite possibilities and dark pleasure spiked through his chest. Josh set his mouth into a grim line and was determined as he walked away. If he had any sense at all, he'd stay away from Amber Hughes. That woman was trouble.

CHAPTER TWO

AMBER GRATEFULLY STEPPED OUT of Tilly's Wedding Shoppe twenty minutes later and headed for Madison's car. As she walked down the sidewalk she became aware of the conversation in the doorway of the yarn store.

"Amber . . ."

"Another wedding . . ."

"That Hughes girl . . ."

"There goes trouble . . ."

Amber balled her hands into fists as she heard the women whispering. She wanted to turn around and confront them. Tell them to get a life. Maybe put a hex on their daughters' future weddings for good measure. Amber's eyes widened with pleasure at the thought.

"I know that look," Madison said softly as she placed a hand on Amber's shoulder. "Ignore them."

"You are no fun," Amber said, but followed Madison's advice. After all, she had no idea how to do a hex. Unless her presence was already jinxing her friend's wedding.

That thought cut too close to the bone. Amber waited

until they got into Madison's car and closed the doors before she faced her friend. "Okay, I know you don't want to hear this, but maybe it's a bad idea that I'm a bridesmaid."

Madison held up her hand to stop Amber from saying another word. "If this is about the dress, don't worry about it. I smoothed things over with Tilly."

"Already?" Madison had more people skills than she gave her credit. "How'd you manage that?"

"She's the best seamstress for any bride on a tight budget, but you just have to know how to handle her. I'll come with you for the next appointment and we'll make sure the dress is perfect."

Great. She needed a chaperone for a gown fitting. It seemed like she found trouble everywhere she turned.

A vision of Josh came to her before she could stop it. Now *he* was trouble with a capital T. Maybe even something more than trouble. The hint of ferocity in his brown eyes had stopped her in her tracks, but the dark sensuality that pulsed underneath his lethal grace beckoned her closer.

Had he always possessed that dangerous edge, and she only now recognized it? Why now? Or had she always known and refused to acknowledge it? Was that why she danced around him all these years? She had secretly yearned for him, but was still afraid to let him catch her.

Amber shook her head, clearing the vision. Her skin felt tight and flushed as she shifted in her seat. Maybe a full-time chaperone is exactly what she needed to keep her away from all types of trouble. "I don't want to take away from your special day, Madison."

"You won't." She turned the key in the ignition. "Everyone will be used to seeing you by next week."

She couldn't believe her friend's naïveté. "No, they'll be watching me, especially right at the part of 'speak now or forever hold your peace.'"

"You have the part memorized," her friend said with a teasing grin.

Amber leaned back on the headrest. "You tend to remember the details when you make a spectacle of yourself."

"Unless you're drunk," Madison said as she pulled the car into traffic. "It's nature's way of softening the humiliation."

Nothing other than mind-wiping the town would have softened the blows that had landed on her. "Think you can remove that objection bit from your ceremony?"

"I haven't asked."

"Really?" That would have been the first thing she would have done had she been in Madison's place. "Acorn Grove didn't ban that passage after my fall from grace?"

"Stop thinking about Bailey's wedding," Madison advised her before honking the horn and waving at a car passing by. "That was three years ago."

"That doesn't matter. Everyone else is still talking about it." A thought suddenly occurred to Amber and she reluctantly faced Madison. "Is Bailey going to be at your wedding?"

She frowned as she shifted gears. "Of course."

Amber lurched forward as panic slapped against her rib cage. "Of course?"

"She's doing one of the readings."

Amber slumped back into the seat and tried not to whimper. How was she going to prevent a scene when someone in the wedding was out for her blood? She had to find a way to avoid Bailey but hide within the bridal party.

"I'm not going to make a spectacle of myself this time.

I promise." She drew a cross over her heart with her finger. "Even if the church spontaneously combusts, I'm keeping my mouth shut."

"Stop worrying. I know you're not going to ruin my wedding."

"You seem to be the only one who feels that way." She slid deeper into the seat. Even her mom found it necessary to have a talk, begging her not to cause problems. That had hurt. Her parents used to be her strongest cheerleaders. "Everyone is surprised you asked me to be a bridesmaid."

Madison shrugged, her eyes on the road. "Let them talk."

"You have enough to worry about."

"No one is going to say anything to me. They wouldn't dare."

The sharp tone alerted Amber. She turned to see Madison's cheery expression falter. "What are you talking about?"

Madison hesitated. "Everyone tiptoes around me these days," she said with a wry smile. "I've already had a few Bridezilla moments."

"You? Get real." Amber scoffed at the idea. Madison never had to raise her voice to get her way. But then she had one of those magical smiles that made the world smile right back.

"It's true." She seemed embarrassed to mention it. "If I start acting that way again, you'll set me straight, won't you?"

"Oh, believe me, I will." She won't cause trouble, but she wasn't going to tolerate any diva behavior.

"I have another favor to ask."

As if making her wear tangerine taffeta wasn't enough. Amber rubbed her aching temple with her fingertips. There had better not be a bonnet to this outfit. "Shoot."

"Tonight is Carl's bachelor party. And I was wondering if you could . . ." She trailed off, unable to finish her request.

"Come to your place?" Amber ventured a guess. There were probably a million things Madison had to do before the wedding and needed help. That should keep her out of trouble.

"No. More like"—she bit her bottom lip—"crash the bachelor party."

Amber sat up straight. "What?" she yelled. "Are you serious?"

Madison hunched her shoulders and cringed. "Yes," she said softly.

"No. Absolutely not." Amber waved her hands in front of her as if she could ward off the request. "Forget it."

Her friend's bottom lip pouted. "Why not?"

"Didn't you just hear me? I'm keeping my mouth shut."

"At the ceremony," Madison clarified. "And that's fine since you don't have any speaking parts."

"No." She slapped her hand against her armrest. "I'm keeping quiet the whole time I'm here."

"You didn't say that. All I'm asking you to do is pop in, look around"—she fluttered her hands above the steering wheel—"and leave."

Amber's eyes narrowed with suspicion. "Why do you need me to do that?"

"C'mon," Madison cajoled. "I'd do it for you."

She snorted. "No, you wouldn't." Because Amber knew she would never ask for such a thing.

Her friend gave a long, bone-shuddering sigh. "Okay, listen." She held up a warning finger. "You can't repeat this to anyone."

"Who's going to talk to me?" Everyone kept their distance as if she were contagious.

"Do you remember Isabel?"

"Vividly." She had been the bridesmaid in the choir room at Bailey's wedding. No matter how hard she tried, Amber couldn't rid the image of Isabel's bright dyed pink shoes crisscrossing Jimmy's hips while he humped her against the wall.

"Carl dated Isabel two years ago."

"Huh?" The image disintegrated. She couldn't have heard that correctly. "I thought he was dating you."

"We were taking a break."

Amber tossed up her hands and looked out her window. "Why do I feel like I'm trapped in an episode of *Friends*?"

"Oh, shut up. The point is, Isabel is sniffing around him again. She always had a thing for unattainable men." Her jaw tightened with anger. "And I think she's going to make her move at the bachelor party. It's the one place I can't be."

"Carl is a big boy." Amber gave a comforting pat on her friend's shoulder. "He can handle it."

"I know."

She didn't sound too convinced. The worried expression didn't disappear from her face. Amber tried again. "Carl is marrying you."

"I know." Madison's voice got smaller.

"If you think—" Amber tightly pressed her lips together. She couldn't say that. Under no circumstances would she suggest the bride and groom needed to resolve this before they got married.

Uh-uh. No. These guys *had* to get married. On time and without any problems. If anything went wrong, Amber knew she would be blamed.

That meant she couldn't question anything. But was that being selfish? Wouldn't a good friend help her find out the truth?

Then again, the last time she tried to be a good friend, everything went horribly wrong. She learned her lesson. Amber was going to keep her mouth shut.

"Carl has been acting a little strange," Madison admitted, caught in her own thoughts.

"Wedding nerves aren't just for brides." Wait, no. Amber bit her tongue and winced. She couldn't say *that* either. Madison would think that Carl was getting cold feet.

Wow, Amber thought as she delicately ran the sore tip of her tongue along her teeth, she's going to cause herself a major injury while keeping quiet.

"No, no, it's more than that," Madison insisted. "He's getting a lot of phone calls lately, and then he goes into the other room to talk."

"I'm sure there's a good explanation," Amber said through tight lips.

"The other day his cell phone rang and I saw Isabel's name flash on the screen."

Oooh. That didn't sound good. Maybe—what was she doing? "Once again, I'm sure there's a reasonable explanation."

"And then yesterday . . ." Madison's voice wavered.

Amber was curious in spite of herself. "What happened yesterday?"

"I drove by the Market Street Café," Madison said and sniffed. "Carl and Isabel were sitting together. So close their heads were *touching*."

Amber started to fidget, trying so hard not to suggest

endless possibilities of what it all might mean. "Did you ask him about it?"

"You better believe I did!"

"What did he say?"

"He said he was nowhere near Market Street yesterday, and that I was wrong." Madison hastily wiped the moisture from her eyes. "But I wasn't. I think I would know what my fiancé looks like!"

Amber crossed her arms. Crossed her legs. Pressed her lips so tightly that they disappeared inside her mouth. She wasn't going to get involved.

Okay, just one question and *then* she wasn't going to get involved. "Did anyone tell you they saw those two together?"

Madison frowned. "No."

Heh. Amber's jaw shifted to the side as she mulled it over. Gossip traveled fast around Acorn Grove. No one said a thing about the lunch? Not even a veiled attempt on getting more information, like one of the old biddies saying to Madison, "I thought you loved eating at the Market Street Café." That was a popular lead-in for the geriatric crowd.

"Amber, I know you would tell me the truth. No matter what. Even if I didn't want to hear it."

"Aw, Madison." She looked away and stared out the window. "Don't do this to me."

"Please go check on the bachelor party. Like you said, there has to be a reasonable explanation. I need to know what that is before I go crazy."

Amber chewed the inside of her mouth. She could just go in, see that Isabel was nowhere around, and leave. No, it sounded too easy. She'd get caught, Carl would think Madison didn't trust her, and she'd cause another wedding fiasco.

How was she going to get out of this mess? "Madison, you haven't even considered the practicalities. What am I going to do if the guys see me there? They'll assume I'm spying for you. And we don't even know where the bachelor party is being held."

"No one would tell me, either."

"Sounds like we're out of luck." Amber sagged with relief. That was a close one.

Madison gasped as the thought struck her. "So you'll have to follow Josh!"

"Josh?" Her stomach clenched. "Josh Griffin?"

"He's in charge of the bachelor party."

Amber thwacked the back of her skull against the seat, lifted the head, and did it again for good measure.

Madison gave her a sidelong look. "What's with you?"

"Oh, nothing." *Just when I thought I had dodged trouble, I ran smack dab into it.* Amber thwacked her head again.

"This goes way beyond the call of duty," Amber muttered to herself as she followed the taillights along the deserted highway through the cornfields. "Even for a bridesmaid."

At least she managed to change Madison's mind on one thing. After all, why follow Joshua Griffin when she could follow Isabel? Madison was worried about the woman's whereabouts, not the bachelor party activities.

Amber was so proud of skirting trouble, she could just kiss herself.

As it turned out, she didn't have any difficulty following Isabel. All she had to do was wait for the unnaturally tanned woman to get off of work from the strip mall where she worked. For as long as Amber could remember, Isabel had the strange ability to find and discard one sales assistant job after another. Isabel probably made more money than she did at her secretarial job, but Amber tried not to think about that.

As she kept driving farther and farther away from civilization, Amber started to get worried. Did Isabel see her and then decide to take her on a wild goose chase? Just when she started to watch the gas gauge in her car every other second, Isabel took an exit. Neon lights and the faint pounding of rock music were off in the distance.

She groaned as her stomach twisted with dread. They were going to the only dance club in the area. It was also a place where many, many bachelor and bachelorette parties were held.

That didn't mean Carl's would be held there, Amber thought as she took the path. Carl and his buddies were probably more creative than that. She waited until she saw Isabel enter the building before she got out of her car.

The music pulsed under her feet in the parking lot. She couldn't hear the bouncer, but knew to show her I.D. The muscular giant grabbed her hand, stamped it with something green and illegible, and shooed her inside.

She paused at the entrance and looked around. A kaleidoscope of colors shone on the live band. The dance floor was packed with gyrating bodies glistening with sweat. The spotlight zigzagged on the customers standing deep in the shadows as they flirted and postured, pretending to be far more exciting than they were.

Amber craned her neck as she looked around. No Isabel. How could she have lost her so fast?

She looked around and considered her next move. The

club had a second level that overlooked the dance floor. It was almost like a mezzanine, and it could pose a problem if she wanted a quick getaway, but she could get a bird's-eye view of the building.

Amber slowly made her way toward the steps. She could have sworn she smelled sex mingling with the scent of beer and perfume. She slid along a cluster of women when she saw a familiar face. Amber did a double take.

Bailey?

Amber ducked her head and flattened her back against the wall. Her heart knocked painfully against her chest. What was she doing here?

She cautiously looked around but didn't see Bailey anymore. She must have moved on. But which way? Maybe she went onto the dance floor. That would be good, Amber decided with a sharp nod. It gave her plenty of opportunity to leave without being seen.

Okay, so she didn't complete her mission, Amber admitted as she pivoted on her heel and headed for the exit. She'd seen enough. It was time to call it a night before Bailey pounced on her.

Getting through the crowd seemed slower this time. Probably because she was going against the current of bodies. She gradually became aware of a group of men cheering at the bar. She squinted, recognizing some of the guys. A lot of the guys, actually. Who were they cheering and why?

Her shoe skidded on the floor as she saw a redheaded man jump to his feet and victoriously punch his fists into the air. His face was pink and glistening from exertion.

Carl.

The bachelor party *was* here. Amber lolled her head back, fighting the urge to scream with frustration. Great. Now what was she going to do?

She should stay. She was doing this as a favor for her friend. Amber reluctantly looked at the spot where she had seen Bailey. But then, the longer she hung around, the more chances Bailey would have to see her.

She really, really didn't want that to happen.

This was all a very bad idea. She wasn't going to spy. It had nothing to do with her. She could leave, call Madison and tell her she didn't see Isabel with Carl at all.

It was technically true. Really, would Isabel and Carl do something so stupid as to—

The image of pink dyed shoes crisscrossing a tuxedo jacket flashed before her eyes.

Okay, Isabel would be stupid. But not Carl. Amber spared a glance at Carl chugging a frosty mug of beer.

At least, not a sober Carl.

She wavered. Should she stay or should she go? *Go.* The decision wasn't the coward's way out. Not totally. It was for the best. For everyone.

Amber took a step back and collided against a hard wall of muscle. "Sorry," she called out, barely glancing over her shoulder. She froze when she felt strong, callused fingers wrap around her arm.

Dread spiraled inside her as she was turned around. She knew who it was before she saw his face. Josh Griffin.

She stared at his white T-shirt. It looked soft and bright against his bronzed skin, stretching against his wide chest. His body heat curled around her.

Amber dragged her gaze up the column of his neck. She

swallowed roughly as she took in the angry set of his jaw and the firm, unyielding line of his mouth. It took some effort to look him in the eye.

She was proud of the fact that she didn't flinch. The guy was not happy. At all. She saw the condemnation in his brown eyes. Josh knew why she was here—but he didn't have to know who sent her.

"Hi, Josh," she said, hating her weak voice. She had to brazen her way out of this. "Uh . . . wanna dance?"

His features sharpened as an unholy gleam flashed through his eyes. Amber took a step back, but his grasp tightened on her arm, keeping her still.

"Sure," he said. There was something about the way he said it that made her skin prickle and flush. "Come with me."

Amber closed her eyes and gritted her teeth. One of these days she was going to learn how to keep her mouth shut!

CHAPTER THREE

JOSH LED AMBER TO the crowded dance floor, keeping a firm hold on her. The initial anger he felt upon seeing the nosy Amber skulking around the dance club had dissipated, but he couldn't control the chaotic emotions swirling deep inside him. Hot, wild and tangled sensations that only Amber could arouse.

The lust and need relentlessly twisted with darker, unsettling emotions he didn't want to examine. He could feel it pushing through his veins and chest like a knot, leaving a scarred path in its wake. He was aware of how it bumped just beneath his skin, determined to break free.

But he wouldn't surrender. He still had command over his body and emotions. Josh thought these feelings had died long ago, but it looked as though they were only dormant. How did such an innocent woman like Amber sneak past his defenses? Then again, she wasn't so innocent anymore. He had to remember that.

What was Amber up to? Josh glanced down at her, noticing how she pressed her lips firmly together. *A little too late to keep your mouth shut.* He never thought she had a malicious streak, but it was obvious she was sniffing around the bachelor party ready to create havoc.

He wasn't going to let Amber ruin the party. Josh knew Carl wouldn't do anything questionable or do something he would regret—other than have a killer hangover tomorrow. But he wouldn't put it past Amber to make her own analysis.

Josh found a small spot on the floor and turned toward Amber. His pulse beat eagerly when he scooped her close to him. As he expected, she went rigid in his arms. Her soft breasts were pressed against him and the lush curves of her hips were just below his hands.

He liked how she fit against him. A little too much, if the way his cock threatened to press against her stomach was anything to go by. Yet he wondered how good it would feel if Amber had sought to be in his arms.

She was doing her best not to offer much body contact. Her hands were gamely twined around his neck, but she couldn't be accused of clinging. No soulful looks or flirty batting of the eyelashes. She wasn't even looking at him. Was she too busy searching for escape routes?

Josh lowered his head, momentarily distracted by the soft waves of her black hair. "What are you doing here, Amber?" he asked against her ear.

A shiver swept through her, but Amber hid it by feigning a casual shrug. "I felt like dancing," she answered without looking at him.

"And it's a coincidence"—Josh hid a smile as Amber shivered again—"that you are here the same night as Carl's bachelor party?"

"Carl's bachelor party is here?" She leaned back in his

embrace and looked at him with surprise. "I had no idea."

"Nice try." She couldn't fake innocence if her life depended on it. That was a surprise considering how she used to be such a good girl.

Amber's hands slid to his chest. "I really didn't know. I was looking for . . ." She stopped and exhaled with disgust, shaking her head.

Josh frowned. "You were looking for whom?"

"Don't worry about it." She gave his chest a pat. "It doesn't concern you."

"Yes, it does."

Amber rolled her eyes. "I'm not trying to crash Carl's party," she said, raising her voice as the music got louder. "I'm not even trying to cause trouble."

"It just comes naturally?" he asked. "More reason for you to leave."

She dropped her arms and any pretense of trying to dance. "I'm not going anywhere."

He wasn't used to such in-your-face stubbornness and it required some hard-won restraint on his part. "You're leaving . . ."

"No, I'm not."

". . . even if I have to carry you out."

Her eyes flashed with outrage. "You wouldn't dare."

She was going to find out fast that he'd dared to do just about anything. "Are you leaving?"

Amber's bottom jaw shifted to the side. "No."

Josh shrugged. He had warned her. He bent his knees and with one smooth move, he had her over his shoulder. By the time Amber squawked with outrage, he had turned toward the exit and was making his way off the dance floor.

"Josh!" Her voice was loud and clear, even over the music and bystanders cheering him on. She grabbed onto the back of his shirt. "Put me down right now!"

He didn't answer, not trusting himself on what he might say or do next. Josh felt like he was skirting the edge of control. The chaos swirled brighter inside him. He didn't cause scenes like this.

"Josh!" Her leg moved back, getting ready for a swift kick.

"Kick me," he warned as he patted his free hand on the tempting curve of her ass, "and you're going to get spanked."

Amber's gasp echoed in his ear. "You . . ." Her voice trailed off but the words hung between them. *Wouldn't dare.*

She learned quickly, and he was thankful. Amber wasn't the type to forgive a spank. As much as Josh wanted Amber to listen and respect what he said, he didn't want her to be disgusted or scared of him.

Amber dug her fingers into his back. "Please put me down."

"Sure," he said calmly as he ignored the people staring at them. "When we get to your car."

"You have no right to do this to me." She swatted wildly at him, the move almost dislodging his hold on her. "Once I find a bouncer, you are in so much trouble."

"There's one right there." Josh nodded at the bouncer approaching them and felt Amber trying to get a look of what was going on. "Hi, Martin."

"Josh." Martin rocked back on his feet and rubbed his chin thoughtfully. "What's going on?"

"Amber is trying to cause trouble at Carl's bachelor party." He shifted Amber more securely on his shoulder. She yelped and grabbed his shirt for dear life. "I'm taking her to her car."

Martin nodded. "Okay, thanks. Just don't drop her."

"I'll try," Josh muttered as he continued his way to the exit. Was it his fault Amber wouldn't keep still?

"I don't believe this!" Amber pushed the heels of her hands deep in Josh's back as she tried to prop herself up. "He takes your word for it?"

"You're known for causing trouble," he said as he walked into the small lobby of the club.

"Josh, please. Put me down."

There was something in her voice that made him pause. As if she was at the end of her rope. "Are you going to be good?"

"Yes."

The word dragged out of her throat, but it was the answer he wanted to hear. He slowly lowered her down. Too slowly as his body memorized the impact her curves made.

Josh took a prudent step back. "Let's start over. Why are you here?"

He watched silently as Amber took a long time readjusting her clothes. Like she needed to stall while coming up with a cover story.

"Amber." Warning threaded his husky voice.

She brushed the hair out of her eyes. "I'm here because . . . I was hoping you were."

Josh tilted his head. Was he hallucinating or did she just say what he thought she said? "What was that?"

"Oh, come on, Josh," she said as she placed her hands on her hips. "You can't tell me that you haven't ever wondered what it would be like. The two of us."

Josh stared, unable to believe Amber was going *there*. She

was not interested in starting anything with him. He could see the big bold caution sign screaming in her head. Why wasn't she listening to it?

"After seeing you again today, it got me thinking—"

He held his hand up, hoping Amber didn't notice the tremor. "You might want to pull back right now and start walking."

She jerked her head back. "Why?"

"You've been warned. You do not want to mess with me."

"I'm not messing with you." She splayed her arms out with frustration and looked around the grungy lobby. "You know, here I am spilling my guts and you tell me to walk away."

"Because you're lying." *Please be lying.* She had no idea how much he wanted her. Her innocence and trepidation helped him keep his distance. If she acted on her curiosity, he was going to discover every weak spot in his iron control, and he didn't know what would hold him back.

"And you're trying to scare me off. Why is that?" She seemed genuinely interested in the answer. "Are you scared of little old me?"

Not quite. More like scared of how he acted when he was around her. "You have the count of three to walk away and go home. If you're still here, I will show you exactly what the two of us would be like."

She raised an eyebrow. "Go for it."

"One."

She folded her arms, mimicking his stance.

The muscle in his cheek bunched. "Two."

He felt the tension crawling through her. She was torn between staying and making a run for it. Whatever made her want to stay in the club had to be a very good reason.

"Three."

Whoa. She stayed. He had thrown down the gauntlet and she picked it up and waved it under his nose.

"I'm still here." Amber found it necessary to point out the obvious. It was the least she could do. Considering the adrenaline shooting through her blood, she really wanted to pump her fist in the air and do a victory dance because she wasn't backing down.

But she just managed to jump out of the frying pan and into the fire. What possessed her to come up with that excuse? It had been instinctual. She thought it would make *him* back down. Instead it challenged him.

Josh clasped his hand on her wrist. Her pulse leapt under his callused fingertips, but she didn't pull away. She also didn't drag her feet like she wanted to when he guided her back into the dance club and headed for the bar.

He strode to the tables that were reserved for the bachelor party. No one was sitting there, but the group of men made their presence known with the overturned shot glasses and half-full beer mugs. Josh chose a table near the corner, pulled out a chair and sat down.

That took her by surprise. It was unlike Josh not to hold out a chair for the woman. Amber was used to the lack of manners thanks to living in the big city, but she hadn't realized how much she took that aspect of him for granted.

It made her wonder what he had in store for her. What had she just agreed to? Amber shut off the list of possibilities scrolling in her mind and pulled out a chair from under the table.

"No," he said as he gently pulled her forward. "You sit on my lap."

She went rigid. "Nuh-uh!" Dancing was one thing, but sitting on Josh's lap displayed a deeper level of intimacy. It was more than pressing bodies and swaying to the same beat. The simple act was one of acceptance and surrender.

"Amber, there are two things you need to know," Josh said coolly as he drew her against his sprawled denim-clad legs. "I am in charge, and if there is anytime you don't like it, I will escort you to your car."

"There's a chair right here." She gestured at the one next to him. No one was using it. It didn't make sense that she should sit on his lap.

"Your choice, Amber."

Amber closed her eyes as she silently begged for strength. She regretted doing this favor for Madison. Her friend owed her big after tonight, and no bridesmaid gift was going to even the score.

She opened her eyes and perched on Josh's lap. The first thing she noticed was his hard, powerful thighs underneath her. She wiggled, uncomfortable, feeling vulnerable and nervous.

Josh reached up and she tensed. Her breath caught in her throat as he captured a wayward tendril of her hair. He rubbed the wavy end between his fingertips, as if the softness fascinated him, before he hooked it gently behind her ear. "Do you want something to drink?" he asked.

Amber shook her head, effectively dodging his hand next to her ear. She didn't want a drink, anyway. The last thing she needed to do was blur her senses while near Josh Griffin. He watched every move she made. It was like he was waiting for her to relax her guard before he pounced.

From the corner of her eye, she watched the club patrons

stroll by. She couldn't concentrate on what they were doing. The people were flashes of color and sound. What was she supposed to do? Just sit on Josh's lap and act like nothing was out of the ordinary?

She tensed as his large hand stroked her back. "Put your arm on the back of the chair," Josh said.

That would require her to lean into his body. How was it that she was sitting on top, but she couldn't shake the feeling that he was surrounding her? "You're enjoying this a little too much," she muttered as she followed his direction.

He flexed his leg muscle under her. "I can tell that you are."

Alarm flashed through her body. She clenched her inner muscles, but it was too late. She couldn't hide the truth from Josh. Her jeans did little to contain the damp heat of her sex.

As he continued to caress her back with the teasing touch of his fingers, Josh reached over and splayed his other hand on her waist. She felt contained. Trapped. Her breathing shortened as he skimmed his hand up along her side. She flinched when his arm brushed her breast.

She looked at his face, needing to know if he was just as affected as she was. Her gaze collided with his and she saw the fire leap in his dark eyes. He was going to kiss her.

Amber parted her lips. She remembered the last kiss they shared. Her bland little world had splintered, revealing the sensual intensity underneath.

She hadn't been able to put it back the way it used to be, and she wasn't sure if she would survive the aftershocks of another kiss from Josh.

Her courage fled and she turned away just as his mouth caught the corner of her lips. Amber froze, uncertain what

Josh would do. She blinked with surprise as Josh placed a soft kiss before sliding his mouth along her cheek.

She exhaled slowly, the last of her breath lodging in her throat as Josh's mouth found a sensitive spot behind her ear-lobe. *Oh . . . my . . .* She had no idea that the swipe of his tongue would go straight to her clit.

Josh seemed to know exactly how the touch made her feel. He traced his tongue along her ear before dipping into the canal. Amber closed her eyes and swallowed as the move made her sex ache and swell. She shifted against his legs as the red-hot need pressed low in her belly.

His hand still rested against the side of her breast. He didn't knead or cup her fullness, but the position teased her. Her nipples beaded against her bra as she considered twisting her torso to fit into his hand.

"Kiss me," he whispered roughly in her ear.

This time she didn't hesitate. Amber turned and he claimed her mouth before she could take a breath. The touch sparked her senses, blooming through her until her fingers and toes tingled. It was as if her body couldn't contain the pulsing hot energy from the kiss.

She grabbed the side of his head and caught his tongue in her mouth. She suckled hard, drawing him. The raw hunger of the kiss made her womb clench. She rubbed her legs to-gether, the denim of her jeans rough and heavy against her flesh.

Josh moved his head away and licked his reddened lips. "Sit up straight."

She did, wondering what wicked thing he had planned. Her nipples stung, the folds of her sex slick and puffy, and her clit ached for attention.

He leaned back in his chair and watched her with hooded, glittering eyes. She couldn't read his thoughts. "What are you doing?" she finally asked with impatience. "What are you planning?"

"Nothing."

She frowned. Nothing? Nothing at all? He got her hot and bothered and showed no interest in finishing what they started. How could he tease her? She wasn't going to put up with it. Amber moved to get up.

"No, not yet." He cupped the top of her thigh with his hand. Her muscles bunched underneath his touch. "Not until I say so."

She squirmed and felt his cock poke against her. He was hot and rock hard. "You get off watching me suffer?"

"You wanted to know what it would be like—the two of us." He caressed her spine with his fingertips, as if calming a skittish animal. "This is a taste of what to expect."

"Unsatisfied?"

His smile reached his eyes. "Anticipation makes it sweeter."

"No it doesn't." People who say that never experienced the heady rush of going for it.

"It sharpens the senses," he said, his fingers now making small circles along her back. "It makes you focus on the one thing you want most."

She had no problems focusing. Her goal was quite clear and it had something to do with him slamming her against the wall and having Josh thrust his cock into her. The image made Amber whimper as she squeezed the muscles of her sex.

"I will touch you any way you want," Josh said in a raspy voice. "But only in one place."

What? Why was he being so stingy? Why couldn't he just go wild? She wanted to tear her clothes off, straddle his hips and plunge down. He wanted to touch her in *one* place!

"Where do you want me to touch you?" he whispered in her ear. "What do you want the most?"

Her core throbbed. Her nipples were begging for attention. Her clit ached. But she wasn't going to tell him any of that. He would tease her until she was an inch of losing her sanity and then back off.

"Where, Amber? Your ear?" He sucked on her lobe.

She shifted against his leg as the suggestive move made her wet. She should stop this. She should walk to the nearest exit and not look back.

"Or maybe your nipples?" His thumb flicked against the furled nipple poking through her shirt and she gasped. "Do you want me to touch you here?"

She closed her eyes as he made slow, lazy circles around her nipples. The circles grew smaller and smaller. She bit her lip as the tips of her breasts puckered stiffly like her clit.

Amber wanted to open her eyes, but couldn't force herself. She knew Josh was watching her. She felt the rise and fall of his chest. The hard cock twitch under her.

"Do you want me to touch your clit?" he asked as his hand drifted down her stomach.

She bucked her hips in anticipation, desperate for Josh to cup her sex. She really, really wished she hadn't worn jeans. She frowned as Josh laid his hand at the top of her thigh.

Don't make me wait . . . Don't make me beg . . .

"Yes." Her jagged whisper echoed in her head. She was vaguely aware of the low, masculine growl vibrating in Josh's chest. All she could think about was how he would rub small, teasing circles against her clit, creating ripples of pleasure, each one feeding the other until she screamed.

But Josh didn't move his hand off her leg. Amber blinked her eyes open and squinted in the dark smoky club. The noise around them suddenly became louder. People walked past them, oblivious to the sexual haze she was under.

Oh, God. What was she doing?

She saw Carl stumble toward them. Amber flinched violently, wondering what he may have seen. Is that why Josh stopped? Or was he still teasing her?

"No one saw," Josh whispered against her ear. "I promise."

Were her thoughts that transparent? All of her thoughts? She looked at him. His face was tight with need, the dull red slashed across his cheekbones. His eyes glittered with lust.

She jumped up and her legs wobbled, her knees threatening to cave. "I need to leave."

"Josh!" Carl called out, swinging a beer mug by means of a salute. "That's where you've been hiding. Oh, hi, Amber."

She sensed Josh standing up and reaching for her. She scurried away and crashed into Carl. Amber gasped as his cold beer spilled onto her shirt and made her skin flush. The bitter scent billowed around her as she saw Carl tumble forward.

Amber's arms and legs felt like they weren't working properly. She awkwardly caught Carl by his arms as he landed face first into her breasts. She staggered back by the impact and knew she was going to go down hard.

Her spine hit something solid and sturdy. *Josh.* His arm banded around her waist as she sagged against his chest.

Carl lifted his head, his chin deep in her cleavage. "Soft landing," he said with a sloppy smile.

"I'm sorry," Amber said as she struggled to get Carl to stand on his own. "I wasn't watching where I was going. I should probably go."

"Already?" Carl asked. "But you just got here."

She pulled at her wet shirt that stuck to her skin. Amber stepped around Carl until he stood between Josh and her. "I'll see you guys around."

Amber turned on her heel and hurried to the exit, her legs boneless and shaky. She heard Josh call her name, but she didn't look back. She hated to admit it, but he was right. She did not want to mess with Josh Griffin.

Chapter Four

THE DOORBELL ON HER parents' front door jolted Amber out of a troubled sleep. She groaned and rolled over to look at the clock. It was ten o'clock. She should get up, but she wouldn't mind a couple more hours of sleep. Especially after the night she had had.

A full blush swept her body. She whimpered and tossed her blanket over her head. What had she been doing last night? What had prompted her to act that way with Josh?

And why had she liked it so much?

That was the part that made her blush. She shouldn't have enjoyed it. She should have walked out earlier. Or the moment he had told her to leave.

But she didn't want to listen to him. No. That wasn't the only reason.

Amber writhed in embarrassment, pulling the sheets free from her bed. She was never going to be able to look Josh in the face again. Because he knew she had liked it and wanted more.

The soft knock on her bedroom door made Amber lift her head. She turned to see her mother peek in.

"Amber? You're still in bed?" Her mom sounded slightly scandalized at the notion. She frowned with disapproval at the oversized T-shirt Amber wore to bed.

She shoved her hair from her face. "What is it, Mom?"

She looked in the direction of the front door and then back at Amber. "Josh Griffin is here to see you."

Amber jackknifed into a sitting position. Josh was *here*? In her parents' house?

"He said it was urgent." Curiosity crackled from her, but Amber wasn't going to appease it.

"I'll be right out." She jumped out of bed as her mom closed the door. Grabbing the first pair of jeans she could find from off the floor, Amber hopped into them and zipped them quickly. She had to get out there before Josh did something she was going to regret.

She bolted out of the bedroom and rushed to the front of the house. Amber skidded to a halt when she saw Josh talking to her mother.

He looked sexy and dangerous. The faded blue bandana covering his head made her think of a sexy pirate. The leather jacket was worn in places and his rock concert T-shirt was so old she couldn't decipher the name of the band. His jeans hugged his long, lean legs, but his intimidating black boots made her want to take a step back.

He looked out of place in the shabby genteel living room, but Josh stood respectfully in front of her mother, his hands behind his back. He dipped his head as he listened to her mother's quiet voice.

"Hi, Josh," she interrupted as she approached him. "I'm sorry I kept you waiting."

He silently turned to her and his brown eyes darkened with anger.

What did she do now? She suddenly wished she had taken the time to pull herself together. Anything to shield the attitude coming off Josh in waves.

Instead she felt vulnerable and caught off guard. Her hair was messy and she wasn't wearing a speck of makeup. It didn't help that she was barefoot and wasn't wearing a bra.

"Let's step outside," he said as he reached for the front door. It wasn't a suggestion; it was an order.

Her first instinct was to refuse, but she caught it just in time. "Sure," she said with a tight smile.

She followed him outside and noticed her mother's look of interest as she remained behind. She wanted to shake her head. Her mom hoped she'd fall for a local boy and move back to Acorn Grove. Nice dream, but she wasn't going to fall for *this* local boy.

Amber closed the door behind her and walked onto the porch. She noticed Josh's motorcycle parked in front. The machine looked dangerous and edgy, much like its owner.

She crossed her arms, hoping it hid her braless state. "What's this about?"

"Have you talked to Madison?" Josh asked as he reached for something in his jacket pocket.

"Not since yesterday evening. Why?"

"Did you plan this?" He held out his cell phone and showed the picture on the small screen.

Amber gasped and clapped her hand over her mouth. The photo showed Carl and her at the bachelor party. He was face-first in her breasts, leering happily as she smiled down at him.

"What is this?" She could barely get the word out. She wanted to double over as the shock punched her in the stomach.

"I thought you would know."

"No." She grabbed the phone and stared at the screen. "Where did you get this?"

"It's making the rounds." Josh's tone was clipped.

"Oh, no." Amber closed her eyes and tilted her head back as she realized what that meant. Madison was already irrational with worry that she was going to lose Carl. Not to mention that she was very insecure about her small breast size. The way Carl appeared to be looking at Amber's breasts would just be another cruel turn of the knife already plunged in her back. If Madison saw this picture, all hell was going to break loose.

"Are you sure you don't have anything to do with this?" Josh asked again as he stepped in front of her and retrieved his phone.

"No!" Josh's distrust twisted painfully. "Why would I? You were there when Carl bumped into me."

"It *looked* like an accident."

She clenched her back teeth. "It was."

"I don't know." He rubbed the dusky stubble appearing on his jaw. "You wanted to be in the dance club real bad. You did things you wouldn't normally do to stay there."

She blushed but held her ground. "I didn't plan this."

"Carl got an incoherent voice mail from Madison this morning, so we can safely say she has seen it." Josh pocketed the phone. "And no one can get a hold of her."

Amber sat down on the steps as her mind whirled. How

could this have happened? She had to talk to Madison and explain.

Realization hit Amber like a cold slap. Oh, she had to do this fast. The last thing she needed was a runaway bride. She would definitely be blamed for it and wouldn't live it down.

Amber felt the panic well inside her. She blinked back the tears and covered her eyes with her hands. No one was going to see her cry. They didn't the last time, and they weren't going to now.

Josh sat down next to her on the steps. "Why were you at the dance club?"

Amber didn't want to break confidences, but she felt it was necessary for Josh to know the truth. "Madison felt that Isabel was making a play for Carl. I followed Isabel to the club, and planned to tell Madison she had nothing to worry about."

"Carl isn't interested in Isabel."

"Try telling that to Madison. And while we're at it, I'm not interested in Carl, either, but the evidence can be damning." She gestured at the phone in his pocket.

"We have to find Madison," he decided. "Do you know where she would run to if she were upset? Somewhere she would go to avoid Carl?"

Amber tossed her hands. "I might. There are a couple of places we used to hang around when we wanted to get away from it all. But that was so long ago."

Josh shrugged. "It's worth a try."

"I'll write down the list for you." She moved to get up and stopped when he grasped her arm.

"No, you're coming with me."

"No, I'm not." She bunched her hand in a fist and tried to pull away. "She's not going to want to talk to me."

"You'll figure a way around it. I have no doubt," Josh murmured wryly.

"Don't you get it?" She broke his hold with a furious tug. "It's all starting again. Everybody thinks I'm wrecking another wedding. I'm not going anywhere."

"You're going to hide in here"—he pointed at her parents' home—"when your friend is missing and everyone in the wedding party is going ballistic?"

She gave a sharp nod. "Yep, that's the plan."

Josh gave her an intense look. "Amber, stop being a wimp."

"Wimp?" How dare he call her that? He had no idea the courage it took to suffer through one wrecked wedding. "I've been through this before. You don't know what it's like to have everyone hate you. People think they have a right to be rude to you. They purposely hurt your feelings because you've made one mistake."

They both stared at each other. "I won't let anyone do that to you," he promised.

Her jaw dropped as her heart squeezed tight. Josh was prepared to hold the world at bay from her. Wow. She almost wished he had that kind of power. Unfortunately, no one did.

"Come on, Amber." His tone was suddenly all business. "We need to find Madison."

"I'm not going." She wasn't strong enough to go through this again. The urge was fierce to run out of Acorn Grove and never return.

Amber paused as she considered the idea. She *could* do it. It would be so easy, but there were consequences to that plan. If she ran now, she would never be able to return.

She couldn't let that happen. There was nothing she'd like

more than to settle back in her hometown. It was a dream she kept close to her chest, not willing to tell anyone. All they would do was inspect the flaws and point out all the reasons she couldn't return home. But Amber wasn't ready to give up that dream, so if it meant she had to weather another storm, she'd do it.

"Amber, I'm giving you to the count of three," Josh announced as he rose from the steps. "Either you get dressed and ready to go, or you're going as you are."

She looked at him in horror. "What is it with you and counting?"

"One." He lifted a finger.

"I'm not a little kid," she said through clenched teeth.

"Then stop acting like one. Two." He lifted another finger.

Amber stood up and marched to the screen door. She swung it open and planned to lock it behind her, but Josh was right at her heels.

"You're learning," he said against her ear with a hint of approval.

"You're not," she replied as she strode angrily to her room. "Don't say I didn't warn you."

"You had to take the bike."

Josh slowed to a stop as the traffic light turned red. He didn't say anything. He kept quiet during most of the search, unlike Amber. She found fault in everything from the old brick streets to the way people did a double take when they saw her.

"I wanted to take a car," Amber continued, "but no. Mr. Macho Man can't be seen in a powder blue hatchback."

Josh smiled and leaned back so Amber could hear him. "That is *not* why I decided to use the bike."

"Yes, it is."

"Amber, I know you wanted to use the car so you can slink down in the front seat and hope no one sees you."

She didn't deny it. "Which is a good plan."

For someone who had lived in Acorn Grove for most of her life, she didn't understand how to play the system. "If people talk, but don't see you, then they're more apt to make a big deal when it comes to your next public appearance."

"So? I'm fine with that."

"That would be the wedding." He paused, allowing for Amber to dwell on the complications that would bring. "You need to go out and be seen as much as possible before the ceremony. It's better to get it over and done with rather than let it drag on."

"Easy for you to say," she muttered.

"Focus on the job," he suggested as he watched the stoplight. "Where else would Madison go?"

"Do you really think I'm enjoying this? Have people point and glare at me, all the time hoping they don't know that the bride has taken a runner? They're going to find out soon, if they haven't already. Why would I want to cruise around for as long as possible?"

Josh crouched over his bike, ready for the light to turn green. "Next stop?"

"I don't know." Amber said with a sigh. "The only other place I can think of is that park on the outskirts of town. I don't know the name of it but it's the one with the pond and the long metal bridge over it."

"I know the one."

He drove to it, trying to ignore the way Amber clung against him. She was right about one thing: he shouldn't have taken the bike.

Her arms tightened around his waist and her legs were wedged tightly against his. Her heat made it difficult to concentrate. He wouldn't mind making a few sudden turns and twists with his bike to make her hold on tighter, but Amber wasn't ready to start anything with him. She made it clear when she confessed the real reason she was at the club. She had been using him.

The knowledge should cool the desire he felt for her, but, man, did last night make him hot and bothered. He wanted to test his boundaries and hers. See how far his restraint would go just before it snapped.

He could never let it snap. Never. The more in control he was, the more pleasure he experienced. He lived too many years in chaos, and had finally mastered the wildness inside him. Letting go would destroy him.

And he already found himself pushing the barrier with Amber. He didn't understand why she challenged him—and on different levels—but he needed to be careful around her.

He found the park Amber mentioned in record time and stopped his motorcycle on the gravel lot. He scanned the quiet park. He didn't see any cars, and it didn't look like anyone was there, but if someone really wanted to hide, there were a few good places nestled in the small hills and clusters of trees around the pond.

Amber swung her leg off the motorcycle, took off her helmet and shook out her hair. Josh fought the urge to sink his fingers in the black silky tresses.

She handed him her helmet and frowned when she saw him get off the bike. "You don't need to come along."

"Yeah, I do." Amber was going to need backup, whether she wanted to believe it or not.

"If I find Madison, she's not going to talk with you around."

"Do you think she's going to open up to *you*?"

She huffed but didn't reply. Instead, Amber turned and marched toward the pond. "What is this sudden interest you have in Carl and Madison?"

"Carl is my friend," Josh said as he followed Madison.

"So?" she asked over her shoulder.

"And I was his wingman at the bachelor party."

"Wingman? What is— Wait a second." She stopped on the slope to the pond and faced him. "Isn't that the guy who 'takes one for the team'?" She angrily made the air quotes as she glared at him. "The one who spends time with the *loser* girl so that his friend gets an open field to go for the hot babe?"

"Usually," Josh admitted with a smile, "but during a bachelor party, the wingman also runs interference of any trouble. Like when one of the bridesmaids tries to crash in on the fun."

Her mouth closed with a snap. She pressed her lips together as if she were trying to contain a comment. She gave up the fight. "So you were in wingman mode last night?"

"I could say you were doing the same." Amber had thrown herself at him to do a favor for Madison. That bothered him more than it should. He wanted to laugh it off, or enjoy the secret pleasure of claiming another kiss from Amber.

He couldn't. He wanted to find another opportunity to get Amber back in his arms. Taste her kisses again, and explore what they had together. It was going to take a miracle to get his wish granted.

"The bachelor party is over," Amber said as she followed the winding path along the pond, "so why are you still here?"

"What happens at the party stays at the party, but this fall-out is still going strong," he said, watching his step as the path curved around a small hill. "I need to clean it up."

"You're taking this wingman thing to the extremes."

"I take all of my responsibilities seriously. When I say I'm going to do something, I do it." He didn't know why it was important for her to understand that. "If I need to take care of a situation, it gets taken care of."

"And if it means complete surrender and public humiliation to the other person, so be it." She tossed her hands in the air, muttered under her breath, and picked up her pace.

He stumbled, surprised by Amber's thoughts. What kind of guy did she think he was? Maybe he didn't want to know the answer. "I would never humiliate you."

"Humph."

"But I do expect complete surrender," he admitted with a smile. The idea of Amber writhing underneath him with abandon made his cock throb.

Her shoulders stiffened. "Keep dreaming."

They walked around another hill and stopped when they saw Madison sitting against the trunk of an old tree. Her knees were curled against her chest and she lifted her head when she felt their presence.

"Amber?" Madison wiped her tears from her face. "Josh? What are you doing here?"

Amber hurried over to her friend. "We've been looking all over town for you."

"Don't talk to me." Madison jumped up and looked like she was ready to make a run for it. "I thought you were my friend."

The accusation stopped Amber in her tracks. "I am."

"I saw the picture from the bachelor party." Madison's face crumpled as her eyes shone with pain. "How could you?"

"That picture doesn't tell the real story." Amber's tone pleaded for her friend to understand. "Carl had too much to drink. He fell and I caught him. That was it."

Madison gave a snort. "Sure."

"Come on." Exasperation and something close to fear burred Amber's words. "You have to believe me. I've never been interested in Carl."

"Why?" Madison jutted out her jaw. "What's wrong with him? He's not good enough for you?"

"No, he is." She held her hands up in a placating gesture. "He's got a lot of good qualities."

"Which is why you wanted a piece of him for yourself," Madison wailed as fresh tears edged along her red eyes.

"No." Amber rubbed her fingertips against her forehead. "That's not what I'm saying."

Josh felt he had seen enough. Amber was not going to get Madison to see reason. Not now, at least. It was time to step in, regardless of how Amber felt about his interference.

"Carl would never touch Amber," Josh declared as he stepped forward. "Even if he wanted to for one second."

She scoffed and made a face. "Oh, gee, thanks."

"Is that right?" Madison said, not believing it for a minute. "What makes you so sure?"

"Because he knows that she's mine." Josh placed his hand on Amber's shoulder. She tensed under his touch. Josh didn't take his hand off, and if she was smart, she wouldn't brush him off.

Madison stared at his hand before she looked at Amber's face for confirmation. "Really?"

He felt Amber's struggle. The way her muscles flexed and tightened, he knew she wanted to shove the lie down his throat. But she also knew he just gave her a shortcut, one that would have Madison returned to the wedding festivities safe and sound before anyone knew she ran away.

"I was there when the picture was taken," Josh said before Amber could back up or deny his claim. "I saw everything. The photo doesn't show me catching them both." He tilted his head and looked at Amber. "Isn't that right?"

"It's true," she dully agreed.

"Whoever sent that to you knew it, too." He felt anger rising within his gut. "I don't know why it was taken, or who took the picture, but I'll find out."

"Oh, Amber." Madison started to cry again as she flung her arms around her friend. "I'm sorry I doubted you."

"It's okay." Amber patted her friend's back. They rotated, huddled together, as Madison swayed side to side, begging for forgiveness.

Josh watched smugly. He sidestepped a crisis and got another opportunity to live out his fantasy. Not bad for a day's work. He caught Amber's vicious glare.

Okay, convincing Amber to go with the lie was going to take longer, he thought with a sly smile, but he was up for the challenge.

Chapter Five

AMBER FELT LIKE SHE was going to explode. She was good and kept quiet while they were with Madison. She didn't do bodily harm when Josh suggested they discuss it privately over lunch. The guy was smart enough to have the talk in a public place where there were witnesses, but that wasn't going to cool her temper.

"I'll listen once I order," Josh said as he flipped through the café's menu. "What do you want?"

She folded her arms and continued to glare at him. "I'm not hungry."

He looked at her from over the menu. "Then I will feed you from my plate."

Amber bristled. Josh would do it, and probably feed her by hand. She'd bite his fingers if he tried. "On second thought, I'll take the special."

He ordered for them, just as she knew he would, and settled back in the booth once the waitress left. "Now, you can tell me all about it."

She leaned forward, her chin just a few inches from the table. "I'm *yours*? Since when?"

"Since Madison thinks she's going to lose Carl to you." He studied her for a moment. "Do you want Carl for yourself?" he asked gruffly.

Amber wrinkled her nose. "No."

"Good." Satisfaction flared from his eyes. "That will make it easier."

"It? What is *it*?" She tossed her hands in the air. "What are you talking about?"

"The wedding is in five days. Madison thinks you are after the groom."

"I'm not," Amber repeated, her patience hanging on by a thread. "And we already convinced her of this."

"This time." He looked away as he mulled over the problem. "I have a feeling whoever did this is warming up."

Dread twisted inside her. The way Josh was talking, it sounded like this wasn't a malicious prank, but a thought-out campaign to hurt her friend. "Who would want to do that to Madison? Everyone adores her."

Josh gave her a level look.

She hated when he did that. It made her feel like she was the only one who didn't know what was going on. "What?"

"Did you look closely at the picture?"

"Yes." She was still trying to shake off the image of Carl salivating over her breasts.

"The focus wasn't on Carl." His gaze held hers, as if waiting for the fireworks to go off. "It was on *you*."

The suggestion hit her like a punch in the stomach. Amber's mouth sagged open and she reared back into her seat. "Someone did this to get to *me*?"

He lifted one shoulder. "That's what I think."

"Why take a picture of me? Wouldn't it be easier to egg my house?" she suggested. "Slit my tires. Trip me on the sidewalk."

"What would that achieve? Whoever did this wants you to ruin another wedding. Or at least, make it look like you're trying to do it."

"Bailey." She slapped her hands on the table. "I saw her there, and she would definitely hold a grudge."

"Or Isabel."

"Isabel?" Amber considered the possibility and reluctantly nodded. "Well, yeah. I did rat her out at Bailey's wedding. Or"—she held up her finger—"she wants to divert attention so she can make her move on Carl."

Josh looked annoyed. "Why do these women suddenly see Carl as a hot commodity?"

Amber waggled her eyebrows. "Envious, Josh?"

"As long as you think I'm hot, that's all I need."

Her pulse jumped as she watched the slow, knowing smile form on his mouth. "I'm immune to your flirting."

The waitress came back with their coffee. Josh waited until the woman left before he resumed the conversation. "Isabel isn't interested in Carl. And Carl only has eyes for Madison."

"But Isabel has been calling Carl, and Madison saw them here with their heads together." She had no idea why she mentioned that detail. It made her sound so unsophisticated. "Carl denies it."

"I'm having lunch with you," he pointed out. "Does this mean we're also having sex?"

"Very funny." Amber paused from retrieving the sugar as it occurred to her. "You know what's going on."

Josh didn't deny it. He set his elbow on the table and propped his chin with his hand. "Do you know what Isabel does for a living?"

She shrugged and ripped open a sugar packet. "She's a sales associate."

"For a jewelry store," Josh added. "Carl wants to surprise Madison with a custom-made bracelet. Isabel is only interested in the commission."

"Oh!" The sugar hit the rim of her coffee mug and spilled on the table. "You have got to be kidding me! Didn't Carl realize how suspicious he was acting?"

"He probably thought he could wing it. If he's smart, he'll tell Madison everything right now."

Amber brushed at the spilled sugar, shaking her head. "And while everyone else comes out smelling like a rose, I'm knee-deep in sludge." Typical.

"I can get you out of it."

He sounded confident, and she was tempted to accept his help, but she had no doubt there were strings attached. "No, thanks, Josh. You've done quite enough."

"It would be very simple. I already said you were mine," he reminded her. "Now I have to prove it."

His claim unsettled her. Her heart pounded hard against her ribs as dark pleasure curled around her chest. She didn't want to be secretly pleased. She wanted to be appalled and toss his offer back in his face.

Amber tried to hide her confusion with sarcasm. "What do you have planned? Are you going to tattoo your name on my butt?"

Josh's sly smile made her skin tingle. "No, we'd want it to be seen, and no one other than me will get that close to you."

His arrogance took her breath away. "*You* won't get that close."

His smile widened, not bothering to argue, which set Amber more on edge. "We need to make it look like we're together," Josh said. "That we are having a mad passionate affair. Very wild and very public."

Was he crazy? How was that supposed to keep her scandal free? "That is not going to solve my problem. It will make me look like a two-timing wedding wrecker."

Josh shook his head. "The people around here know that I wouldn't tolerate it."

"Oh, is that right?" Josh Griffin was not exactly citizen of the year. What made him think he had that kind of power?

"They also know that I protect and take care of my own."

The way he said it made it sound like a pledge. "Are we still talking about the women you date?" she asked lightly. "Because it's beginning to sound like you're talking about your property. Are you lumping me in with your motor-cycle?"

Josh ignored that. "All of Acorn Grove knows how the women I date treat me, so you have your work cut out for you."

Amber braced herself. "This I have to hear."

"They are"—he considered his word carefully—"respect-ful."

She looked down at her coffee mug when a memory flashed before her. She remembered one of his ex-girlfriends would add cream and sugar to *his* coffee before she fixed her own. Another one of Josh's former lovers always seemed to lower her eyes in deference to him.

That had been years ago, but the women's actions had

surprised her. They hadn't been obvious or overly demonstra-
tive, but it had roused her curiosity. These women had been
smart, successful and sexy. What had Josh done to warrant
that kind of behavior?

At the time she had wondered if he gave them mind-
shattering orgasms, so irreversible that they turned into clinging, docile creatures. It was something they couldn't get from
any other man, so they put up with it for as long as they
could. Amber still wasn't ruling the theory out.

"Respectful?" she asked hoarsely. "Don't you mean sub-
servient?"

"Attentive," he corrected. "The agreement was very clear.
I take care of her and she takes care of me."

Amber leaned back and stared at him, determined to
maintain eye contact from now on. She was not a submissive
woman, and he was going to have to get used to it.

"I would have never guessed it." She studied him from his
faded bandanna to the worn leather jacket. "Joshua Griffin is
an old-fashioned man."

The accusation didn't bother him. "There's nothing old-
fashioned about it."

"If I have to fake being your girlfriend, I am not going to
wait on you hand and foot."

"I'm not asking you to." The look he gave made her wonder if one day she'd beg to serve him. "I am telling you to
show your allegiance to me."

She shifted uncomfortably in her seat. "This is not a feu-
dal battle."

"If you don't show it then whoever is trying to smear your
name will succeed."

"My show of respect isn't going to help." A wicked

thought occurred. "Now if you served me, that would be different. How about if you get down on your knees and grovel a little?"

Josh didn't appear amused. "If that ever happened—and don't count on it—the protection I give would be worthless. I would be seen as weak. That would defeat the purpose."

Amber dipped her head and grumbled. "This whole idea is stupid."

"Why are you so afraid?"

Her jaw locked and she made herself look up at him. "I'm not afraid."

He lifted an eyebrow in disbelief.

"I happen to be an independent, modern-day woman. I can support myself"—she started ticking the list off on her fingers—"I have a life of my own, and I can be happy without a man. Especially a man telling me what to do."

"Then you have nothing to worry about. This will only last for five days. Unless . . ." Amusement gleamed in his eye.

Amber hunched her shoulders as the tension crawled up her spine. "Unless what?"

"You're worried that you will enjoy it too much."

She stiffened at his teasing statement. Her safe, peaceful world that she had painfully pieced back together three years ago took a hit. A jagged rip revealed the dark fantasy that she had tried to ignore. It went against the good-girl life she was trying to get back. The fantasy was stronger, too, and building momentum. It wouldn't take much to knock her wholesome existence to smithereens.

Amber knew she had to get away before it was too late. "I'm out of here," she announced, tossing her napkin onto the table and rising from her seat.

Josh's sigh was long and heartfelt. "Leave and I will bring you back."

He'd do it, too. Or at least, he would try. "I don't listen to threats." She walked away quickly before he could reach out and catch her.

Josh noticed the reckless swing of her hip as Amber walked away. How long would it take for Amber to realize that he always meant what he said?

Or maybe she felt the compulsive urge to test it. To test *him*. Did she need to see how far she could push him before he gave up on her? Amber was in for a long wait, because that wasn't going to happen.

"Natalie," Josh said to the waitress as he got up from the table. "We'll be right back."

The waitress clucked her tongue. "You've met your match with the Hughes girl."

She might be right. "I like to think of it as she met her match with me."

"Better hurry." Natalie nodded at the door. "She was walking fast."

He noticed that, too. As if Amber had been silently taunting him with a you-have-to-catch-me-first. He would catch her. It was a matter of who would tire first. And he wasn't planning to quit.

He stood at the café entrance and looked down the sidewalk. Amber was already on the next block. Josh followed, noticing a car on the street was slowing down to match Amber's pace. Josh immediately recognized the car. Isabel.

He walked down the sidewalk, watching every nuance of Amber's body language as she talked to Isabel. The rigid line of her spine. The hands flexing and bunching at her sides. He could imagine what Isabel was saying.

Amber suddenly stopped and turned toward Isabel. The car crawled to a stop. Josh quickened his pace before Amber lunged through the open driver's window.

"Amber," he said casually as he reached her. Josh turned to the driver in the car. "Isabel."

"Hi, Josh." Isabel greeted him in a high, friendly tone.

Josh wrapped his arm around Amber's waist, hoping she wouldn't pull away, and was somewhat surprised when she didn't. "What's going on?"

"Just catching up," Isabel said with a dazzling smile that she reserved for men. "Have you seen the pictures of the bachelor party?"

"One of the pictures," he admitted. Josh decided to press his luck and curled Amber's stiff body closer to his. "Why didn't you keep me in the shot, Isabel?"

She blinked her long lashes, looking slightly confused. "I had nothing to do with it."

He didn't believe her, but now wasn't the time to drag out a confession. He just wanted it stopped. "I'm glad to hear it. If you find out who did, let them know I'm not happy."

"You?" Isabel's eyes widened when she finally noticed his hand on Amber's waist. "What do you mean?"

"I'm not tolerating any rumors about Amber." Josh allowed the bite in his tone.

Isabel looked at Amber, then at Josh as the realization slowly dawned on her. "I see. When did the two of you hook up?"

"It's been a while," Amber said.

Josh was glad to see Amber finally backing him up. He had been getting a little worried about her silence. There was nothing more dangerous than a quiet Amber Hughes.

"Huh." Isabel's eyes narrowed into slits, and Josh knew she wasn't taking it at face value. "I never would have thought it. She's a little too vanilla for your taste, Josh."

"How would you know?" Amber asked.

Isabel's secretive smile set Josh's teeth on edge. "See you around," she said before giving a fluttery wave and driving off.

Amber waited until the car disappeared from sight before she relaxed. "Thanks."

"What was all that about?" And had she realized that he backed her up without knowing the fight?

"The usual," she said as she untangled herself from Josh. "Isabel seems determined to prove that she's smarter, sexier and all around better than me."

"Are you okay?" It was like Isabel managed to find chinks in Amber's armor.

"Oh, yeah. It's no big deal, just annoying stuff. But you are so going to regret telling Isabel that we've hooked up."

"I'll be the judge of that."

Amber made a face. "Don't you think you're taking this wingman thing a little too far?"

She thought he was doing all this because of the bachelor party? "My wingman duties are over."

She closed her eyes and sighed. "Then what is this about?"

Josh hesitated. If he told her he appointed himself as her defender, she was going to cause more trouble trying to get him to quit. So he needed to give her one of the other reasons. "I'm taking an advantage of an opportunity."

Amber's forehead wrinkled with a fierce frown. "What

kind of opportunity would you find in pretending to have a fling with me?"

He slowly ran his gaze over her curvy body. "How good are you at pretending?"

"Listen to me." She folded her arms, covering her breasts from his view. "We are not going to have an affair. Even if we did, no one would believe it."

"Why not?" The idea of the two of them together made perfect sense to him.

"You heard Isabel." She motioned to where they had last seen the car. "I'm too 'vanilla' for you."

Josh scoffed at the accusation. "She doesn't know what she's talking about. You are not the good girl everyone thinks you are."

Amber didn't look happy with that assessment. "She's going to do what she can to prove we're faking it."

He shrugged, not too concerned about that. "Then you are going to have to fake it really well. You can start by listening to me."

"Oh," Amber growled with frustration. "I knew you were going to say that!"

"We need to finish eating." He pointed at the restaurant they had just left.

"Forget it. I'm not going back."

He reached out and hooked his fingers around the front of her jeans. His fingers grazed the soft skin of her abdomen. Josh felt her muscles clench from the intimate touch.

She gasped and stared at his fingers. "W-what are you doing?" She swatted at his hand.

"I'm taking you back to the restaurant," he replied as he walked backward, guiding her along the sidewalk.

She arched back, trying to slip away from his grasp, but the move allowed his hand to dip further. His fingertips skimmed the lacy edge of her panties.

Amber encircled his wrist with both hands, trying to pull him off, but he didn't budge. "Josh! This is totally unacceptable behavior."

"No, walking out on our meal would fall into that category."

"I'm sorry." She sounded like she really meant it. "Now will you let me go?"

"No." He led her across the street, the heels of her sneakers squeaking as she refused to pick up her feet.

"Let go immediately or I'll—I'll . . ."

"You'll what?" He stopped at the corner and looked at her flushed face. "Take your jeans off and walk home half-naked?"

She glared at him.

"Yeah, I thought you'd see it my way."

"Josh." Natalie poked her head out the door. "I saw you coming back down the sidewalk, so I refreshed your coffee."

Josh ignored Amber's growl low in her throat. "Thanks, Natalie."

"Great," Amber muttered. "Now everyone's going to hear how you dragged me down the sidewalk."

"And how you walked out on me." He let go of her jeans, immediately missing her body heat. Josh stepped behind her and she reentered the restaurant. "Everyone will hear that I chased you down a couple of blocks before I caught you."

Amber didn't answer. She kept her chin up and walked to their table. He knew she felt the interested gaze of the other patrons, but kept her eyes firmly ahead of her as she returned to her seat.

He also knew she was blaming him for the embarrassment. He wasn't trying to do that, but she couldn't believe it. "Don't worry about what others think," he suggested as he sat across from her. "And think of it this way; the gossip will help us establish our red-hot affair."

"We are *not* going to have an affair," she whispered harshly, a blush staining her cheeks.

"Of course we're not." Her consistent rejection of the idea was getting to him. "But they don't need to know that. It's a matter of illusion."

"Okay, now you're talking." She gave a snap to her napkin before laying it across her lap. "Illusions. I can handle that. Hey, what do you mean by 'of course not'?"

He smiled. She didn't want to know the answer.

"C'mon, Josh." She said through clenched teeth. "What does that mean?"

Josh leaned back against the booth and draped his arm over the vinyl. "We won't have sex until I say so."

Temptation flared in her eyes for an instant before she glared at him. "And that will be when hell freezes over."

"No, Amber." The corner of his mouth slanted up as anticipation danced in his blood. "It will happen sooner than you think. I promise."

Chapter Six

"THIS IS NEVER GOING to work," Amber muttered as she strode down the quiet street in the early morning to pick her car up from Josh's home. Her heels seemed to echo on the cracked sidewalks, and for a second she fought the urge to slip them off and walk the rest of the way barefoot before someone heard her.

The plan had seemed ridiculously simple last night—and safe. That was always a selling point for her. Yet why spend the night at Josh's—which would never have worked in a million years—when she could simply park the car at his house and walk home to retrieve it the next day?

It was too simple. No one was going to notice her car or think she spent the night at Josh's. Or maybe, she didn't *want* it to work, Amber thought with a wry twist to her mouth as she looked around the street, looking for signs of life. Maybe she didn't want people to believe she had succumbed to Josh's charms.

She was suffering from feminine pride. She liked it when the citizens of Acorn Grove did double takes when she was out with Josh. She practically preened when Josh focused all his attention on her. Yet she wanted to think she hadn't fallen under his spell. That she was different from the other women. Special.

A part of her was horrified by her love-struck behavior. How bad would she be acting if she had believed it all to be real?

But it wasn't. It was *fake*. She needed to remember it was a five-day act before life returned to normal.

Too bad she kind of wished it was love. Every raw emotion she had experienced years ago had come back in a rush. She had to keep it just below the surface. It pushed against her, gaining strength, ready to burst through her at the worst possible moment.

Just three more days. Amber picked up her pace, as if that would hurry up time itself. She could hold it together for three more days before she left Acorn Grove.

It would help if she kept her distance from Josh, but she couldn't seem to do it. She had to ration her phone calls to him, fighting the need to share every trivial detail with him. She caught herself walking around with a stupid smile on her face, usually thinking about Josh. Any unexpected sighting of him made her nerves jangle and got her heart pumping.

Those were definite signs that she had it bad. It showed the necessity of keeping away. After all, it's all about illusion, Amber reminded herself as she turned the corner of Josh's street. She immediately spotted her hatchback parked next to his duplex.

Her old good girl tendencies immediately kicked in. She scanned the other cars on the street, wondering if anyone had already left for work. Had anyone noticed her car parked out front of Josh's home? Or realized it had been there *all night long*?

That was the whole point of the exercise, Amber reminded herself fiercely as she made a quick check along the street, noticing everyone seemed to still be home. She was *trying* to make it look like she stayed overnight at Josh's.

Had she done it for real, she wouldn't be upright and walking this early in the morning. She winced as longing pulled deep in her belly.

Amber stood by her car and paused, wondering if she should just get in the car and drive off, or if she should go inside Josh's home and make her exit when everyone was leaving for work.

A spate of nerves gripped her stomach as she imagined the frowns and glares she would receive. She didn't think she could handle the neighbors' condemnation. Josh may think this would help, but it would make it worse.

What was she doing following Josh's idea? She was completely out of her mind! There were different rules and expectations for men and women. She had to get out of here before someone saw her.

Amber hunched her shoulders when she heard the slam of a screen door. *Too late!* There was no time to hide. It was time to apply the ancient technique of "If I can't see you, then you can't see me."

"Amber?" The raspy voice of one of the Fillmore sisters cut through the early morning silence. "Little Amber Hughes?"

Amber reluctantly turned to face the octogenarian. She couldn't tell which sister it was. The two looked alike with their white permed hair, floral housecoats and cigarettes dangling from their mouths that were always bright red and greasy with lipstick.

"Hi, Miss Fillmore. How are you?" She thought fast and

latched her attention on the Pomeranian dog relieving itself on the small patch of brown grass next to the elderly woman's blue-veined leg. "Spike is looking as cute as ever."

The Fillmore sister didn't grab the bait. "Were you at Josh's house all night?"

Sheesh, did she have to say it so loud? "Me? Uh . . ." She couldn't do this. She didn't trust this maneuver. "No, no. Of course not."

The old woman squinted at her and blew out a puff of smoke. Hell, even Spike was giving her a look of disbelief.

"I had asked Josh to look at my car." She patted the hood, which was stone cold. Boy, she hoped no one hunting for gossip checked that damning piece of evidence during the night. "It was making a funny noise."

"Uh-huh. I thought he was a handyman, not a mechanic."

"Well, he's good with his hands." She winced. "I mean—"

"I didn't know you and Josh were together. Martha always thought it would happen."

Martha needed her medication checked. "Yeah, well . . ." There was no way to respond. "I should be going."

"Just like that?" Josh asked, his amused voice coming from his front door. "Is that the thanks I get?"

Amber closed her eyes in defeat. He *would* be up, waiting for her. Did he have to make that comment sound so . . . suggestive? Indecent?

Admit it. You are thrilled. You couldn't wait to see him again. Just the sound of his voice made your day.

"Morning, Josh," the elderly woman called over as her dog yapped a greeting. "How are you doing?"

"Better than ever."

Oh, God. Could he *be* any more obvious? Amber reluctantly

turned to face him. Her heart beat stopped when she saw Josh standing by the door, wearing nothing but an unbuttoned pair of faded jeans.

He stood there like a wild beast stirred awake. She wanted to get closer and drag her hand along his ruffled hair before skimming the dark shadow of whiskers on his jaw. But the glitter of his brown eyes stopped her. He looked grumpy and should be handled with great care.

He raised one arm against the door frame and Amber couldn't help but notice the sculpted muscle. Josh was a lean and sleek animal. He might look civilized, but there was no telling when he was going to do something outrageous.

There were too many moments when he made her feel outrageous. She eyed the unfastened button of his jeans. Her hands tingled with the need to reach past the denim and explore.

Nope. No exploring. Not now. Not ever. She balled her hands until her nails bit into her palms. "Josh," she said with a fixed smile. "What are you doing up?"

"Were you going to leave without telling me?"

She blushed at the lazy sensual tone. She felt it sizzling on her skin. She decided the best antidote was to march up to his porch.

"There's a little thing called overkill," Amber whispered, and immediately relaxed when she heard the Fillmores' screen door slam shut.

"Just playing a part." He looked at the V-neck of her yellow wraparound dress. "Nice outfit."

Her nipples tightened when she saw the wicked gleam in his eye. It was like he was planning a strategy to strip her free from the cotton. How could he make her feel naughty when she wore her most proper dress?

"I have to go to a bridesmaid luncheon after my dress fitting," she primly informed him in case he got any bright ideas that she was dressing for him. "Which is why I'm getting the car."

"Bridesmaid luncheon?"

"Yes, while you guys got to have a fun bachelor party, I'm stuck remembering which fork to use and trying not to fall asleep."

He leaned closer. "Are you going to need help?"

She took a step back. "You don't need a wingman for a table setting, but thanks for the offer. See you around, Josh."

Josh smiled. "I meant is Bailey going to be there?"

His concern stopped her. "No, she has to work, thankfully." She really liked how he looked after her and she didn't want it to end. It could dangerously become a habit to rely on him, and he wasn't promising it would last forever. "Isabel is not going anywhere near the luncheon, so I think I'll be okay."

"I don't know, Amber. You have a talent for finding trouble." He reached out for her and she felt a mix of triumph and excitement from his touch.

She tried to play it cool. "What is it now?"

"You forgot to kiss me good-bye." His hooded gaze dropped to her mouth.

Amber swallowed roughly as her lips stung. "Excuse me?"

"Don't look now," Josh murmured, not taking his eye off her, "but the curtains are twitching all over the neighborhood."

"They are not," she denied in a whispered rush.

"Okay, only one from across the street," he admitted as he lowered his mouth closer to hers.

She looked at his mouth and felt the need to purse her lips. "That doesn't mean I have to give them a show."

"Then give a teaser. Come on, Amber." He winked at her. "Give me your best shot."

She knew he was going to delay her until she did what he asked. The last thing she needed was to be late for the dress fitting with Tilly. Sure, that was her excuse. It had nothing to do with the fact that she wanted to get close and touch him.

Reaching on her tiptoes, she gave him a peck on the cheek. She liked the bite of the stubble against her lips. "I gotta go. See you."

His brown eyes gleamed. "Amber, that was pathetic. You can do better."

She tilted her head, as if considering his words. "Mmm, no. That was it."

"Need to control all that passion simmering beneath the surface, huh?"

She froze, her lungs shriveling with panic. Was it that obvious? She had tried so hard to conceal it.

"Too afraid you won't be able to keep your hands off my body?" he teased. "I understand."

Oh, he was kidding. For some reason, that didn't make her breathe easier. Josh had no idea that his teasing was too close to the truth. Was he really that clueless that she was holding back, or did he think she had ice in her veins? Maybe he needed to know that she wasn't someone to be trifled with, either.

Amber reached up and cupped the back of his head, holding him in place before slamming her mouth on to his. He didn't utter a sound as she kissed him. Excitement and desire tripped along her nerves as she tasted the latent danger on his lips.

She wasn't going to hold back. She wanted a response, even if she had to yank it from him. Amber decided to go up another level, rubbing her breasts against his hard chest, throwing in a throaty purr for the fun of it.

He parted his lips, but Amber chose not to accept the invitation. Once she darted her tongue in his mouth, he would take over. Instead she caught his bottom lip between her teeth and sucked hard.

Josh's hands clamped on her hips. She felt the possession vibrating from his fingers through the thin layer of her dress. When the back of her shoe hit something solid, she realized he had turned her around. She lifted one foot against the wall behind her, fighting for balance as she drew Josh closer.

She trembled, her mouth softening against his, as he skimmed his hands up her body before reaching her breasts. He palmed her nipples, rubbing circles until they tightened painfully. The sensations tugged deep in her pelvis like a ribbon ready to break.

He was going to drive her wild before she had a chance to do the same for him. She had baited him and now she was getting caught in her own trap. She had to do something before he took her right there against the side of his house.

Not that that was a bad thing . . .

She slid her hands down his stomach before drifting to his jeans. His stomach muscles clenched from the light touch. She smiled against his mouth as she smoothed her hands to his lower back before slipping her fingers past the denim.

Amber cupped the tight, compact muscles of his buttocks. Her sex felt hot and slick as she rubbed against his cock. She clenched the bare muscles with her hands, wanting to get closer.

His control suddenly snapped.

He bucked into her, sliding his mouth down her throat and sucking the pulse point. She leaned back, allowing him more access as he branded her skin with his mouth.

She didn't care that he bunched her skirt high up on her hips. She wanted to cry with relief when he ground his hard, thick cock against her sex. She shivered at his low, sexy growl when he found her hot, wet and ready for him.

His unbuttoned jeans and her panties were the only barriers. Her hands dug into the hard flesh of his buttocks and she loved the feel of his muscles flexing and tightening at every thrust.

Josh lifted his head and their gazes collided. His brown eyes were blurred with lust, his face ruddy as he breathed hard.

She could lure him into his bed right now. She could have him any way she wanted. Make him beg for her to feed the primitive hunger that pounded in his blood.

The sense of power made her dizzy. She felt strong and ultrafeminine.

She knew he wanted to take her. Claim. Mate. It was going to be rough, wild and untamed. Oh, she couldn't wait.

But then saw the fear flicker in his brown eyes. She frowned. But that was impossible. What did he have to be scared of? She wouldn't hurt him, and he would never hurt her.

Then she understood. Amber instinctively loosened her hold. Josh was afraid of losing control of himself. He wouldn't let the wildness inside him break free.

She wanted a taste of that wildness. She could get it, but he would never forgive himself.

She lowered her leg and reluctantly removed her hands from his body. He stood completely still, his breathing ragged.

She sidestepped him, tugging the hem of her dress. The tense silence was palpable.

Amber licked her swollen lips. "Is that better?" she asked as coolly as possible, but her voice came out husky.

Josh didn't say anything. He didn't look at her. He was holding on to the last of his control. It was as if the sight of her would send him over the edge.

She placed her hand on his arm and he flinched. She quickly withdrew. "I have to go," she said quietly. "I'll see you around." She walked away, her legs shaking, determined not to look back. It was only when she was in her car and driving off that she looked back. He was already gone.

"There's no reason to drive me to the rehearsal dinner," Amber told him two days later. She sat in the passenger seat of her car, her arms and legs tucked close to her body.

"Yes, there is." Josh parked the hatchback next to the church. "We are a couple."

He liked the sound of that. Amber didn't seem to care one way or the other. She lowered the visor and checked her appearance and he caught a glimpse of the love bite he had left on her neck.

The mark bothered him. Dark pleasure bloomed in his chest at his branding. A part of him wanted to take his thumb and swipe off the makeup she had applied to conceal it. The other part of him was disgusted by his lack of sophistication. The mark was a glaring reminder of how his iron control deserted him.

"Couples have a tendency to show up at parties together," he said as he turned off the engine.

"Not always." She snapped the visor back and unhooked

her seat belt. Every move was careful and precise. She was making certain there'd be no accidental touching in the small car.

"Usually," he argued. "But we don't have the luxury of time. The wedding is tomorrow and I'm not taking any chances."

One more day. He pulled the key from the ignition with more force than was warranted. Josh couldn't believe it. He barely had enough time with Amber. He hadn't gotten her alone, and never anywhere near a bed.

Time was running out and he was nowhere close to reaching his fantasy. Josh closed his hand over the keys, welcoming the bite of metal against his palm. If only Amber made a move and acted on her desires. That would go a long way for him.

She was torturing him as it was. Amber watched him with a hunger that made him hot, but whenever he got close, she bolted. And he let her get away, not sure if he was willing to have a repeat of what happened on his porch. He did *not* want to lose control again and scare her.

Amber had caught a glimpse of his weakness, but hadn't used it against him. She could have—made him a slave in her bed—and she knew it.

But instead, she pulled back and let him regain control over himself. He wasn't sure why she had done that. Did she want him in control? Or did she not want him that badly?

No, that couldn't be it. Please don't let that be it. He glanced over at her. Amber wore a bright red sundress that hugged her curves. Her black hair was wild and free, and the fire in her brown eyes made him ache.

She wanted him. It was killing him not to act on it.

Amber looked away sharply and pushed open the car door. She got away fast, just as she had for the past few days. Her heels clacked against the sidewalk as she headed for the church. Josh sighed and unbuckled his seat belt. He wondered what it would take for her to stay by his side.

As Josh got out of the car, watching the flirty red dress swish against her legs, he noticed her abrupt stop. She tensed, like an animal scenting danger. He looked in the direction of her stare and saw Bailey heading straight for Amber.

Uh-oh. Josh slammed the door closed and strode toward Amber, who was looking around, unsure of where to go. She looked over her shoulder and her expression twisted his heart. He picked up his pace, but there was no way he could get there in time.

"Amber?" Bailey called out as she made a straight path for her.

Josh saw Amber roll back her shoulders. She braced her feet, as if she was finding her center of balance so the first blow wouldn't knock her down.

She wasn't going to run. The woman had more strength than he gave her credit.

"Hi, Bailey." Amber sounded almost defiant.

Bailey raised her arms and Josh got there just as she wrapped her arms around Amber's shoulders.

Wait a second. Josh skidded to a halt. Bailey wanted to *hug* Amber? The gesture was brief and awkward, but still shocking. Why would Bailey hug the woman who wrecked her wedding?

"I've been looking all over for you," Bailey admitted as she took a step back.

"Really?" Amber's voice was thready and weak. "I thought you would want to avoid me."

"I used to," she admitted bluntly.

Amber looked at Josh, her eyes mirroring his own look of confusion. She returned her attention to her former friend. "What changed?"

Bailey sighed. "Me. It's time to move on and stop getting stuck in the past."

"I hate to say this," Amber said, wincing, "but Acorn Grove won't let that happen. Believe me, they are *still* talking about your wedding."

Bailey looked over at Josh. "Isn't that just like Amber?" she asked wryly. "Tells the truth whether you want to hear it or not."

"I'm trying to break her of the habit," he confessed.

Amber glanced at him in surprise. "Oh, are you?"

"Good luck on that," Bailey said.

Amber held her hands up. "What's going on here? You should be hating my guts."

"I did. I hated everyone." Shadows swept along her face. "Especially those who knew about Jimmy and Isabel, but never tried to tell me."

Amber patted her shoulder. "I'm really sorry I made a mess of it."

"I know, but you shouldn't have suffered for it. I'm sorry about that. Maybe someone"—she gave a look at Josh—"will convince you to move back."

His world shifted at the suggestion. Amber back in town? He liked that idea. Too much, in fact.

"We'll see," Amber said with a polite smile.

Bailey turned when someone called her name. She searched

the small group of people on the church steps. "My date is looking for me." She turned back to Amber. "We'll talk later?"

"Definitely."

They watched Bailey leave. "How about that?" Josh asked as Bailey climbed the steps and out of earshot.

Amber shrugged. "My mom kept saying time heals all wounds, but I didn't believe her."

"Are you okay?" He curled his arm around her back and she didn't try to escape. Something must be wrong, Josh decided grimly. "You look shaky."

"Oh, yeah." She pressed her hand to her head. "I thought I was going to get punched. A black eye at the very least."

Josh would have never allowed the hit to land. "That oughta teach you to never leave my side." He heard Amber's scoff, but let it slide. She'd learn.

CHAPTER SEVEN

THIS IS IT. AMBER's mind was going full-speed as she focused her eyes on her friend's frothy white veil. Carl and Madison were one minute away from being pronounced husband and wife. One more minute and her past would be erased.

The young, dynamic minister looked before the congregation, studiously avoiding eye contact with her. "If anyone believes that this man and this woman should not be wed in holy matrimony . . ."

Oh, boy. She could feel the attention shifting to her like a wave. Did they notice how her flower bouquet shook? Or the sweat beading on her lower lip?

"Speak now," the man's voice rang to the rafters, "or forever hold your peace."

Amber clenched her teeth. She wasn't going to move a muscle. Not even blink. Something tickled her throat, but she refused to cough.

She could feel every pair of eyes on her. Some were expectant, others curious, while a few dared her. Amber wanted to close her eyes and ward off the attention.

What she really wanted to do was seek out Josh in the crowd and look into his eyes. Let him be her anchor while the storm passed.

But she couldn't move. *Wouldn't.* Josh was seated far back in the church, and any move she made to find him would be misunderstood.

She really didn't have to look for Josh. She felt his attention on her. It was strange that she could sense it from the rest of the stares. But his gaze felt warm and supportive. Trusting. Loving.

Oh, yeah, right. Amber curbed the urge to roll her eyes. Loving. That was wishful thinking.

"I now pronounce you husband and wife."

She made it! Amber exhaled slowly, wanting to melt into a puddle of tangerine taffeta. As the guests cheered Madison and Carl, Amber turned to find Josh in the church.

He looked straight at her and a wild, hot sensation pierced her straight through. She turned away, off-balance, which could have been the result of relief knocking at her bones or the slightly altered bridesmaid dress cutting off her circulation.

Who was she kidding? It was the aftershock from falling for Josh Griffin. Hard.

The end of the wedding seemed to move at warp speed while her mind wrapped around Josh's expression. Did he love her? She thought about it as she took the groomsman's arm and walked down the aisle. Enough to share his life with her?

She shook her head, trying to clear her mind. She couldn't dwell on that. Because she didn't know, and it was going to gnaw away at her until she found some kind of evidence to support her fantasies.

She had to concentrate on the wedding, but it was difficult to focus. Her duties weren't over and one slipup would still cause her grief. Amber silently took her position in the receiving line, forcing a smile on her face.

Amber did her best chatting briefly with each guest. Most of them had snubbed her three years ago, and now they were all smiles. *Imagine that.* She slowly noticed an alarming pattern of what they were saying to her.

"Josh is keeping you out of trouble?"

"You needed a good man to keep you in line."

"He's a keeper. Don't lose him."

Whoa. What was going on? Suddenly she was acceptable because Josh kept an eye on her? What about all those years when she was the epitome of proper behavior? What about all those years when she kept her eye on Josh? Hmm?

Amber sighed with relief when the last guest left the building. She didn't think her smile was going to last much longer.

She stepped outside of the church, vaguely aware of the guests taking small sacks of rice to toss at the happy couple. She didn't feel like joining in as troubling thoughts whirled in her head.

What if she made another mistake like speaking when she shouldn't? No matter how hard she tried to prevent it, random acts of clumsiness and the run-of-the-mill disasters would occur. Would public opinion turn on her again? Would Josh's opinion change?

Maybe the dream of returning to Acorn Grove wasn't a good one, Amber thought as she ventured to the edges of the crowd. Or perhaps, not realistic. She wouldn't like to be public enemy number one again, but she would survive. Josh's change of heart would be devastating.

Josh was suddenly at her side. Her weariness evaporated, the energy roaring back in her.

"You did good," he said, pride shining from his brown eyes.

Amber smiled wanly. She had kept her mouth shut and stayed in the background as much as possible. She had been the proper woman of her past and found it fit about as comfortably as her bridesmaid dress.

His eyes darkened as a serious look overcame his face. She stood still as the world started moving in slow motion. She held his gaze as he lifted his hand and placed it on the top of her head. His palm rested authoritatively above her forehead.

Her heart started to gallop. What was he doing? The gesture should have been comforting, but it shattered her world. The simple touch was meant to claim her. She was his.

He didn't need to say a word. She knew. Amber closed her eyes to hide the unexpected shimmer of tears. She wanted to earn his respect and pride. The right to carry his name.

That wasn't going to happen any time soon. She wasn't the proper woman everyone expected her to be. It was kind of ironic. The one man who uncovered her wild streak was probably the one man who wanted to tame it.

She needed to show that she couldn't be tamed—even by Josh. She had to do it now, by tonight, before anyone started to hope or get a crazy idea about the future. Especially her.

It was time to misbehave.

She was up to no good.

Josh watched Amber on the dance floor as she gyrated wildly to the rock music. He hadn't been concerned when she kicked off her shoes and whirled them around her head. He hadn't raised an eyebrow like the other guests when she bunched her bridesmaid dress scandalously high so she could kick up her bare legs.

But then he started to notice that every move and loud laugh was designed to gain attention. The only thing missing from her repertoire was flashing the band. The way she was acting, he wouldn't dismiss the possibility.

But when Amber found every opportunity to dance with every man at the reception, Josh knew he was getting played. She was directing this outburst mainly at him. The question was why?

Did she feel his claim on her too constricting? Did it frighten her? Or didn't she understand? She was his and he didn't share.

She was playing a very dangerous game, Josh decided as Amber danced a little too close to one of the male guests. He set his jaw. She had already seen him lose control—and that had been when she touched him. Imagine his mood when she touched another man.

A movement in the corner of his eye captured his attention. Josh turned and saw Isabel on the other side of the dance floor. She was sitting down at one of the tables, aiming her cell phone in Amber's direction.

The woman never learns. Josh sighed and made his way through the crowd. Isabel hadn't been at the wedding ceremony, but she made an entrance when she walked into the reception hall on her date's arm. The noise level went from silence to a sudden buzz of whispers. Josh wasn't sure if the guests had been commenting on her choice to wear a strapless white minidress or if they were shocked at her audacity to show up where she was not invited.

He had kept an eye on Isabel throughout the dinner, knowing that she would not be content with simply showing up and making a grand entrance. His instincts told him that she wasn't trying to wreck the wedding. Her interests were still on Amber.

And Amber was giving Isabel a lot of material to work with. Josh looked back on the dance floor and saw Amber move her hips in such a way that made every man stop and stare. He reluctantly turned away and reached Isabel. Josh snatched the phone from her.

"Hey!" Isabel's frown immediately transformed into a flirty smile. "Oh, Josh. Hi."

"Hi, Isabel," he said as he scrolled through her phone menu and viewed the pictures. All of them were of Amber, documenting her wild behavior growing as the night went on. She looked sexy, naughty, and just a little bit dangerous. Josh secretly liked the pictures and wished he could keep them for his private viewing.

He glanced at Isabel. "I know you were the one who forwarded the picture of Amber and Carl."

She tipped her chin proudly. "What of it?" Her eyes grew wide when he began deleting the pictures. "Josh! Give it back to me."

He held the phone out of her reach. "Why does she fascinate you so much?"

Isabel snorted at the claim. "Hardly."

"Then why take her picture?" He held the phone up high as Isabel made another attempt to retrieve it.

She shrugged. "Can I help it if she's making a scene?"

"Can I help it if I talk to your date and tell him to take you home?" He knew that he had that kind of influence over her date, and from Isabel's hesitation, she knew it, too.

"Don't waste your time."

"I like to think of it as investing my time." He deleted the last picture before turning his full attention on Isabel. "I will do whatever necessary to keep you from bothering Amber."

"Fine. I get the message. Who cares anyway? Amber is leaving after this weekend."

"Think again."

Isabel held up her hand. "Wait. You think she's going to move back to Acorn Grove? For what? For you?"

Josh didn't answer. Hearing his secret wish spoken out loud like that hurt. Was it as ridiculous as Isabel made it out to be? He wondered if he was setting himself up for a fall.

Isabel laughed and shook her head. "You guys are all alike. Believe it or not, good girls have weekend flings, too. They are just hypocritical about it."

"I'll keep that in mind." Josh handed the phone back to Isabel. "Leave Amber alone." He didn't stay around to hear her response. Josh headed for Amber, needing some reassurance.

The music ended with a flourish. Amber stepped off the dance floor and walked directly to him. He noticed the provocative sway of her hips and the glitter of defiance in her eyes.

She was definitely up to something.

"Don't you want to dance?" Amber asked as she lifted her

hair off her neck. Her breasts threatened to spill from the low neckline.

"What are you doing, Amber?" He wanted to sound firm, but it came out rough. It didn't help that his attention kept dragging back to her cleavage.

She shrugged. "I'm having fun."

He narrowed his eyes. "Are you testing me?"

Amber bit her bottom lip and watched him from beneath her lashes. "Maybe I am."

"Maybe you shouldn't." His chest tightened at the way she flirted with him. That move worked. She had to know how it affected him. "You won't like the consequences."

"I'll take my chances." She boldly stepped closer and laid her hand on his chest. "Anyway, you don't need to keep a tight leash on me anymore."

The image flared in his mind. He swallowed hard and pushed it aside. Amber did that on purpose.

"The wedding is over," she continued. She patted her hand over his heart, but it felt like a stroke. "No need to pretend."

"And this is your way of breaking up with me." It kicked him in the gut. He felt sick. Weak.

She looked away, the first instinctive move she made all night, and it was telling. "Why prolong the inevitable?" she asked lightly.

"Inevitable?"

"Okay, fine." The naughty tone in her voice disappeared and she removed her hand from his chest. "I'm going to give it to you straight."

He braced himself. "Can't wait."

"If you're looking for a submissive, quiet woman, you're

not going to find her in me." She put her hands on her hips. "I'm not nice, I'm not sweet, and even when I try, I'm not all that proper."

Josh said nothing. He was still waiting for the shocking revelation. Was she going to keep him in suspense, or was that it?

"I could try," Amber continued as she blew a wave of hair out of her eyes. "It's tempting if it means coming back home and being with you. But it won't last."

"You think I want someone wholesome?" A thin ray of hope warmed his chest.

"Well, yeah."

"Amber, I used to think you were sweet and innocent. That's why I never touched you. I didn't think you could handle me."

She scoffed at the idea. "Say what?"

"I like it when you're wild." He was drawn to her spirit. Why would he want to break it?

"No, you don't," she argued as a blush crept up her neck. "What was all this counting to three and dragging me in and out of places?"

"I'm sorry. I was trying to keep you from getting in over your head. You kept going straight into trouble and I was trying to keep you out of it." He offered a sheepish grin. "I don't usually act like that."

"That's too bad." She pouted her lips and genuinely looked disappointed.

"It . . . it is?"

She pressed against him and whispered in his ear. "I like it when *you're* wild. Especially when it's directed at me."

He reared his head back as her words jarred him. He

wanted to take Amber without holding back. "There you go again, heading straight into trouble that's over your head."

She clung to his shoulders. "Josh, I don't expect you to be in control all the time."

"It's better that way." He reached for her hands and carefully removed them from his shoulders.

"I promise I won't let you do anything you'll regret," she pledged and made a cross over her heart.

"What are you saying?"

"Let me put it to you in a way you would understand." The gleam in her eyes should have warned him. "You have the count of three to take me to bed."

"Excuse me?" He wanted to take her to his bed, strip her naked and cover her body with his. His cock swelled as the image flickered in his head.

She held up a finger. "One . . ."

Amber had the uncanny ability to make his head spin. "A minute ago you were trying to break up with me, and now you want to have sex?"

"Two . . ." She held up two fingers.

"You are not in charge," he said through clenched teeth.

"Thr—"

He grasped her hand. His hold wasn't tight, but firm as the raw emotions rolled through his blood. "Come with me."

They entered his bedroom with a crash. Amber's shoulders banged against the door. She gasped against Josh's mouth as he kissed and nipped her lips. The doorknob poked her lower back. She shifted to the side, and Josh followed, trapping her against the wall.

Amber pushed at his tuxedo jacket and let it fall to the

floor. She pulled his black tie, her fingers fumbling as she felt his sure hands glide the zipper down her back.

Great. She couldn't even take his tie off. She really did get in over her head with Josh. She talked a big game, but she had nothing to back it up.

She wasn't *that* experienced, and she wasn't all that wild, either.

He was definitely going to notice. She couldn't let him think she was good and sweet, but she didn't think one could fake something like that.

All thoughts fled as her bridesmaid dress fell to her waist. He tugged at the taffeta, but it didn't budge. *Damn hips.* They were always getting in the way.

But was she grabbing for her dress and pushing it past her thighs? No, she cupped her breasts, trying to cover them from Josh's eyes.

Typical good-girl behavior.

Josh took a step back and Amber held her breath. Was he going to ask her to drop her hands, or drop the act?

She should let her hands drop to her sides. Or, hey, here's a thought—finish undressing the sexy and turned-on man in front of her.

Josh tugged hard at her dress. The sound of a ripping seam splintered in the air. The taffeta fell to her feet in a whoosh.

Amber glanced up and noticed Josh's startled gaze. "I wasn't going to wear it again," she assured him.

He didn't answer as he hooked his fingertips along the waistband of her panties. Her stomach trembled as he slowly drew them down her legs.

She silently stepped out of them, her legs shaking as Josh

knelt before her. Huh, he was in the submissive position, but she was the one naked and vulnerable.

His hands cupped her bare bottom as he kissed a trail down her pelvic bone. Her sex grew slick as he got closer. He didn't seem to be moving quickly, but everything was happening so fast for Amber. She didn't want to call it to a stop, but she felt like she needed to catch up before someone wound up disappointed.

Josh slid his hands down the backs of her thighs. Her knees tingled and weakened. She gasped as he hooked one knee over his shoulder.

"What—?" Her voice died as he pressed his mouth tantalizingly near the slippery folds of her sex. She pressed her hands against the door and hooked her other knee around him.

Her muscles twanged as Josh inhaled her scent with obvious pleasure before he burrowed his face into her sex. Amber groaned as he licked his tongue against her clit.

His hands held her hips still as she tried to buck against his swirling tongue. The door creaked and shifted against her spine.

She felt the climax building in her core. Every flick of his tongue made the pressure grow stronger and brighter. It sparked in her legs and belly. The gentle orgasm took her by surprise, her soft cries dragged from her throat as the pleasure rippled through her.

Amber felt like she was flying as the sensations crackled in her body. She opened her eyes and saw Josh grab her legs and wrap them around his lean hips.

"Uh, Josh . . ."

His slanted grin made her heart pump harder. "Hold on tight," he said.

Hold on tight to what? Josh rose, taking her with him. She slapped her hands against the door, but there was nothing to hold on to.

"Stay right there," he ordered as he unzipped his trousers.

Where could she possibly go? She didn't say it out loud as he grabbed her hips, his cock pressing against her wet entrance.

She groaned, loud and long, as he gradually stretched her. She felt his legendary control shimmer and weaken as he finally filled her to the hilt. Amber squeezed her inner muscles as he withdrew, only to thrust back into her tight channel.

The hot, glittery look in his eye warned her. His control was slipping. One more aggressive move on her part and he was going to go wild.

Did she push him over the edge, or choose to be good?

Was she wild or sweet?

She was both, Amber realized as she closed her eyes. One didn't dominate the other. She was everything she wanted to be when she was with Josh. She didn't need to pretend. Not with him.

Amber surrendered to the moment, to the hot intensity building inside her. She raised her hands over her head, rolling her hips as the pleasure crashed against her.

Josh paused, his muscles shuddering. He slammed into her, thrusting at a ferocious pace that left her breathless. He burrowed his face into her breasts, groaning, as he strained against her.

The door rocked against her back. She kept her hands up,

trusting Josh wouldn't let her fall, when she felt his callused fingers entwine with hers.

And she wouldn't let him fall, either.

She held his hands tight, grasping his hips with her legs as he hunted for the elusive release. It was like he couldn't reach it, and she wished she knew how to help.

Suddenly he arched his back before ramming his cock in her one final time. She moaned as he shouted against her breast.

Amber lay against the door, gasping for breath. Sweat dripped from her skin as her muscles shook from exertion.

"You are coming back to Acorn Grove," Josh mumbled against her breast.

"I don't know." Amber smiled lazily. "I seem to find nothing but trouble around here."

"I'll keep you out of trouble."

She looked at the bed and her pulse kicked up a notch. "I'd like to see you try."

ABOUT THE AUTHOR

Susanna Carr lives in the Pacific Northwest. Visit her Web site at www.susannacarr.com.